Ploughing Through
Rainbows

Anne E. Thompson

The Cobweb Press

This edition published 2019

All the events and characters in Ploughing Through Rainbows
are fictitious.
Any resemblance to real persons is coincidental and not intended
by the author.

The views and actions of the characters do not represent the
author's own views. It is a work of fiction.

Published by The Cobweb Press
www.thecobwebpress.com
thecobwebpress@gmail.com

ISBN 978-0-9954632-6-4

Cover by M. Todd

For Bob Beffins

Chapter One

She didn't realise that she was being watched. Busy in her kitchen, it didn't occur to Susan that he might be standing there, outside of the window, looking in. The morning sunshine was searing through the window, the expanse of the yard hidden by the dazzle, so although Susan was well-lit, almost like an actor on stage, everything beyond the window was shadows and smudges.

Susan reached for her recipe book, unaware of the wild eyes watching – her head full of meals to cook and ingredients to buy. She didn't see him when he shifted his weight from one foot to the other, and she was humming – the jingle from an advert that had got stuck in her head – so Susan didn't hear his ragged breathing, or his steps when he came even closer to the window for a better view. Her back was to the window, and she was reaching into a cupboard, straining to reach the large china dish at the back.

The family was coming home for the funeral, and Susan's thoughts were full of potatoes and casseroles and changing bedding.

"It's always lovely to see the boys, but I'm not sure they always appreciate that as my life grows busier, it gets hard sometimes to fit in all the work that a visit entails. Sometimes, I think they assume I just sit around, waiting for them to come home, with nothing else to do all day..." Not that she didn't want to see them, Susan thought, as she reached into the cupboard for vegetables. Nor did she mind the extra hours spent cooking and washing. It was simply hard sometimes, to find the time.

It wasn't until Susan heaved the dish onto the hob that she noticed the shadow, and became aware of the danger. Large and grey, it flickered on the wall in the periphery of her vision. Susan was turning, picking up an onion, when she noticed the movement. The shadow moved, crossing the wall. Followed by another. In panic, Susan spun to face the window, just in time to glimpse the back of the head as it hurried away.

She gave a cry of alarm, and dropped the onion.

Another head appeared, stared at her, moved past. Then another. She could hear them now, uneasy moans and snorts of panic.

She ripped open the kitchen door and yelled up the stairs.

"Tom!" she shouted, "The cows are out!"

Susan didn't wait for him to answer, rushing to the back door and jamming her feet into wellies. Seconds later, Tom was by her side. They glanced over to the enclosure, where the gate was swinging uselessly in the wind. Thirty cows, heifers and steers, almost full grown, were heading towards the lane – the lane which was usually quiet but where the odd car hurtled at speed, confident the road would be empty.

Susan, starting towards the herd with the dogs at her heels, felt Tom's hand restraining her. Then he was off, calling to the cows, marching *away* from them, while Susan kept very still, called the dogs close, splayed her fingers so they waited, not moving, next to her. A cloud passed over the sun, and the yard softened into greys and blue, the stark shadows dissolving. Susan shivered, watching Tom as he shouted again, calling to the herd, still walking away from them.

Susan saw the lead steer stop and raise his head, listening. Susan knew he would recognise Tom's voice. That was the voice that fed him, had raised him from a calf. That voice represented security, and she knew that being out was frightening for the herd, they liked security. She guessed that when the gate had swung open, the lead steer had walked through it, keen to explore, and the herd had followed. But now all the cows were in panic, saliva dripping from mouths, eyes rolling; they were on unfamiliar territory, wary of predators, shying from danger. Tom's voice offered safety.

The herd paused.

Susan held her breath, then pressed into the wall as the cows turned. Mooing and snorting, eyes still rolling, they streamed past her. Hooves clattering on cobblestones, steam rising from their backs, they hurried towards Tom. Towards safety.

Susan waited until they had all passed, then followed at a distance, shutting the gate behind the last one. Tom was in the pen, moving amongst the herd, rubbing shoulders and backs, his voice soothing, checking they were all there.

"How did that happen?" said Susan.

"Something must've caught on the chain," said Tom, lifting the gate mechanism to see if it was broken. "Perhaps it was him," he nodded towards a badly polled head that still had the remains of a single horn. "I'll check it later," he said, looping the chain across the latch and securing it with a padlock. "Back to my bath now."

Susan looked at him, in blue towelling dressing gown, bare feet thrust into wellington boots. She grinned.

"Surprised that seeing those legs didn't send them into complete panic," she muttered.

"What's that?" he said, half turning.

"Nothing," she smiled, "I just said I love you."

Tom snorted, and stomped towards the house.

As she walked past the Land Rover, parked next to the house in the yard, Susan remembered to look at it, to see if it needed to be hosed down. It was, she decided, clean enough. Although it wasn't exactly gleaming, the car wasn't too dirty, and would be fine for the drive to the funeral and back.

***

Susan felt overwhelmed by mental lists of things she needed to prepare before the boys arrived. Now that the cows were safely back in their enclosure, she felt irritated by their intrusion, and resented the time she had lost. All the ingredients for the casseroles were lined up on the counter, ready for her to cook: vegetables and spices, and beef and bacon and herbs. They were sitting there, looking neat and orderly, waiting to be turned into something delicious. She picked up the onion she had dropped, and added it to the line.

"Now," Susan thought, "where did I get to? I need to plan the other meals...and decide what shopping I need." Her mind drifted again, and she thought of her boys, smiling.

Ben would stay for a couple of weeks, as he only had coursework to do and could miss a couple of lectures. A sort of half-term holiday, he'd said, a well-deserved rest. Susan felt the rest was probably not deserved, at all, and she shook her head, her expression wry as she thought of Ben. Susan doubted much in the way of hard work had been accomplished throughout the term, but felt disinclined to probe further. He was in his final year at university, and Susan knew that real life would all too quickly sneak up and sink in her teeth.

Her other sons had emailed to say they would arrive for the funeral on Thursday, and then stay until the Monday. They had each emailed her during the night. Susan had read them while she drank her morning coffee, surprised by their promised attendance.

"I wonder if they're coming just because Uncle George has died," she thought, "or if they planned to come anyway." Sometimes the family had a life of its own, and Susan felt that she was left on the periphery, learning plans after they had been arranged.

"Ben and Jack will be there...Even Ed is coming – that really *is* a surprise! And Neil – though he would probably have come anyway, he'd want to be there to support me and Mum.

"It's a shame Neil is bringing Kylie," thought Susan, with a sigh. She thought of Neil's wife, and frowned, knowing that she disliked the young woman but not feeling she could admit it, even to her closest friends, because Kylie was black.

"Though that's not why I dislike her," she thought, reaching for a recipe book. But people would think that it was, whatever she said, they would assume that she was racist. She wasn't, she was fairly sure. She didn't actually have any close friends who were black, but that was because she'd grown up in southern England, there were not many black people amongst her peers.

"But if there had been," Susan thought, turning the greasy pages of the recipe book while not really looking at them, "if there had been some black mums at the school gate, or at the village market, I would have been friends with them; if they were nice." But Kylie was not, in Susan's opinion, nice. "She's too...strident," thought Susan, thinking about how the younger woman spoke, remembering her very long fingernails which were always painted. "And she refuses to cook decent food for Neil; and everything that I suggest or advise, anything I try to help Neil with, Kylie automatically takes the opposite view. And Neil always sides with Kylie, always. He barely listens to me any more..." Susan felt a mixture of sadness and anger bubbling up inside her, and pushed it back down. She took a breath, forcing herself to think about meals and jobs, and not waste time on self-pity.

"I raised my boys to be independent, strong-minded adults," Susan reminded herself, "and occasionally they might make decisions I don't like, but I can respect that, can't I?" Susan closed her book with a thump. "It's not as if they're likely to choose something radically different, or wrong, is it?"

Tom reappeared after his bath, dressed in his normal jeans and sweater.

"That was bit of a shock, the cows getting out like that," Tom said, "lucky you noticed." He went to the back door and began to pull on his wellies. "I need to check that bred heifer," he said. "You making tea?"

Susan watched as Tom walked across to the barn, where he was keeping the heifer. He'd decided to breed from one of the Friesian heifers – mating her with an Aberdeen Angus, so the calf's shoulders should be small enough for a nice easy birth. It was nearly time for the birth, and Tom was checking the heifer regularly.

"I hope this experiment works out for him," thought Susan, as she filled the kettle. It was always bit of a risk, changing the way they did things – they usually bought-in all their stock. But Tom fancied trying to breed one himself, and talked about possibly entering it in the show in the summer. His father had occasionally calved, but like today, the farm had usually bought-in new calves. Tom's experience was very limited, and although Susan knew he'd spent hours talking over warm beers in the pub, with more experienced breeders, she could tell he was feeling nervous. They couldn't afford to lose the heifer, and losing the calf would be a hit they could do without. It was only a whim really, something Tom fancied doing, to see if he could win a prize at show, earn the herd some credence. Plus, there was always the chance the heifer might have a male, a decent animal that he could leave intact, that could be used to sire more young. There was money in that, especially if it won a prize. It would be full grown by August, would be plenty old enough to show. So,

Susan had supported Tom when he'd first mentioned it, had told him it was a good idea, and why not give it a try?

"But I hadn't realised how completed obsessed with the whole thing he would become," she thought, turning from the window.

Susan sat down with a new heap of recipe books and tried to think about what she needed to cook. She had also agreed that she would provide food after the funeral. They weren't expecting many people, so she had filled the freezer with cakes and would spend the morning of the funeral making trays of sandwiches.

"I have absolutely no idea how hungry people will be, I don't even know how many people will come back to the farm after the service." Susan frowned as she turned the pages. Perhaps she should concentrate on family meals, that was easier.

***

Neil too was in agonies of indecision. The invitation – though as it was unavoidable it felt more like an order – to give the eulogy at the funeral was proving a heavy burden. He had sat at his desk, uninspired, for nearly an hour when Kylie put her head round the door to enquire how he was progressing.

"Not at all, actually," he said, miserably honest. "I don't even know where to start. It's not as if any of us actually *liked* Uncle George, but I can hardly say that, can I?"

Neil looked up at Kylie, feeling almost desperate. "I think this might be too hard for me," he admitted, "I don't want to let Mum down, but really, I just don't know what to say. And I hate giving speeches, I wish they'd asked Ed, he's much better at things like this."

Kylie snorted. "Ha! Can you imagine what he would say! It would be entertaining, that's for sure – but not exactly appropriate..." She came into the room, and kissed the top of his head. "Look online," she said, turning to leave, "you might find something there.

So, Neil looked. He was sure a Google search of "Eulogies for Uncles" would come up blank, but after a while, and with a few tweaks of the initial search words, his computer began to fill with lyrical remembrances and poetical phrases. True, they were all about other people's uncles, who bore absolutely no resemblance to his own truculent relative. But did that matter?

As far as Neil could see, what was needed was a speech that people would listen to, and afterwards say, "Ah, that was lovely." He felt he had two clear choices: either he could write a speech about Uncle George that would reflect the life of a cantankerous nasty old man – which would make for unpleasant listening and no one would benefit. Or, he could write a nice speech, which would be about a mythical uncle, but would fill the time and not offend anyone.

"Surely," Neil thought, "the truth of the words in this situation aren't important? Surely, it's more important that Mum and Gran feel comforted, and know that they've 'done the right thing' by George, given him a respectable funeral."

Neil found two eulogies which he found particularly touching, and copied and pasted them onto a blank document. A little fine-tuning, in the way of name changing and the alteration of dates and places, and he was ready. He had a speech. One, he felt, that would do both himself, and his deceased Uncle, proud.

Neil spent some time reading it through, varying his tone of voice, pausing for effect, trying to remember all the things he'd been taught many years ago about public speaking. He began to feel more positive, allowed himself to think that maybe this wouldn't be so bad after all, he wouldn't let anyone down, it was actually rather a good speech. He wasn't sure it was quite long enough though, so he added a few sentences to the end, then with a flourish he sent the document to his printer.

He pressed print, and stood, watching the white pages splurge squeakily from the printer, then folded them and took them upstairs to pack. He couldn't face looking at it again, he had stressed about it enough already. He had a speech. He was ready.

Chapter Two

Ben was the first to arrive home. As he walked towards Netherley Farmhouse, he could hear noises coming from the barn, so veered off to look. Long shadows stretched across the yard, the autumn sun low in the sky. Ben stood in the near dusk of the doorway, watching Tom as the forklift truck jerked backwards, then lurched forwards, manoeuvring between the grain store and the crusher mill. The new feed must have arrived earlier in the day, and Ben knew it needed to be moved somewhere dry, so the damp wouldn't encourage mould to grow. Before university, it had been one of his jobs, and as Ben watched his father narrowly miss a bale of hay, he grinned. There weren't many jobs he'd enjoyed on the farm, but negotiating the little truck, with its fierce clutch and unreliable steering, had been quite fun. Ben wondered if he should offer his father some advice, but decided it wasn't a discussion worth having.

As he watched his father, Ben felt that small knot in his stomach again. The one that was so easy to ignore when he was away, but which had become a regular feature of his life at home. He knew he had to tell them, knew he couldn't keep putting it off. It made him feel slightly sick, and he turned away, to look at the barn.

The barn was huge. It was really three barns, knocked into one for ease of movement, and it towered above Ben, dust motes drifting over his head. To one side was the grain store, the barley held in a huge vat with a pipe reaching towards the crusher mill, reminding Ben of a one-armed robot. Beyond it were the sacks of protein, extra goodness to add to the grains they could grow. The protein pellets were ordered regularly, and stored in a small mountain to one side. At the back were stacks of straw and hay, reaching up towards the ceiling, hopefully enough feed to last the winter. The sweet smell was filling the barn, warming the air. A secure smell, familiar and comfortable. Ben lowered the bag from his shoulder, letting it thump to the floor.

In the middle of the barn were the pens, empty now, ready for the next lot of calves. Ben guessed they'd be arriving soon. On the far left were the larger calves, half-grown, still kept inside for some of the day, turning their big heads towards Ben, staring with their big round eyes, their jaws lazily chewing. Outside would be the full-grown cattle, those big enough to get most of the nutrients they needed from the grass. If the weather turned wetter, they would have to be moved inside too, away from the damp clay soil.

Ben turned from the cows to watch his father's back. He was a solid figure, someone who usually inspired security. But not now – Ben now had no idea how he'd take the news, no clue to his reaction. Ben felt the knot of tension yawn wide in his stomach and split into a thousand dancing judders of panic. He swallowed.

Tom caught sight of Ben, and shut off the engine, raising his arm to wave, grinning.

"Hello there, didn't hear you come in," he said. "Do you want to give me a hand with the mill?"

Ben sighed, and arranged his face into what he thought of as his 'home face' – the one that people expected to see.

"Sure," he said, walking over to the big funnel, thinking there was always something to do on the farm, you didn't stand still for long before you were given a job.

Tom dragged over the long pipe from the barley store, directing it into the base of the hopper. The machinery was coated in fine dust, fat blobs appearing wherever Tom's fingers landed, as he guided the funnel, tipped barley into the top. Inside the metal barrel was a fat steel drill, and when the machine was switched on, it turned, steadily drawing the barley up to the top, where it could fall down, between the mill stones. The machinery was noisy, shuddering as the drill wound its way upwards, sending plumes of barley dust over Ben as he stood, watching the ground barley as it was spat from the stones to the receptacle below. As it filled, he removed the ground barley, filling the empty sacks that rested by his feet.

The noise of the machinery filled the barn, too loud for talking, and for a while father and son worked side by side, not talking, grinding the barley and filling the sacks. Ben knew the barley had to be ground, otherwise it would pass straight through the cows, all the nutrients expelled with the husks. It was a boring job though. Boring and noisy and dirty. Like most of the jobs on the farm. He was glad he was getting out, wouldn't be trapped there forever.

When the last sack was filled, Tom switched off the machine. The silence rushed back into the barn, their ears momentarily deaf to the tiny sounds of cattle breathing and the wind outside.

"Does Mum know you're back?" said Tom.

Ben shook his head, a cloud of dust falling from his hair, tickling his throat and drying his eyes. "No, I heard you in here, so stopped off to say hello on my way in."

"Ah, well, you should go on into the house. Dot's here – with Elsie."

Ben thought of his grandmother and her sister, and smiled. He knew they would welcome him, smile with their crooked teeth, pleased to see him; and he enjoyed listening to them, so decided to go into the house. Plus, Ben thought, it meant that there wasn't time to talk to his father, gave him an excuse for another delay. He'd tell him another time.

"Can you bring me a cuppa?" Tom called after him, as Ben heaved his bag back onto his shoulder, wiping away more dust, and lumbered off towards the house.

***

Susan and her visitors were in the little sitting room off the kitchen. Susan yawned. She worked in the coffee shop on Wednesdays, and had arrived home to find her mother and aunt waiting. Susan made tea, and took them into the sitting room. It was warm in there, being next to the kitchen, heated by the oven and a radiator, even when the tiny fireplace was empty. They sat on chairs either side of the brick hearth, and smiled when Ben walked in.

"Hello stranger," said Susan, rising to kiss him. She stood on tiptoe and reached up, pulling him into a hug. There was something physical about her love for her boys, even now when she had to stand on tiptoe to hug them, and they smelt of aftershave and deodorant rather than the little boy smell of wind and sunshine. Ben was the most like Tom, the same broad shoulders, and compact strength. He was dark too, like his father had been before he lost his hair. She pulled back to look at him, took note of the pale cheeks, the grey beneath his eyes, the slight weight loss.

"Journey okay?"

"Yes, thanks, the bus was running late, so it was still there when the train got to Marksbridge. Saved me some time."

Susan smiled, anticipating the arrival of her other sons, knowing that she always felt complete when the boys were at home. She was secretly looking forward to the weekend. "Not that I've finished most of the jobs," she thought, gazing at Ben, glad to have him close again.

Ben was the youngest of her sons − the first son had been born two years after she married Tom. They were born into farming stock, so the first three boys had been welcomed as potential muscle for the farm, boys to work alongside their father. But when Susan had fallen pregnant for the fourth time, everyone assumed she was hoping for a girl. They were wrong. Susan knew boys by then, she understood about worm sandwiches and grubby fingernails, and how hilarious anything concerning poo or bottoms was. She was used to their sweaty bodies climbing onto her lap, their complete acceptance of her, the physicalness of their anger when they were cross. She knew boys, and wasn't at all sure she would cope with a girl. She watched her friends combing their daughters' hair, and thought it looked as tedious an activity as brushing the dogs when they were moulting. She saw toys of pink plastic, and boxes of fake jewellery, and feared that she might find it rather hard to relate to a little girl. So when Ben had been born, Susan had been contented. He was everything she had wanted, and he slotted onto the end of the family as a perfect fit.

Ben was now nodding towards the teapot.

"Is there enough in there for me to have a cup? And Dad wants one too." Ben slumped into the sofa next to his grandmother. "All right Gran?"

"Well," Dot began, as Susan stood to carry the teapot into the kitchen to add more hot water. "I'm fine, but Elsie's got a saga, haven't you Els?" Dot nodded towards her sister, who placed her cup, very carefully, on the small table beside her and leant forward, as if keen to tell her news. Aunty Elsie's eyes sparkled, and she waved her palms towards Ben, preparing to speak.

Susan was smiling as she went into the kitchen, shaking her head as she refilled the kettle and set it to boil. Her aunt's voice could be heard, above the bubble of the kettle, as it drifted through the doorway, and Susan could hear her excitement as she began to tell her story to Ben.

"I was just telling your mother; I'm thinking of going on a holiday. With June from Bingo. She's got a nephew who's got a house in France, and we could get there on the coach. June wants to fly, but I'm not holding with that. It isn't safe, not anymore, not with all these foreign terrorists blowing things up. Did you know, you can't even take plastic bottles on board these days?"

"You do know," Susan heard her mother interrupt, "that France will be full of foreigners, don't you Elsie?"

Susan paused, straining to hear the conversation over the noise of the kettle as it began to boil, steam rising furiously from the spout.

"Yes, well, you have to expect that if you travel," she heard Elsie reply, her tone snappish, then softening as she returned to her conversation with Ben.

"So, I said to June, I said, 'No, I don't mind coming to France with you, it might even be nice to have a little break, but I'm not flying. It's too dangerous.'

"I mean, Ben, you've got to be sensible about these things, haven't you?"

Susan refilled the teapot and carried it back to the lounge. Her mother was smiling widely, clearly enjoying teasing her sister. Ben was sprawled on the sofa, his bags dumped next to him. Susan searched his face while he chatted to his elderly relatives, checking he was eating enough, that his hair was clean, that he was bothering to shave. His eyes looked tired, and she wondered if something was worrying him, though he seemed relaxed enough.

"Sounds lovely," Ben was saying, his voice full of laughter. "You not going too Granny?"

Susan poured tea into a mug for Tom, and added a spoonful of sugar. She glanced at her mother, who was shaking her head and smiling at Ben.

"No, not this time," she said, "I think June can look after Elsie this time, I'll stay at home." She glanced at the clock.

"Talking of home, we'd better make tracks in a minute. Drink up Elsie, I don't want to be driving when it gets dark, I might bump into something. My eyes aren't what they used to be."

Susan picked up the tea for Tom.

"There's tea in the pot Ben," she said, nodding towards the tray. "I should let it brew for a minute if I were you. I'll just take a cup out to Dad."

Chapter Three

While Ben was drinking tea in the sitting room, Neil was still packing. He'd managed to take a couple of days holiday from work, though his boss had made unhappy noises and raised his eyebrows and pretended to check the calendar for important reasons so he could refuse. But he'd had to agree in the end, it was a quiet time of year, and Neil was one of his best people, so he owed him a few favours.

Now Neil was searching through his wardrobe for a black tie. He was sure he had one.

"Kylie," he shouted towards the bedroom door, "have you seen my black tie?"

Kylie appeared in the doorway, carrying a pile of washing. She dumped it on the bed and came over to the wardrobe.

"It must be here somewhere, not likely to be anywhere else is it?" she said as she began to look under each tie on the rack behind the door. Then she knelt down and began to rummage amongst the shoes and boxes on the floor. "You ought to keep this more tidy," Kylie said, sounding irritated. "Ah, here it is, under a box of trainers. It must have fallen there without you noticing." She pulled it out with a flourish. "There! Anything else?"

Neil was watching her bottom as she searched. It was rather excellent.

"Nothing we've got time for," he said, curling the tie into a ball and putting it into the corner of his case. "Are you ready to go?"

Kylie nodded.

Neil picked up her black dress and jacket that were hanging on the door, wrapped in plastic from the dry cleaners. He carried them downstairs, and found her travel bag and matching make-up box were waiting by the front door. The make-up box held all her lotions and potions, and it was somewhere that Neil never ventured, though he sometimes wondered why it needed to be quite so large. Next to it was a smart presentation box, which he knew held her new hairdryer.

"Not cheap at £329, but quality is worth paying for," she had told him. Neil hadn't said anything at the time, because he could see Kylie was excited, and he didn't want to disappoint her. But, he thought, lifting it now with his spare hand and carrying it to the car, it was a complete waste of money. He stowed it safely in the boot and went back into the house.

He found Kylie sitting on the bed, examining her nails. They were very long and shiny, though Neil was pleased to see they were no longer the dark red she had worn yesterday. Kylie looked up and noticed him watching her. She grinned, as if guessing his thoughts.

"Yeah, well, I thought red might not be right for a funeral, and I don't want to annoy your mum, so I went with a French polish. Classy, don't you think? Even your mother might approve of these..." She frowned.

"Neil, I wish you'd let me buy her a present, a little '*thank you for having us*' gift. I found a little china vase when I was shopping, it was really pretty, I'm sure she'd have liked it. Things like that might help her to like me a bit more too, not see me as a threat."

Neil crossed the room to sit beside her, and picked up her hand. He leant over and kissed her forehead.

"Kylie, my mum does like you. And if she's got a problem, then it's not your fault and she'll have to sort it out herself. But I honestly don't think buying her gifts would help."

He paused. He wanted to say that actually, gifts would only make things worse, because his mother would see it as a complete waste of money. On the farm, money was tight, and every penny was accounted for. Things were only bought if they couldn't be hired, and only hired if they were essential.

But Neil thought that might make his mother look bad, and he desperately wanted the two women he loved to find some kind of a truce, so instead he squeezed Kylie's hand and stood up.

"Mum already has vases; she doesn't need another one.

"Are you all ready to go? I've loaded the car."

As they drove from their little two-bedroomed house, with its tidy rooms and modern fixtures, towards the farmhouse, Neil thought again about his mother and Kylie. He sighed. The two women were very different, he thought, edging into the traffic as they joined the main road, as different as the homes they lived in. Kylie liked things to be neat and clean and organised, and she tended to panic when their plans changed. She wasn't very keen on dirt or animals – had even refused to let Neil buy a kitten, saying they didn't have room for one. Yet his mother seemed to thrive on the farm, to hardly notice the smells and mud. He frowned, slowing to a stop at a red light, wondering if the women would ever find a common ground, ever learn to appreciate each other.

"What are you thinking about?" asked Kylie, and Neil realised she was watching him.

"I was wondering what we'll have for dinner," he said.

"Yeah well, we both know it won't be a ready-meal, don't we," said Kylie, with a wry smile. "However busy your mum is, she always makes time to cook. I don't know why really, all that effort, and then it's gone in half an hour."

"She likes cooking," said Neil, not wanting to encourage a tirade.

"You have told her, haven't you?" said Kylie, "She does know what we decided, doesn't she?"

Neil frowned, pretending to concentrate on the road.

"No, not yet. Hasn't been the right time. I'll tell her today, when we arrive."

"Great," said Kylie, sighing, "because her getting ready for her uncle's funeral, after she's probably already prepared something for dinner, is an excellent time to tell her. Honestly Neil, you can't keep putting it off. She has to know sometime. It will be worse if they guess and one of them asks me. You should tell them. Otherwise it'll be me who gets the blame. Like I do for everything else..."

"I already said I would," said Neil, speaking more sharply than he'd intended to. He knew that Kylie was right, knew that he needed to tell his parents, have the conversation and get it out of the way. Normally, he tackled issues head-on, and was very direct. But he simply was not sure how they would react this time. He suspected his father would be livid – not that he'd say much, because he never did. He would become silent, be extra polite whenever he spoke to Neil, let his son know by his general frostiness that he took it as a personal insult.

Neil had no idea what his mother would say. Lots probably, in a rush of emotion, as she told him it was rude and silly and insulting and immature. And Kylie was right, his mother would blame her, think it was all her idea. But it wasn't. He was sure he'd made the right decision. It was what Kylie wanted anyway, and he wanted to make her happy.

He glanced across at Kylie. Her hand was outstretched, and she was admiring her rings. He'd given her most of them, she had one for each finger, and even one on her thumb. Not very practical, but pretty, different, stylish. He liked that about Kylie, she was different. She was about as different to his mother as you could get, Neil thought. Kylie was like a little china doll, fragile somehow, until you got to know her and realised that actually she was very strong, very decided about things. But physically she wasn't exactly muscle-bound, she was more interested in walking properly in very high heels than being able to carry things. Neil couldn't imagine her humping sacks of hay around, she'd break one of those pretty nails. But he liked that, liked that Kylie was delicate and needed to be looked after. Neil knew she didn't quite fit with his family, but that was all right, it was time to grow up and make his own way in life. Though telling them about some of his decisions was still proving difficult.

Neil sighed again. He would have to tell them, Kylie was right. He wished now that he'd done it on the phone, or emailed them. Too late now, he'd have to tell them when they arrived.

Kylie glared at him, and Neil knew she was cross at how he'd spoken to her. He reached across and squeezed her knee.

"Sorry love. You're right, I know you are. Am just a bit tense about this whole visit, having to make a speech and everything. But I will tell them."

"Today? Soon as we get there?"

"Yes, I promise," said Neil, knowing that he wouldn't. He let go of her knee and held the steering wheel very tightly.

Kylie turned on the radio and looked out of the window.

***

Edward did not have anything to tell his parents. In fact, as he set off towards the farm, he was very much hoping they would never find out too much about how he was living his life, because he knew they wouldn't approve.

Edward was a salesman. His day job was to travel vast swathes of the country, persuading builders' merchants and DIY shops to stock the tools produced by the company he worked for. It was boring work, but the persuading part was fun, and the travel part was useful, as it allowed him a lot of freedom. Freedom was important to Edward.

He didn't think that Emily really understood, but that was okay, she'd survive. When he'd told her that he was going to a family funeral, planned to stay with his parents for a few days while he was there, Emily had made all sorts of fuss. She'd wanted to come, of course, and then sulked when he'd said no. Edward wished now that he'd just said it was a work trip. Emily wouldn't have known, but he'd worried she might notice him packing his black suit, so he'd had to tell her. Then there had been sighs and curt sentences, and reproachful looks. But she'd get over it. He'd buy her something on the way home, she was easily bribed into better moods with gifts.

They'd been together for about ten months now, which was bit of a record for Edward. But Emily was good company, had a sharp sense of humour, and she had a better job than him, so paid most of the bills. He'd moved in with her six months ago, and so far, the arrangement was proving to be very satisfactory.

Edward set the Sat Nav as he drove. His parents' house was still listed as 'home' – Edward supposed he should change that really, it was the sort of thing that Emily got stroppy about. But the farm would always be his home, in a weird way, even though he hoped he'd never live there again.

The funeral had been a good excuse to go back. Edward didn't actually have any feelings for Great Uncle George, he didn't think anyone did really, George had been too horrible to all of them over the years, there was certainly no affection for him.

"And," thought Edward as he adjusted his speed to slightly higher than the speed limit but low enough to escape a fine, "he smelt bad – and left damp patches on chairs." Edward shuddered, thinking that he wasn't sure he wanted to be old, not if he ended up like Uncle George. But George was Gran's brother, and he'd never married, so had turned up for most of the family events that Edward could remember.

Edward knew his mum would be pleased that he was going back for the funeral. Pleased and a bit surprised, because Edward didn't usually do family things unless it was convenient. But he'd fancied a break, bit of a rest from work... and Emily; so it was a good excuse. Edward smiled, realising that he was rather looking forward to being with his brothers again.

***

Jack was also hoping to not reveal any secrets. He was walking to the station, his suit bag slung over his shoulder, a leather bag swinging by his side.

The last of the light had faded from the sky, and he walked in the yellow glow of streetlights. As he passed the park, the indigo blobs of bushes lowering behind the fence, he noticed that an owl was hooting. He missed that, living in the city, mostly he heard traffic, a steady drone through his bedroom window, a continuous whoosh as he walked to the bank. Of course, once Jack was actually inside, safe in the cubby hole assigned to him and his computers, there was only the whir and hum of machines and the murmur of voices. Jack didn't really miss the sounds of the farm, only tended to think of them when he was actually there, thought that he was only now noticing the birds because he was on his way home. On his way back.

Jack felt that the farm was stuck in the past. They all reverted to type when they were there: Neil trying to look after them all, Ed doing the opposite to whatever Neil said and cracking jokes, Ben laughing. And him sort of stuck between all of them. Less than a year younger than Ed, Jack had always felt as if he was trying to catch up with his older brothers, and they were always trying to leave him behind. He was too often lumped together with Ben, the baby, whilst he was desperate to keep up with 'the big ones'. Growing up, he'd spent a lot of time with his father, helping with the animals, trying to be what his parents wanted him to be.

Jack arrived at the station and bought his ticket, stuffing it into his pocket. The price had gone up since he'd last been home. Jack hoped the weekend wouldn't turn out to be too expensive.

He frowned, working out if there was anything else he'd have to pay for.

There weren't many people on the platform, and he managed to get a seat on a cold metal bench, moving his suit onto his knee and putting his bag down next to a puddle. Jack wasn't sure if he wanted to be going home, but he didn't want to be the only one not there. He would enjoy seeing his brothers again, watching them, listening to their conversations. He always felt slightly detached, was happier with the animals when he was young, and his computers now he was an adult. He smiled; it would be nice to see everyone though. When the train drew into the station, Jack was already standing. He found an empty carriage and settled back against the window as he sped towards Marksbridge.

Before he arrived, Jack sent a text to his brothers, asking who would be able to collect him. Ed didn't reply, of course, but Neil said him and Kylie were nearly at Marksbridge themselves, so they would wait at the station and drive him. As Jack left the station, he saw the Golf, neatly waiting near the entrance. He grinned and walked across.

"Hi guys, thanks for the lift," Jack said, as he slid onto the back seat.

Kylie half turned, and blew him a kiss. Neil smiled at him in the rearview mirror and turned the key.

They drove to the farm.

***

Dinner was a noisy affair. They all sat around the long oak table in the kitchen, the same one Tom's parents and grandparents had used when they'd lived at the farm. Susan heaved a second casserole dish onto a mat and raised the lid. The steam rose up, warming her hand and scenting her hair with spices and herbs. She spooned some onto a plate for Tom, stuck a spoon into the thick gravy, telling everyone to help themselves, while she put the plate of food back into the warm oven. Then she sat, enjoying the scene, happy to listen as the conversation went back and forth. Her boys were back.

Edward was sitting to her right, swinging back on his chair – a habit she had never managed to break him of when he was young, despite many tellings. He was watching Neil as he heaped mashed potatoes onto his plate, then turned to Ben and asked him if he'd have to empty his university room for the Christmas holiday.

"No, I've got that sorted," said Ben, spooning peas onto his plate and ignoring the few that slipped off the spoon and rolled across the table. "Uni will allow us to rent our rooms during the holidays, so I've booked one. I'll leave all my stuff there."

"Sounds expensive," said Jack, "how much is that costing?"

"Ah well, that's where my cunning plan comes in," said Ben, taking the potatoes from Neil and almost dropping them because the dish was hot. Susan passed him a cork mat.

"Sounds like Baldrick," muttered Edward, "didn't he always have a cunning plan?"

Ben ignored him. "I've agreed, for a small fee, to store everyone else's stuff in there, as I don't plan to actually be living there during the break. So, if you think about how much stuff you can fit into a room, it's a pretty big storage unit. I'm hoping to make a tidy profit."

"In other words, you're ripping off your friends," said Edward. He turned to Neil.

"How's the speech coming? Have you planned it yet?"

"What speech?" asked Jack, ladling casserole onto his plate.

"The eulogy," said Edward, "Neil was selected to give it."

"Ha, rather you than me!" said Jack. "Are you going to list all the swear words George could fit into a single sentence? Or tell the story of when he ran over the cat and then pretended it was Ben?"

"I'd forgotten about that," said Ben. "That was terrible – I was only a learner at the time."

"I'm trying not to think about it," said Neil.

Susan saw him start eating, though he hadn't taken any casserole. She offered it, but he said he was okay.

"Poor Neil," thought Susan, "he must be nervous already." Kylie too was picking at her food, pushing it around her plate, looking unhappy. "I wonder," thought Susan, "perhaps I've got a grandchild on the way." The thought was a good one, even if she didn't like Kylie, and Susan smiled at her.

They had almost finished eating the casserole by the time Tom arrived. Susan got his plate from the oven while he sat in his place, at the head of the table, and nodded at his sons. She knew he liked having them all home too, it felt right.

There was a knock on the back door, and they all stopped eating and looked at it. Susan started to rise, but Ben stopped her.

"Don't worry Mum, I'll get it, I've finished. You finish your meal..." He went to the door and pulled it open. It had dropped on its hinges slightly and Susan heard it scrape the tiles as it opened.

Ben opened the door wide, and Susan felt a rush of cold air, and saw Josie, their neighbour, fidgeting on the step.

"Oh, hello Ben," Susan heard Josie say, all in a rush, as if she had rehearsed a speech. "I heard about your uncle – and I'm very sorry to hear your news – and I wondered if your mum would like any help with the refreshments after the funeral, at the wake...or whatever it's called." Josie stopped and looked across the room, pink cheeked, with hair that refused to stay tied back and had escaped from her hairband to curl wildly around her face. She pushed it back and stared past Ben, towards Susan.

Susan got up and came to the door, smiling.

"Hello Josie, that's very sweet of you. I'm hoping the boys will help me, but another pair of hands is always useful, if you're sure you've got time?"

"Oh yes, I asked for the afternoon off – I'm working at the hairdressers at the moment, that over-priced one in Marksbridge with the unfortunate name – and they said it's fine. Great, well, okay, I'll see you tomorrow then."

Susan watched as Josie looked past her, towards the table, and knew she was looking for Edward. She saw the girl blush a deeper red, and guessed Edward had seen her.

"Thank you, Josie," Susan said. "Have you eaten? I made plenty..."

"Oh, no. I mean yes, I have. Thanks anyway. See you..." Josie was already turning, rushing away to where she couldn't be seen, couldn't embarrass herself further.

Susan closed the door. As she walked back to the table, Edward started to speak.

"Soo..." he began.

"Don't," said Susan. "Poor girl, and she's lovely, so don't say a word. And tomorrow, be nice."

Edward raised his hands in surrender. "Hey, I'm always nice." His chair scraped the floor as he pushed it back. "In fact...Be back in a minute," he said, and walked out the back door.

"There's apple pie for pudding," Susan called after him, knowing he wouldn't be back until the rest of them had finished eating. She shook her head. Family meals had always been like this, Tom late because he was with the animals, the boys rushing to go somewhere afterwards. The time they all actually overlapped, were all seated at the table at the same time, was sometimes tiny.

The rest of the family were looking at each other, laughing. Except for Jack, who was sighing, and looking down at his plate. Susan began to clear the empty dishes.

***

After dinner, while Susan loaded the dishwasher and Ben loitered next to her in an effort to be helpful, Neil carried his and Kylie's cases into their room. Kylie wasn't speaking to him.

The meal had been an effort. Susan's casseroles were one of the family's favourite meals – shin of beef tenderised for several hours in a sweet gravy of allspice and bay leaves, served with carrots and peas and heaps of soft mashed potato. But Neil had still not told his parents – he told Kylie that it had been 'the wrong time' – and he knew that all she had eaten were the vegetables and potato.

Neil opened the door to his old bedroom and juggled the cases inside. There was no room for them really, as most of the room was full of bed. His parents had bought the double bed when he married Kylie four years ago, a sort of token gesture of acceptance. Now when they visited they could share a bed, but the wardrobe door didn't open fully and they had to sit on the bed to open any of the drawers in the large oak chest.

Kylie followed Neil into the room and sat on the bed, kicking her heels onto the floor and curling her legs underneath her.

"So, that was great," she scowled.

Neil put the cases on the bed beside her, and opened the large one which was full of his clothes. Kylie had folded the shirt for him, and he shook it out, then moved to the wardrobe to hang it.

"Yes, it was nice to see everyone," he said, pretending to not understand.

"Neil, you *have* to tell them," said Kylie. "This is stupid. And I'm starving hungry. Go down now, while your mum is in the kitchen and tell her. It'll be easier without your dad there." She reached into the case for a pair of jeans and her trainers, and started to pull them on.

"I'm going for a walk," she said. "Make sure they know by the time I get back."

Neil nodded, and carried on unpacking. When she got up to leave, he followed her out, and went into the kitchen.

Susan was still in there, wiping surfaces. She had piled plastic containers of cakes onto the table.

"Those are for tomorrow," Susan said, as Neil went in and sat down. "I hope I've made enough."

Neil looked at them. There seemed to be about a hundred cupcakes and three loaf cakes of different colours.

"How come you got lumbered with the catering anyway?" he asked.

His mother moved to the table and sat next to him.

"Well, there isn't really anyone else, is there?" she said. "And I don't mind. Granny and Elsie started to get into bit of a tizz about it, started worrying about booking caterers, and saying they wanted it done properly, that there should be some refreshments after the service. I don't think Uncle George would've cared one way or the other actually, but it's not really about him, is it? The funeral is about the people left behind, it's for his sisters really. So I said I'd do it. I don't expect there'll be many people anyway, I've probably made far too much.

"Do you want a drink?" his mother asked. "You and Kylie hardly ate anything at dinner."

"No, thanks" said Neil, his heart sinking, "Actually Mum, I need to talk to you about that..."

Susan looked at him, waiting, her face expectant as if she was about to receive good news of some kind. Neil saw her mouth twitch into a smile, then become serious again as she waited.

"Yes?" she said, sounding eager, "what do you want to tell me? Have you got some special news? I did wonder..."

Neil swallowed. He stood up, walked across the kitchen and picked up a tea-towel, and swirled it around his hand like a bandage, trying to think how to phrase his next sentence.

"The thing is Mum, we've, well, we've been thinking and we've decided," he paused, not looking at her. Neil's mouth was dry, and he felt like a little boy again. He flicked the tea-towel at the work surface, as if swatting a fly. He glanced up.

Susan was nodding, smiling, leaning forwards. "Yes?"

He coughed. "We've decided that we're going to be vegetarians."

Susan stared at him. Her mouth opened, then shut, and she recoiled, as if slapped.

"Vegetarians? As in, not eating meat?"

He nodded.

"Oh!"

It was quiet, only the sound of the clock in the parlour piercing the silence.

"Oh," said Susan again. She was sitting completely still, and Neil waited, hardly daring to breathe, waiting for the storm of words which he felt certain would come.

When Susan finally spoke, her tone was very controlled, overly calm, which Neil thought was worse than if she'd shouted.

"You should have told me before dinner," she said. "Then I could've given you both something different. Do you eat cheese?"

He nodded. "I do. But Kylie doesn't. She's a vegan."

"Of course she is," said Susan, her voice terse.

She stood up.

"I need to get on," she said, and left the room.

Neil sat there for a few minutes, not quite sure what to do. He went to the fridge and looked for something he could take for Kylie to eat when she got back from her walk – a sort of peace offering. There were eggs, she would probably eat those as they came from free-range chickens, but he didn't fancy staying in the kitchen long enough to cook them. He wanted to give his mother time to cool-off. In the end he cut some bread, and spread it with marmalade. He could pop out and buy some margarine tomorrow, but for now it was the best he could do.

Then he went back upstairs to continue unpacking. He moved the shoes to the corner of the bedroom, and put socks and pants into the top drawer. The speech was safely in his suit jacket pocket. He was ignoring it, trying not to think about it until he had to. It was all printed out; he hadn't needed to practice it because he'd kept it very simple. Even thinking about it made him nervous. He looked for his tie, but it didn't seem to be in the corner of the case where he'd put it. Neil frowned. Maybe Kylie had moved it, though he couldn't think why.

Neil emptied the case and then slid it on top of the wardrobe, out of the way. Then he lay on the bed with his laptop and started to scroll through emails. He'd stay out of the way for a bit, he decided, give everyone a chance to settle down.

***

Downstairs, Susan was in the parlour. They had always called the larger sitting room that, probably it had been named by Tom's great grandparents when they had lived in the house and run the farm. Her mother had told her that she should rename it, that historically 'parlours' were for laying-out dead people, and when commercial funeral parlours appeared, household parlours were called 'living rooms'. But Susan felt it fitted somehow, plus she had always tried to slot into the farm, to not cause ripples in a way of life that had existed for centuries. So 'parlour' it remained.

It was a sunny room during the day, with patio doors to the south-facing back garden. But outside was dark now, the trees and flowerbeds hidden, a draught of cold air seeping down the chimney. Susan looked at the window, saw the black night pressed against the glass, and felt suddenly cold. She dropped into the fat armchair in the corner – the chair where Uncle George would undoubtedly have sat if the funeral had been for any other family member – and she sighed. Susan realised she hadn't handled the conversation with Neil very well. But she had been so disappointed, had been so sure he was going to tell her they were expecting a baby, instead of this, this *insulting* news.

Susan shook her head, trying to make sense of it. Neil knew that they cared for the animals on the farm, that they ran their lives around making sure they were well fed, and happy, and secure. He knew that when it was time to send them to the abattoir, they did everything they could to make it painless and stress-free.

"It feels like he thinks we're cruel," she thought. Susan took a breath, and forced herself to think instead about the funeral, knowing deep inside that the real problem wasn't Neil, or Kylie.

Susan knew that she was tense, and was snapping at people more than she intended to. "It's because of Dad," she told herself, "every funeral has an echo of my first one, and however much I tell myself it's different, those same feelings start to rise up again, that feeling of despair, of helplessness." She sat back in the chair, the solid leather sides supporting her arms, and allowed herself to remember. She remembered being eight years old, wearing a black dress with a collar that itched. The memory flooded back in a rush: standing between her mother and Cassie, who was clutching her hand, squeezing her fingers too tightly, in a hand damp from tears. The coffin being carried slowly to the front, Susan following, carefully keeping step with her big sister, holding her breath, knowing that her father was inside, but not quite believing it and wanting to open the lid and look, but knowing that this was an impossible request and one that should never be voiced. She recalled the confusion of that day, the emptiness that remained with her whenever she thought of her father, remembered the feel of his hugs, the smell of his aftershave, the strength of his arms when he carried her.

"It was a long time ago," she thought, "but I still miss him, I still want to tell him things sometimes.

"But the worst thing," she thought, "is that sometimes I can't quite remember his face. I know from photos what he looked like, but in my real memories, I only have snippets, the odd glimpse or smell or feeling. I'm afraid I might be forgetting him, even though I loved him, I seem to be forgetting him..."

She straightened her back and swallowed. It *was* a long time ago, and her attachment to Uncle George had been tentative at best.

"This funeral will be entirely different," she told herself, pushing herself up from the chair. "I just need to protect Mum and Aunty Elsie, and make sure everyone has enough food after the service. It will all be fine."

Susan gathered the last of the ornaments from the top of the sideboard and carried them upstairs. They could stay in a heap in her bedroom until everyone had gone. She wasn't sure who would come back after the funeral, or what flowers there would be, but she had agreed with her mother that one of the arrangements from the church could be transported back to the house. It seemed a waste of money to leave them in the church, and it would be nice to have a display afterwards, for the funeral reception.

Then she went back to the kitchen, and opened the fridge. "Kylie hardly ate anything for dinner," she thought, "I'd better make her something to eat, she must be starving." Susan stared at the food, wondering what a vegan would eat.

"Not ham, not cheese, probably not eggs, not butter..." Susan stopped. "Not much, in fact. Ah well, it'll have to be a marmalade sandwich."

She pulled out the marmalade and went to find the bread.

***

Susan had left the kitchen when Edward returned, but Jack was in there, making a drink. Edward opened the latch softly, hoping to slip upstairs without being seen, but his brother was standing next to the kettle, waiting for it to boil.

"Making coffee?" said Edward, smiling, trying to appear casual.

Jack scowled at him. "What's going on with you and Josie then? I thought you were still living with Emily?"

Edward grinned, hoping to take some of the heat from Jack.

"Yeah, I am. I just thought, I'd walk Josie home, you know, being neighbourly and all that. Why? What's it got to do with you? You like her yourself or something?"

Jack flushed. "I just don't like how you treat people; they're not objects," he said. "And you know that Josie's always had a thing for you, seems a bit mean to start messing her around if you're not serious."

Edward decided the whole conversation was getting too serious.

"Changing the subject," he said, "how's your new job working out? Will you get a car do you think?"

Jack stared at him, his face became stony, and Edward wondered what he'd said wrong – he'd clearly touched a nerve. Jack chose to not answer, and turned back to the kettle, tipping the boiling water over coffee granules. The water gushed out, bubbling from the spout, spluttering over the work surface. He wiped the underside of his wet mug on the cloth and moved to the door.

"Kettle's hot if you want a drink," Jack said, and carried his coffee from the kitchen.

Edward puffed out his cheeks. "What, exactly, was that all about?" he wondered. Then he went to the kettle, and made himself a drink.

Chapter Four

The day of the funeral was grey, the sky an awning of thick clouds, and the world damp with a fine drizzle – which seemed appropriate to Susan, who was finding it quite hard to feel suitably subdued. The trouble was, she thought, as she pulled on her black tights, Uncle George had been very awkward when he was alive, so really, no one was sorry that he'd died, and having the boys at home made it feel more like Christmas than a sad occasion.

Susan walked to the wardrobe and found her black dress. She'd bought it years ago, but it was rarely worn so still looked smart. On the floor were her jeans and tee-shirt, worn earlier while she fed the poultry and topped up their water before taking the dogs for a run in the field. As she strung pearls around her neck, Susan noticed some straw in her hair. It was hard, she thought, to ever really forget the farm. She scooped her casual clothes from the floor and slung them over a chair. She could change back into them later, when she went to check the birds for the night.

Tom opened the door and sat on the bed. He was still in jeans, and Susan saw that he'd made a dirty mark on the cover. She frowned.

"You'd better get a move on," she said, "we need to leave soon."

"Yes, I know," Tom said, heaving himself to his feet and starting to strip. "But I'm worried about that heifer; she'll go into labour soon and I really ought to be there."

Susan turned to look at him. "Are there any signs that she's started?"

Tom shook his head. "No, but you never know with these things, I was hoping to stay around for these next few days, just in case."

"Well, it's only about an hour," said Susan, feeling cross. "Uncle George hardly chose when to die, I expect the cow will be fine for one hour. She probably won't do anything for several days." She frowned, knowing that if he could find a good enough excuse, Tom wouldn't go with her. But Susan had endured too many events on her own, too many occasions when the farm had taken precedence. She had always known when they went on holiday, that if he was called back, Tom would leave her and the boys to cope on their own. There were too many school plays, and concerts, and parents' evenings, when Susan had been the sole parent in attendance because of a lame cow or an ill calf. She might not have cared overly for Uncle George, she thought, as she drew a pencil across her eyebrows, but this was a family event and her husband should jolly well be there.

"And these are too tight," said Tom, struggling to fasten his black trousers, "they must've shrunk."

Susan was saved from answering by a bang on the door. It was Neil.

"Can I borrow a tie Dad?" he said. He glanced at Susan's face and added, "I definitely packed one, you can ask Kylie. But I've looked everywhere, emptied the whole case, and it's gone."

Tom grunted and went to his wardrobe. "I've only got one black one, and I'm wearing that," he said, looping the tie around his neck over his vest, as if worried his son might take it. "There's a navy one, will that do? Or dark grey?"

"It has elephants on it," said Neil.

"Navy then," said Tom, passing it to his son. "Though I expect George would've rather appreciated the elephants," he muttered.

"Thanks Dad," said Neil, and moved to the mirror to tie it. "Is Granny meeting us there?" he asked.

Susan noticed that his hands weren't quite steady, and it took him two attempts to tie the knot. She took a step towards him, smelt something rather unpleasant, and stepped back. She wondered if she should offer him some Imodium – nerves always went to Neil's stomach.

"Yes," said Susan, trying not to breathe, "her and Aunty Elsie will go together. Ben said he'd collect them." She glanced at the clock. "I hope he hasn't forgotten."

She went onto the landing and shouted towards Ben's door: "Ben! Are you ready? You ought to go and get Granny now."

Ben answered from where he was standing in the hall. "I'm going now Mum, you don't need to worry. I'm all grownup now, can tell the time and everything..."

"Well that's debatable!" came a shout from Edward's room. He emerged, tall and handsome in his dark suit, his fair hair combed back.

Susan smiled at him, thinking how nice he looked.

"Is that my tie?" said Neil from behind her.

"Nope," said Edward, moving quickly down the stairs before his brother could check the label. "Why, did you forget to bring one? Ask Dad, he's probably got a knitted one you could borrow."

Kylie appeared on the landing. She wore a short black dress and impossibly high heels. The dress was low cut and lacy and showed a lot of leg. Neil told her she looked beautiful, and moved to kiss her cheek. Susan thought she looked like a tart, and went back into her bedroom.

"Oh no, is that the best tie you could borrow? Is it polyester?" Susan heard, as she shut the door.

***

Ben slammed the front door behind him and walked to the car, jangling his mother's keys, looking forward to driving her car. As he passed the Land Rover, he noticed it was covered in thick brown mud. He'd heard his father muttering earlier about having to drag a tree that had fallen in the corner field, and he now understood the implications of that comment.

"That's going to cause a row later," Ben thought, wondering if he should give it a quick hose before he left. But he was already slightly late, and he was in his posh clothes now, he decided he'd leave it for his parents to sort out.

Ben drove to the next village and drew up outside his grandmother's house. All the curtains were shut, and he wondered if the two old ladies had overslept. He opened the gate, and walked up the garden path. The front door had an owl shaped knocker, and he gave three loud raps – loud enough, he hoped, to wake them if they were still in bed.

Almost immediately the door opened, and his grandmother glared at him.

"There's no need to make all that noise," she said, "you'll break the door down."

"Sorry," said Ben, "I thought you might've overslept. All the curtains are shut."

"Yes, well, that was Elsie's idea. She said it was a sign of respect, seeing as our George has died. I'm not sure George merited much respect myself, but Elsie's gone all sentimental. She might start crying in the car, so brace yourself."

Ben smiled at her. "Okay Gran. How are you – you feeling all right?"

She paused for a moment, as if considering. "Well, I'm not looking forward to this morning much," she admitted. "But George was ready to go, and he wasn't an easy man when he was alive."

His grandmother collected her handbag and gloves from the dresser by the door and called to her sister.

"Elsie! Ben's here; are you ready?"

Elsie emerged from the sitting room. "I just need to pop to the little girl's room," she said, "I won't keep you a minute."

"You've already been a hundred times," said her sister, raising her eyebrows, "we'll be in the car. Slam the front door when you come out.

"Honestly," she said, as she followed Ben to the car, "Elsie's driving me potty. We knew what time you were coming; I don't know why she has to wait until you're actually here before she gets herself ready."

Dot opened the car door and glanced at the front seat. The whole car smelt strongly of dogs, and there were hairs on the seat. Ben noticed, and began to sweep them off with his hand.

"Sorry Gran," he said, "I forgot everyone would be in smart clothes."

"Yes, well I don't suppose George would care a jot," she said, easing herself onto the seat. "In fact," she confided, when Ben had sat back in the driver's seat, "I'm a bit worried about this whole thing. George left very detailed instructions in his will – which I haven't seen – about how he wanted this done, and you know George. I don't at all trust that this is going to go well..."

Elsie appeared. She closed the front door and seemed to be walking particularly slowly down the front path. Ben wasn't sure if it was because she was dreading the funeral and hoping to delay, or if she was enjoying the power of making them wait for her. He supposed that at her age there were very few times when you could manipulate people, and if Gran had taken second place to George, Elsie was definitely below Gran in the pecking order. As she approached, Ben remembered that old people like a show of manners, and got up to open the door for her. Elsie nodded at him as she climbed in, which made him feel like a chauffeur. Eventually she was in the car, seat belt on (that took another half hour while Elsie debated whether it would crease her coat, and Ben told her he was not allowed to drive her unless she wore it) and finally they were off.

The service was to be held in Marksbridge Anglican Church. Ben didn't think Uncle George had ever actually attended, but it was the nearest church, and where he would be buried. Ben sometimes accompanied his mother to the Baptist chapel, but he knew where the Anglican church was, and it was easy enough to park in the line of cars against the church wall. There were not likely to be many mourners.

They walked along the path, stepping carefully as roots had pushed up over the years, causing lumps and bumps that were easy to trip over, the tarmac split open in places like unhealed scars. A few other people were drifting towards the door, but Ben only recognised Josie, the rest merged into the 'old person' category, barely distinguishable from each other with their grey curls and dark coats. People walked slowly, as if not wanting to be late yet also unwilling to sit in a dank church for longer than was necessary, in case someone spoke to them.

They were met at the door by the vicar, a diminutive figure with more grey curly hair, and a rather artificial smile. Standing next to the vicar was Aunt Cassie, speaking in a quiet urgent voice, so Ben gave her a smile and escaped into the church before she could kiss him. Funerals were funny things, you never knew what strange behaviours might emerge, and Ben felt that having deposited his relatives safely at the church door, his duty was done.

Ben walked down the aisle towards his family, feeling the height of the ceiling above him almost as a tangible weight that somehow cowed him into silence. His brothers were sitting at the front — a long line of black-clad shoulders. Ben sat next to Edward. Then, when the two elderly ladies arrived, there was a moment of reorganisation, as there wasn't room for all of them in the same row, and his mother said the boys should support their grandmother.

"Mum, you sit here," she whispered, standing up. "Tom, come back with me, to make room for Elsie."

They rearranged themselves, Ben sitting in the front row with his brothers, grandmother and Elsie, and his parents sitting behind with Kylie and Aunt Cassie. Ben wasn't quite sure why Kylie had joined his parents, perhaps she was trying to make amends. Or maybe she and Neil had had an argument.

It all seemed like a lot of fuss to Ben. He didn't think it made any difference at all, very few other people were likely to come. He was also nervous, having not yet managed to chat to either of his parents. They had both been tense, probably because of Neil and Kylie announcing they no longer ate meat. His father took this as a personal affront, a slight on his profession, as if blatantly accused of cruelty. His mother was simply using it as another reason to not like Kylie. But it all made his own situation much harder. Ben didn't feel he could tell them, not now, not when they were already smarting. He sighed, leaned back on the unwelcoming seat, and looked around. He could hear people, shuffling into place behind him, the click of heels on the stone floor. He turned to Edward.

"Do you think many people will come?" Ben whispered.

Edward didn't answer, because at that moment a smell wafted towards them, putrid and strong. The brothers' eyes met, and they grinned at each other.

"What died?" said Ben, wrinkling his nose.

"Probably not the best question to ask today," said Edward.

The absurdity of the conversation struck them suddenly, and they both began to giggle, their shoulders shaking in their suit jackets. They looked away from each other, at the floor, struggling to compose themselves.

"Perhaps it's him," said Edward, nodding towards the vicar who had appeared at the front of the church.

The vicar stood in front of the altar. He seemed nervous, and kept swallowing.

"Ladies and Gentlemen," he began. His voice was deep and melodic, almost as if he were chanting the words. "Ladies and Gentlemen, thank you all for coming today to pay respects to our brother, George Heath. Before we begin, I should like to explain that many aspects of today's service were decided in advance by George. We have done our best to accommodate his wishes, though some of his requests..." he paused, clearly not sure how to phrase his explanation. "Some of his requests were somewhat irregular...However, much of the music and order of service was decided in advance by George..."

The vicar stood up straighter, as if relieved that he had made his introduction and was now absolved from any blame. In a deep voice, he boomed:

"Welcome. Please be upstanding for the coffin."

The congregation rose. Behind the family were a smattering of colleagues and neighbours. Ben half turned to look, and thought there were probably about twenty people in total. He noticed his mother, who was watching her own mother and aunt, ready with tissues in case the arrival of the coffin should provoke a rush of emotion.

Everyone was tense, waiting for the music and sombre procession, Ben felt as if no one was breathing, everyone holding their breath, waiting for the coffin.

There was a click, as a CD player was turned on, a shuffle of feet from the rear doors as the pall bearers arranged themselves.

Ben turned back to the front, squared his shoulders, stared straight ahead, waiting.

Booming through the quiet church came the unexpected chords from a well-known pop song. The music was loud, the singer's voice clear. The congregation shuffled, as one after the other recognised the opening stanza, braced themselves for the chorus. Ben stared hard at the floor, not daring to look at his brothers, knowing his mother would be in agonies behind him.

The pall bearers were processing down the aisle, the coffin heavy on their shoulders, their faces contorted as they tried to look solemn, to pretend they were walking to some other, more appropriate music. One was shuffling, as if trying to keep step with the music.

"Come on, hurry up," thought Ben, knowing what was coming. "Please," he thought, "get to the front before the chorus."

Halfway down the aisle, and the song continued, the words and music building towards the chorus.

The pall bearers were nearing the table at the front, Ben could see them in the periphery of his vision. He looked up, stared ahead, still not trusting himself to look at his brothers, knowing they would all be standing, like him, as if statues.

"Hurry up, hurry up," willed Ben as the pall bearers began to shift the weight of the coffin, to move it from their shoulders to their hands, glancing at each other to ensure they were all in sync, all ready at the same time. As though there was anything at all dignified about their entrance. They seemed to Ben to be moving in slow motion. He couldn't breathe, as the music approached the refrain and then, clearly, defiantly, filling the church, was the line that Ben had been dreading, the words, from Rod Stewart's *Da Ya Think I'm Sexy*...telling the world that the singer was sexy, inviting them to take his body.

"As if," thought Ben, "anyone would have wanted to take Uncle George's body, even when he was alive."

It was too much. Ben felt Edward begin to shake beside him, glanced down the line to see Jack and Neil both quaking with silent giggles, and lost his own battle to remain sombre. The absurdity of Uncle George being described as sexy, the double meaning of offering his body – now a corpse – was too much. As the laughter bubbled up inside him, shaking his body inside his suit, Ben tried to remain upright, to keep silent, to stare ahead. It was the best he could manage.

The vicar's head was bowed, his expression hidden.

Everyone waited, as torturously, the song was played in its entirety, the pall bearers in their black coats and gloves standing to attention, heads bowed. Finally, it ended. With relief the congregation sat back in their seats, the pall bearers left, managing to maintain their decorum and walk sedately to the exit rather than following their inclination to flee at speed.

The vicar was back in position, ready to continue. The next few minutes were pleasantly mundane, a few words of condolence, a prayer of thanks for George's life (though there were conspicuously few "*amens*" said at the end) some liturgy. Then the vicar introduced one of "George's great-nephews" who had, "prepared a few words to help us remember George."

"Though," thought Ben, "that entrance had been all the reminding that any of us needed."

Neil had stood, and was walking to the lectern, pulling a sheet of paper from his pocket. Ben could see Kylie leaning forwards slightly, as if wanting to appear especially attentive. He settled back in his seat, and waited to hear what his brother would say.

Neil stood at the lectern, which was shaped like an eagle. He grasped hold of it with both hands. The eagle began to tremble, as though about to take flight. Neil cleared his throat, glanced at his notes, and coughed again. He glanced up, towards his brothers, and looked back down quickly. Ben grinned, knowing Neil had avoided looking at them.

"Good morning," said Neil, his voice cracking. He swallowed. He seemed to be staring very hard at his paper, not daring to look up. "I am honoured to be invited to say a few words about Uncle George. We all loved him, and he will be sadly missed."

Someone shuffled in the front row to Ben's left, but Neil did not look up. He continued:

"Uncle George was in many ways, different to the rest of the family. He loved to joke, and tended to be slightly loud at times. He was rather outspoken, but always honest. You knew you could trust him."

This did not quite tally with Ben's own recollection, and he looked with interest at his brother, wondering what he was going to say. Ben was glad he hadn't been asked to speak, and was happy to let Neil's words wash over him.

Neil was talking about George's past, his time living with his sisters. He seemed to have got into a nice flow, and Ben began to wonder how long Neil would speak for, his mind wandering to his own problems, the news he needed to share with his parents like a nagging itch in his mind.

"But not today," Ben told himself, "I can't tell them today. The funeral has given me another day's reprieve."

He sighed, and forced herself to concentrate, to listen to what Neil was saying.

"Uncle George loved to tell us tales from his time in the navy. Growing up, we heard many stories about his times in other countries, and we were always proud to have such a brave uncle. He was a very kind man —"

Ben heard someone snigger, and glanced around, feeling cross that someone was distracting his brother. Whilst he wouldn't mind if Neil messed up a bit, and actually it would be quite funny if he did, Ben didn't want anyone else to mess things up for Neil.

Neil had continued to speak, ignoring the disturbance, speaking slightly faster as he drew towards the end of his speech, "— he always was willing to help if someone had a problem. I feel that his advice has been a source of inspiration in my own life, and I'm sure that each of us here today, feel that life without Uncle John will be slightly harder."

"*John!*" thought Ben. "Neil said *John!* Did I miss something?"

Neil was speaking quickly now, the words running into each other, barely audible as he read the final part of his speech.

"So, we now remember —" Neil paused, as though choosing his words, "— our dear relative, and lay him to rest. Thank you."

Neil was already leaving the lectern as he finished speaking, folding the paper and hurrying back to the congregation. He kept his eyes low, not looking at his family. He ignored the seat he'd been in, and went to where Kylie was sitting, slunk into the seat next to her. She reached out, took his hand and he squeezed it.

"That was lovely," Ben heard her whisper.

"I got the name wrong..." Ben heard Neil mutter, followed by something about "downloaded the speech" and "no time to practise it properly." Ben grinned, understanding what had happened. He turned to Edward, who beamed back at him, a glint in his eye.

"No one noticed," Ben heard Kylie whisper. But they had, he thought to himself, they most certainly had.

The vicar was standing again. He announced a hymn: *"All Things Bright and Beautiful,"* — which Ben didn't feel was very suitable for a funeral, but was much more suitable than the music his uncle had chosen earlier.

The organ sounded, the tune swelling to fill the ancient church, a few people forcing the song out, their voices weak and unused to singing. Most people simply stood there, reading the words, moving their mouths, but not producing any volume. Everyone remained standing after the hymn for a final prayer, the words familiar and safe.

The vicar cleared his throat again, as if forcing himself to make another unwelcome announcement.

"In lieu of flowers, there will be a collection for the *Core Charity*, who work for the relief of constipation."

Someone giggled, but most people by now were resigned to being inflicted with Uncle George's warped sense of humour. Everyone stood, waiting for the pall bearers, glad the service had finished.

The distinctive music of *"I want to break free"* by the band *Queen* echoed through the church, and Uncle George's body was finally, loudly, removed from the church.

Chapter Five

It was with some relief that the congregation followed the coffin from the church. It had rained while they were inside, and the air was damp, as if the sky hadn't quite decided whether it had finished. There were puddles on the path, and water droplets clung to leaves and dripped from branches.

Susan held her mother's arm as they picked their way along the path, and then through the maze of graves to where Uncle George was to be buried. Their heels sank into the soft mud, which clung to their shoes and dirtied the grass. As they stood next to the hole, waiting for everyone to arrive, Susan watched the other mourners, interested to see who had come, wondering again who would come back to the farm for refreshments. Josie was there, walking with Edward, head bent low.

There were a few people who Susan didn't recognise – possibly George's neighbours, or friends from the club he had attended. There were a couple of younger women too – they might be workers from George's residential home; they looked the sort, with capable, no-nonsense faces, and practical hairstyles. They all filed towards the grave, each one nursing their own thoughts or daydreams. There was, thought Susan, something about a funeral that made you retreat inside yourself a little, to want to hide. Whether it was being faced with death, or simply due to the more mundane reason that you wanted everything to be 'right', to not offend, she wasn't sure. But she was glad she had a large bottle of whiskey to serve alongside the pot of tea. She felt everyone could do with some today.

The exception were two elderly ladies, who Susan noticed walking together, arm in arm, chatting as if on a day-out. They weren't smiling, and looked suitably sombre, but something about the way they walked, engrossed in conversation, stopping to look at flowers on other graves, pointing at headstones, made Susan feel that they were rather enjoying the occasion.

Most of the congregation had arrived, and Susan and her mother shuffled around slightly, to make room. People were speaking in whispers, snatches of conversation drifting to where Susan stood with her mother:

"Lovely speech, I thought, that was his great nephew you know, does something in the city..."

"I couldn't look at the vicar's face, I just couldn't..."

"More here than I thought, considering..."

The coffin was lowered on strips of cloth, into the earth, while more damp earth clung to their shoes. Although the grave was surrounded by green matting, there wasn't enough to stand on, and Susan, noticing, was glad her floors were tiled and easily cleaned – she didn't feel she could ask people to remove their shoes, not after a funeral.

The vicar said his final words, another prayer, another reminder that they had come from dust and would return to dust. The funeral director proffered a box of dirt so that Elsie and Dot could both take a handful and throw it into the grave.

"It's very clean-looking dirt," thought Susan, "as if the thought of coming from 'dust' and returning to 'dust' was only acceptable if it was sanitised in some way; we say the words, but we don't want to get our hands dirty."

Her thoughts were broken as the two women she had seen earlier, deep in conversation, jostled to the front of the group. One of them posed in front of the grave, looking serious, while the other lifted her phone and took a photo.

"I've seen everything now," muttered Tom.

"Perhaps she fancied him, and this was her last chance for a photo with them both in," said Edward, laughing.

Susan felt that laughing at the graveside was inappropriate, whoever happened to be in it.

"Come on Mum," she said, "we'll take you home for some tea.

"Though try not to notice the state of the car," she added, shooting a look at Tom, "I did my best."

***

Susan began to pour tea into china cups. Elsie was sitting next to her sister on the sofa, and the boys were milling around, offering plates of sandwiches and cakes. She had no idea where Tom was – probably checking that bred heifer again. Josie was helping Susan, taking the cups round to people and directing them towards the food. There was an open bottle of whiskey on the sideboard. An elderly woman appeared at her elbow, and Susan recognised her as the one who had taken the photograph at the graveside.

"Well, this is all lovely, isn't it?" she smiled up at Susan. "It's so kind of you to have everyone here, and such a lovely array of cakes. Did you make them all yourself? I do love homemade cakes."

Susan said she had, and offered her a cup of tea. The woman took a sip, holding the saucer in her other hand.

"And how are you feeling dear?" she asked, gazing up at Susan. "Were you very close to your uncle?"

"No, no, not really," said Susan, wondering if she should try to appear sad. She had no idea who this lady was, but she seemed very sweet natured, very caring. The woman reached out, and patted her arm.

"Well dear," the woman said, "make sure you don't forget to eat something yourself. I'm sure one of your lovely boys could take over here for a minute, give you a break."

"Yes, thank you," said Susan. "How did you know George?" she asked.

"I'm Nell," the woman said, as if that explained it. She put down her cup and saucer, gave Susan another pat, and moved away.

Susan watched as the woman left, walking towards Elsie. Nell sat next to Elsie, said a few words and squeezed her hand, offering a clean tissue as Elsie started to cry again. Then she rose, went over to where the two care-home workers were standing and started talking to them. Susan poured more tea, and her mother came for a cup.

"I'm glad that's over with," Dot said, blowing on the tea before she took a sip. "It was bad enough, though knowing George, it could've been even worse.

"The flowers were nice though," Dot added, looking towards the arrangement that Ben had transported as directed and placed on the sideboard. "George asked for them to be shaped like a cricket bat and balls, and I think the florist did a pretty good job. Not an easy thing to make flowers into, I'd have thought."

"Oh *that's* what they were meant to be!" said Susan. Then, when her mother looked up sharply, added, "I wasn't really sure. But yes, they are very pretty."

The door from the kitchen opened, and Tom sidled into the room, walking around the edge, as if hoping no one would notice he had only just appeared. Susan saw Nell go towards him, offering a plate and napkin, gesturing towards the cakes.

"Who's Nell?" Susan asked her mother.

Her mother raised her eyebrows and shook her head.

"Over there, look, talking to Tom."

"Oh, said her mother, "I have no idea. Possibly another of George's fancy women." Dot lowered her voice. "That lady there..." she said, nodding towards a tall thin woman who was balancing a tea-cup and plate in one hand while she smoothed her white curls, "that woman thinks she was George's girlfriend.

"And so does that one," she said, pointing to a chubby woman sitting next to Elsie and holding her hand. "I don't know whether or not to introduce them," Dot added with a grin.

"Best not," said Susan, and went to rescue Tom, who appeared to be trapped in a corner by Nell while she explained, in an intense voice, why it was important for the council to provide more litter bins in the park. As Susan approached, Nell smiled and moved away.

"Everything all right?" Susan asked Tom, her tone sharp.

"Yes, thanks, just went to check that heifer again, you know, just in case." Tom took his plate and looked at the cakes. "These all look good, you've worked hard for this, haven't you? Well done."

Susan saw him lift the paper napkin from the plate, and surreptitiously use it to rub at a patch on his suit trousers which looked suspiciously like mud. She decided to not comment, she had enough to worry about already today. Edward joined them at the cake table, followed by Neil.

"Ah, David, great speech," said Edward, looking up at his brother.

Jack overheard and moved over to join in. "Yes Peter, can't fault you on what you said, really moving it was."

Neil smiled, but didn't reply.

Susan watched the boys – "Though really they are men now," she reminded herself – as they loaded their plates with sandwiches. Jack and Edward were both teasing Neil, who looked resigned and wasn't bothering to defend himself. Susan knew they would tease him anyway, so ignoring them was probably best. She thought Neil looked much less strained now his speech was over, and thankfully he had stopped emitting those awful smells.

It was hot in the room, the small hearth billowing heat, the guests producing even more. Susan wondered if she should open a window, thought about the flies that would then come inside with the cool air, and decided not to. The heavy drapes were open, the misted windows showing the fading light of an autumn sky. There was a quiet hum of voices, people were tired, glad to sit and eat too much sugar, to add a dash of whiskey to their tea when they thought no one was looking. Their smart clothes looked crumpled now, the too tight waistbands beginning to dig uncomfortably, the stiff shirt collars itchy. People had pink cheeks and lazy eyes and their minds were numb, talking about nothing. Susan was ready for them to leave, and was glad when the first person came to thank her and ask for their coat. She turned to Jack, and asked him to collect it. They had thrown all the coats on one of the beds as people arrived, and Jack had agreed to be 'coat monitor'.

Within a few minutes, Jack returned with a heap of coats slung over one arm. People noticed and took it as a cue that they should leave. They each went to where Susan stood with her mother, thanked her, offered condolences, before collecting their coat.

Susan felt she was beginning to wilt. She leaned back, supporting her weight against the back of a sofa, and watched Jack as he handed out coats.

"He looks tired too," she thought absently, "his face looks grey. I'm sure he didn't look like that earlier, I hope he isn't going down with something."

"Thank you so much," Susan heard the tall, curly haired, lady say, as she collected her coat from the mound on Jack's arm.

"Yes, thank you all so much," said the shorter, chubbier lady, arriving to collect her coat at the same time. Then she added proprietorially, "I know George would have loved it. He liked his cakes."

"Well," frowned the tall curly haired woman, "I'm not sure about that. He told me that he was trying to cut down. But perhaps that wasn't common knowledge..."

"Oh, I would know if George had decided a thing like that!" declared her rival.

Tom stepped forwards, his face puzzled. He opened his mouth, but before he could speak, could ask how the women knew George, Susan called to him from across the room.

"Tom!" she said, slightly too loudly. They all turned to her. "Tom, please could you help Jack? I think he's struggling. I need to go to the kitchen, to collect a tray."

***

As Susan entered the kitchen, Edward and Josie jumped apart. They were both standing by the cooker, and Josie stared, red faced, at the floor. Edward smiled at her.

"Everything okay Mum?" he asked, completely unfazed.

Susan gave him a stern look. She hoped he wasn't messing around with Josie, she was a nice girl, but Susan had no illusions about her son. She knew Edward preferred 'pretty' to 'practical' and would leave Josie without a thought when his visit ended.

"People are leaving," she said, "and I need a tray to collect the empties.

"Could you go and help Jack with the coats?" she added, not wanting to leave them alone when she left.

"Sure, be right there," said Edward, not moving.

Josie was still staring at the floor. Susan frowned, and went back to her guests.

***

Later, when everyone had left and Susan was sitting by the remains of the fire with Neil and Ben, she told them about the two women. Susan giggled as she explained, saying how Tom had nearly caused a row, just when it was almost over.

The only light came from the fire, and it cast shadows that leapt around the room, like echoes of the people who had so recently stood there. Susan could feel it warming her cheeks as she chatted with her boys.

"They're all grown-up now," she thought, her heart swelling with emotion, "they barely need me anymore. It will all get easier from now on."

"How," Ben was saying, "did someone as awful as Uncle George manage to have *two* lovers?"

"I'm not sure that 'lovers' is the right description," said Neil. "And who was the old biddy called Nell? She came up to me at the grave, asked if she could have a lift here, then didn't stop talking the whole way here. Was she another one of his women?"

"Oh, I spoke to her too," said Ben. "I'm not sure that she actually knew George, if I'm honest. I think she just came for the tea. And at the end, when she thought no one was looking, I noticed her filling a plastic bag with left-over cakes. I didn't think you'd mind Mum, so I let her get on with it."

Susan wasn't really listening. She had flicked on the lamp next to her, and was going through the cards that had arrived, reading the messages of condolence, mostly from people who she didn't know. She would give them all to her mother when she saw her, and they could join the ones that had been sent directly to the two sisters. But these had been left on the sideboard by people who'd come to the funeral, and she'd decided to look through them. Suddenly, she giggled.

"Oh dear," she said, laughing again, "look at this."

Susan passed the card to Neil.

"What is it?" he said, confused, "Who's it from?"

"I think it must be the old people from his care home," said Susan, taking the card back from him. "Some of them must be blind, which is why they've written across the middle. But read the one in green pen. Do you think he was in a muddle about what the card was for? Or did he know Uncle George and was deciding to be truthful?" She giggled again, and passed it to Ben.

Ben began to read the messages aloud:

"So sorry for your loss.

"Thinking of you at this time.

"May God be with you.

"Many congratulations, Arthur x.

"Ah, see what you mean," said Ben, laughing. "Do you think Gran will be upset, should we keep this one back?"

"No," said Susan, "I think she'll laugh.

"Oh golly," she said, stretching her legs with a sigh, "I'm not sure I want to get old."

"Get?" said Ben, as he handed her the card.

"Oi!" she said, and went to put them in a pile in the kitchen. She would take them to the sisters in the week. For now, she was done.

Chapter Six

The day after the funeral, Susan woke to the sounds of the farm oozing through the window, harsh and insistent, impossible to ignore. Her eyes itched and her head was thick with sleep. She glared at the clock and forced herself from bed to make tea.

There were letters in the hall, and she picked them up on her way to the kitchen. There were two bills for Tom, a letter for Ben, and one for Neil. Susan went to put them on the mantlepiece, then in a fit of temper, went back into the hall and threw them onto the mat. Why should she pick up other people's mail? There was no reason why Tom and Ben couldn't pick up their own letters, and why the heck had Neil *still* not informed everyone that he'd moved out? Susan felt as if everyone relied on her to do all the chores they didn't fancy doing themselves, because it was easy for her, because she didn't have a life of her own...not one that mattered anyway.

She walked round the house, looking for evidence. It wasn't difficult. There was Ben's sweatshirt slung on the back of the chair. An empty cup left on the desk, boots that had been kicked off, the mud left on the floor for her to sweep up. Newspapers read and discarded, the pages scattered across the kitchen table for her to put in the recycling bin.

Susan went upstairs. The bathroom sinks were pock-marked, dried white spots scarring the surface where people hadn't bothered to swoosh them round after cleaning their teeth; there were empty toilet roll tubes waiting for her to throw them away, and a new roll balanced on the cistern, waiting for her to thread it onto the holder. As Susan passed the room which had been Neil's, and which he now shared with Kylie, she noticed the door was wide open. They'd told her they were going out early, wanted to get to Bluewater before hordes of shoppers arrived. The bed was a tangle of sheets, with damp towels, a hairdryer and a brush thrown on top. The floor was littered with shoes, old tissues, a magazine. It was like having teenagers in the house again.

Edward was also out, though she didn't know where he'd gone, she hoped it had nothing to do with Josie.

Ben's door was shut, a statement of his late night and not wanting to be disturbed. No help there then. Jack had left after the funeral, saying he needed to get back to work. Susan paused, her anger momentarily on pause as she thought about Jack – there was something wrong there, he was paler than usual, and some of his humour had felt a bit forced, as if he was playing a part. She sighed, shaking her head. Jack was a grown-up, she couldn't keep worrying about him.

Susan noticed a mark on the carpet, where someone had spilt a drink on their way to their bedroom, and her anger rushed back, heating her brain, making her want to hit out. She knew that when the family left to go back to their own flats, there would be dirty linen left on beds – no one would strip the bed when they left, and certainly to carry the washing downstairs, to possibly put it into the washing machine, was way beyond their ability.

"It's not fair," she said to the empty house. "I never offered to be the family's general servant. I never said I wanted to do all the jobs that they can't be bothered to do. I am worth more than this, and I'm not doing it."

Susan walked back into her bedroom and began to get dressed, pulling on clothes, any clothes – she didn't pause to consider what she should wear, simply pulling them from the chair piled with worn clothes and dragging them onto her body, in a hurry to get out, to be far from all the mess, all the thoughtlessness that her family had dumped on her. She shut the dogs into the utility room, deciding that they were just as bad as the family when it came to creating jobs for her to sort, and she left. It was as easy as that. She pulled on her coat and boots and left, marching to end of the path unseen and into the lane.

After stomping for a few minutes, she left the lane, climbing over the stile into the field that bordered the land that Trevor farmed. As she walked, Susan felt her mood lift, some of the tension unwound from her head, her breathing became more even and her shoulders less hunched. She began to notice the birdsong, the sunlight filtering through the grey clouds, the sweet tang of fermenting silage wafting through the moist air. The grass underfoot was damp, wetting her boots, but the mud was relatively firm, and Susan marched forwards, her lungs full of fresh air, her footsteps sure. She felt better, but she also wanted to stay out for longer.

Susan reached into her pocket, pulling out her phone. She would call Esther, see if she had time for an impromptu coffee. Esther was a good friend, and her boys were a similar age, so she would understand.

"Hello Esther? It's Susan. Oh yes, I always forget you can see that. How are you? I wondered if you had time for a coffee this morning? I've just stormed out of the house in a temper, and I don't feel like going back yet." Susan was shouting into the phone, the slight breeze taking her words and carrying them away, across the field. She pressed the phone close to her ear, closed her eyes, straining to hear.

"No, no, nothing important. Family stuff – you know...

"You can? Oh, that's great. No, no, that's fine, I can go shopping afterwards if I still feel I need to avoid everyone.

"Really nothing, I'll tell you when I see you. I'd just rather avoid them all for a bit than burst and tell them what I'm thinking. Better to calm down a bit first, I think. See you in a few minutes. Bye."

Susan smiled and slipped the phone back into her pocket. She returned home long enough to throw some food to the poultry, collect a smarter coat and her car keys, and to exchange the boots for shoes. No one was around, and she managed to leave again unseen. She would text Tom from the coffee shop. He would moan about the money, ask why she couldn't have invited Esther home, say it was five pounds they couldn't afford. But she didn't care. For once, she was going to put herself first. As she drove along the lane, she realised she was smiling, and leant down to switch on the radio.

***

Tom was in the barn when the text arrived. He grunted, reached for his phone, and swore. That was very bad timing, he wished Susan had popped out to tell him she was leaving. He needed her here.

Tom was looking at the heifer they'd decided to calf. She had a pinched nerve, and was refusing to stand. The cow looked at him, and Tom could read the pain in her eyes. He stood next to her, hypodermic needle in hand, watching her, hoping the painkiller he'd injected would help, while he considered his options. The heifer groaned, a guttural sigh of pain that filled the barn, seeming to echo from the cobweb-laced beams. Tom had spread fresh straw in the pen, and it smelt clean and warm.

The heifer was restless, regularly kicking towards her belly. Tom was pretty sure she would calve soon, he'd been checking her as often as time allowed, and yesterday evening the heifer's teats had filled, a sure sign she'd birth within a day. First thing this morning, Tom had dragged himself from bed, leaving Susan asleep, so he could check the heifer before he fed the cows. Now he was back, deciding that things were imminent, and that he'd probably need another pair of hands. Tom glanced at his phone again, considered using it to call the house, decided it was easier to run in. He had time. The calf was coming, but not this very minute.

Tom raced across the yard and flung open the kitchen door.

"Ben!" he shouted, "Ben, are you here?"

He heard something stir upstairs, but no reply. Typical. Ben was probably still in bed, hoping that if he didn't respond, his father would give up and ask someone else or do it himself. Some things never changed. Tom ran into the hall and shouted up the stairs.

"Ben! Ben, wake up boy. I need you."

There was a thump, a pause, a sleepy reply.

"Uh, Dad? I'm asleep. What's the matter?"

"I need you. Now! In the barn. My heifer's calving, and your mother's disappeared. Can you come? Now? There's not much time."

There was a mutter, which was probably swearing, and another thump. Tom tapped impatiently on the wooden bannister rail, his tension released through the steady tapping of his nails on wood. He could feel time ticking past, the seconds stretching before him as Tom waited for Ben to answer.

Then the door opened, and Ben's voice could be heard more clearly. Ben spoke slowly, as if forcing himself to be polite:

"Right, okay Dad. Give me a minute to get dressed and I'll be down."

"Might not be time for that. Come as quick as you can," called Tom as he began to run back along the hallway – then stopped, ran back to the bottom of the stairs: "And don't have a shower. There isn't time!"

Upstairs, Ben groaned. Life was always like this on the farm. The animals and the weather and the crops dictated the rest of life. You could never decide to have a lie-in, never get completely wasted and hope to nurse a hangover the following day. Ben reached for his jeans and pants, pulled them on, grimacing – horrible not being able to shower first. But if Ben delayed, his father would know, and if the calf died, it would be Ben's fault, even if it would have died anyway.

When Ben was dressed, he trudged across the yard, glad he had worn a thick jumper. Dark clouds were scurrying across the grey sky, and in the yard, puddles filled the dips where the concrete had worn away. Ben knew his father had high hopes for this calf, hoped to show it at the farm show in August; he knew his father would have already spent money on the venture, so losing the calf would be a financial loss. Ben had never helped at a birth before, though he knew the theory – they all did, as his father had talked about little else recently. They usually bought in the calves, so Ben found he was quite excited, now he'd recovered from being woken so suddenly. He went into the barn. The heifer was moaning, kicking at her belly, her eyes looking madly in all directions – Ben wondered if the heifer would survive.

"She going to be okay?" he asked his father.

Tom grunted. "She will be unless we're unlucky," he said.

"They always look a bit frantic when they're in labour," Tom continued, plonking a bucket of soapy water in the corner; suds slithered down the outside and steam rose from the surface. "It's because in the wild they need to watch for predators all the time. A newborn calf has no protection, and it can make the herd vulnerable. It's why she'll try to eat the placenta as soon as she can too, so the scent doesn't attract lions.

"—Not," Tom added, "that Kent is particularly well known for its lions. But she doesn't know that."

"You planning on torturing her if it goes wrong?" said Ben, glancing towards his father's feet, staring at the items, some of which looked as if they had been borrowed from the dungeons at the Tower of London. The equipment was spread out on the straw. There was rope, and gloves, and a squeezy bottle of disinfectant. A dark bottle of iodine sat on a heap of old towels, and a box with a lock, which Ben knew contained medicines bought from the vet for an extortionate price. There were tubes, and a suction bulb, and a battered hair dryer and even an old shovel handle. Ben didn't like to think too much about what they could all be used for. He wasn't squeamish, but some things were best not thought about in advance.

Tom grinned. "I'm hoping we won't need most of it, but best to be prepared."

A complicated device of chains and pulleys caught Ben's eye, and he stared at it.

"What's that?" Ben asked, not sure if he really wanted to know.

"A ratchet," said his father, glancing at Ben. "We can try using ropes to pull out the calf if it gets stuck, but that can get tiring, so I've borrowed a ratchet from Trevor, just in case."

Ben sensed his father was only half listening, he was staring at the heifer, considering what to do.

"How big are your hands now?" asked Tom, holding up his own for comparison. Ben placed his palms against his father's, glad to see that his own were much bigger. He had a feeling that this would absolve him from the worst of the jobs that might become necessary.

"I do wish your mother was here," said Tom frowning.

The cow at their feet was straining, and Tom knelt next to her, ran his hand over her flank.

"All right old girl," he said, calming her with his voice, "soon be over."

"Is that normal?" asked Ben, as a gush of amber fluid flooded the pen. It had a faint metallic smell, and Ben was glad he was wearing boots. His father's jeans were soaked.

"Yep, that's her waters," said Tom, stooping nearer to the ground, staring at where the liquid had pooled in a dip. "Is it clear enough?" he muttered, "This is our first clue if something is wrong. We're meant to check it's not too dark, doesn't smell wrong..."

Ben shrugged. He hoped his father was thinking aloud, and not actually asking for an opinion. Ben had absolutely no idea what any of this was meant to look or smell like. He harboured a suspicion that neither did his father.

After an age – after his father had explained in great detail everything that might go wrong – after Ben had gone back into the house to make them both coffee (though still not a shower, he hadn't dared to suggest there might be time for that, even though there had been time for about a hundred showers) – the heifer began to strain in earnest. Ben watched, fascinated, as the bulge was forced along her swollen abdomen. The cow was silent, her body arching as she strained, her mouth dripping frothy foam. Within minutes the feet, covered in slime, appeared under her tail.

Ben watched as his father checked again.

"Feet first, that's good," Tom muttered. "We want it to dive out, front feet followed by head. The hips are the biggest part, so we need to start timing her. If the calf isn't out in an hour, we'll need to pull."

Ben checked his watch. Pulling sounded unpleasant.

They waited. The heifer lay there, sometimes panting, sometimes straining. Ben could hear the cows in the big barn as they jostled each other, the chickens in the yard, the occasional car as it sped along the lane. At one point a dog appeared, looking for Tom, who told Ben he should've shut the door, the last thing they needed was dog germs infecting everything.

"I think I'd better get scrubbed up," said Tom, as the hour neared its end. He took off his coat and hung it on the fence around the enclosure, and began to roll up his sleeves. "I'd hoped this wouldn't be necessary," he told Ben, "though I've been keeping my nails short, just in case."

Ben didn't want to consider the implications of that statement. He watched as his father prepared to wash his arms in the bucket of disinfected water – which would now be cold.

Just as his father was about to plunge his arms into the tepid water, there was a sound. The heifer gave a final heave, her back arching slightly, and the calf slid out, onto the wet hay, followed by a gush of yellow liquid. The heifer half turned towards it, then stopped. Ben guessed the pain in her back still bothered her, and she was tired. She looked at her calf for a long minute, then lay back.

Tom was already moving forwards. "We need to start it breathing."

Ben watched his father rub away the slime from the amnion sac, ensuring the nose was free. Tom shook his hand, drips of slime falling onto the hay, then he wiped them on his overalls.

Ben was ready with straw to tickle its nostrils, but it wasn't necessary, the calf was strong, it shook its head, droplets of fluid flying from the nose, and started breathing freely.

"It's a bull," Tom said, and Ben could tell he was pleased.

Ben moved closer, then stepped back hurriedly as a gush of blood and liquid was expelled from the mother. He wrinkled his nose, knowing that he would never be accustomed to the smells and gore that came with keeping animals.

With a final shudder the placenta was expelled, the smell strong and metallic, the heifer began to writhe, struggling to reach it, every instinct tuned to eating it before the odour put her calf in danger. Straw and blood and gore were scattered, as the heifer struggled, her frantic kicking achieving little other than nearly wounding both the calf and Tom. The umbilical cord broke, a long snake trailing from the calf. Tom moved out of range, taking the calf with him. He knelt, and used both hands to pull apart the cord attached to the calf, so just a couple of inches remained.

"Quick, pass me the iodine," Tom directed Ben.

Ben turned to where his father had laid out his equipment and found the purple bottle. Tom took it with bloodied hands, and dipped the cord stub into the bottle, disinfecting it.

"The iodine will also act as an astringent," Tom told Ben, "helps the navel stump to dry up. We might need to dip it again if the calf lies on wet hay or gets dirty."

Ben took the smeary bottle from his father, who moved to pick up the calf, struggling to move the slimy burden round to its mother's head.

"Come on, come on, lick your baby to dry it off and warm it up," said Tom.

Ben and his father both waited, hoping that instinct would take over and the mother would lick her calf. She didn't.

Tom tried holding his hands, covered in calf slime and smelling of the calf, close to the mother's nose. But she turned her head away, refusing to be persuaded.

Ben could see the heifer was tired, and in pain, and she wasn't moving.

The calf was standing, but it was shivering, all the enthusiasm it had shown after birth was seeping away, and Ben realised that this little bundle of life had no reserves, that it was cold and damp, abandoned by its mother. Ben jumped, as Tom sped into action, grabbing the towels, scattering equipment.

"Quick! We need to get him dry," Tom said. "Grab the hairdryer and plug it into that extension lead, then bring it over here so I can warm him up a bit. And put on the red lamp. And hurry up, don't just stand there."

Ben hurried to do as directed, but when he turned on the dryer, something popped and there was a smell of burning. No heat.

"It's broken Dad," he said.

Ben looked across to where Tom was vigorously rubbing the calf, trying to make the blood circulate, drying the fur.

"You take over here," Tom said, standing, throwing the towel towards Ben, already moving away. "I know where your mother keeps hers...

"We need the heat," Ben heard, as his father rushed from the barn.

Ben knelt next to the calf, and continued to rub the damp fur, feeling the bony legs, the hard head. The towel was old and rough, worn thin by repeated washing, the colours – faded now – were gradually obliterated by the dirt and slime from the calf.

"All right boy," Ben whispered, "you'll feel better in a minute." He felt the calf tremble beneath his hands and rubbed harder, faster, trying to cover the whole body, increasing the friction, drying the fur, stimulating heat. He rubbed over the hard head, the knobbly ribs, the fat knees. "Hurry up Dad..."

***

Tom was hurrying. He raced into the kitchen, through the hall, and up the stairs two at a time, all the time shouting for Susan.

But she wasn't back. He was pretty sure he knew where she kept her hairdryer, not that she used it very often. It was kept in her drawer, below the one where she kept her socks and tights.

Tom reached the top of the stairs and was about to run across the landing, when, in the corner of his eye, he saw that Neil's door was open. There, on the bed, was a hairdryer. He'd seen Kylie using it yesterday, otherwise he wouldn't have even known it *was* a hairdryer, it looked like something from a science-fiction film. But as long as it worked, produced hot air, that was all that mattered.

Tom didn't even think. In one movement he'd entered the room, grabbed the dryer, and was leaping back down the stairs, the lead dangling behind him, the plug bumping down the stairs like an enthusiastic puppy. He dashed across the yard, charged into the barn, snatched the plug from the socket and replaced it with the one from the new hairdryer.

"Here we are," Tom said, breathing heavily, "this should do the trick."

"What is it?" said Ben. "Oh, I see. A space-age dryer!"

Tom slid the switch to *on*, and directed the warm air over the calf. The appliance was light but surprisingly efficient. The warm air soothed and dried the calf, and after its initial shock at the noise, the calf stood, as if enjoying the warmth. Ben continued to rub the legs, and the head, and the back. Tom waved the hairdryer gently across the body, careful not to burn the animal, using his other hand to ruffle the fur and comfort the new-born. Before long, the calf had stopped shivering, and was looking for milk.

"Here, you keep going with this," said Tom, passing the dryer – now covered in bloody fingerprints – to Ben.

Tom knelt, and extracted some milk from the mother, then pushed the calf's nose towards her. Hardly daring to breathe, he watched as the infant latched on, its tail wagging as the milk flowed into its belly.

"Well, at least the heifer got that bit right," Tom said, relieved. He went to get some clean straw, spreading it across the damp dirty bedding.

For a while, Tom and Ben sat and watched. The calf fed, then nestled next to its mother on the warm straw. The heifer turned her head, her long grey tongue stretched out, and licked the calf. It was a peaceful scene, and Tom felt very contented, as if the mood of mother and calf had infected the air around them. There was something intrinsically *right* about the scene.

***

It was much later, when Susan was serving dinner, that Kylie mentioned the hairdryer. Susan had enjoyed her day, her bad mood of the morning forgotten. She'd met Esther and had a good chat over coffee, then wandered around the shops and bought vegetables and pasta for dinner. Susan didn't know much about vegetarian cooking, but she thought if she roasted some peppers and courgettes, they could eat those in place of the chicken the rest of them were having. She picked up a jar of onion gravy mix too, realising that her gravy made with meat juices would also be deemed unacceptable.

Susan had arrived home, and been ushered to the barn, shown the calf and told, in great detail, the story of its birth. Ben was smiling, chipping in with comments, explaining what had happened. Tom had been curt, never actually voicing that he thought she *should* have been there, but letting it be known that although everything was fine, and Ben had done his best, and the calf had survived, it *might* have been a different story. He had *thought* that Susan would've been there. Especially with him giving up a day's work yesterday to be at her uncle's funeral and everything...

Susan admired the calf and decided not to respond to the barbs. She knew that Tom was mainly angry with Neil, that the decision to be a vegetarian felt personal, a criticism of his way of life. So she ignored the sarcasm, and the moment had passed, and the day had been peaceful.

Now the family were at the table, the conversation muted while they ate. They were all there, and Susan had just carried the last dish to the table, when Kylie mentioned the hairdryer.

"Has anyone seen it?" Kylie asked, slicing through a courgette. "I assumed at first it must've slipped behind something, and I know it's a daft question, but I've looked everywhere in our room, and I just can't find it. Has anyone borrowed it? You should've asked first really, because it's new, and it's the latest model, rather expensive. But the box is still

59

there, which is why I'm assuming one of you borrowed it? Like I said, you should've asked first."

"It's red," added Neil.

Tom's chair scraped the floor as he rose from the table.

"I need to check that calf," he said and walked from the kitchen.

Ben was staring hard at his plate.

The rest of the family looked up from their food and stared at Kylie, as though surprised by the question.

"Er, which one of us do you think might have borrowed it Kylie," asked Edward, laughing. "Honestly, look at us, do we look like we dry our hair with fancy hairdryers? Even Mum goes for the 'windswept' look, don't you Mum?"

But Susan didn't answer. "Oh no," she was thinking, "surely not..."

Chapter Seven

Susan stuck her head into the doorway and shouted: "Ben! Are you ready? Give me ten minutes and I'll meet you in the yard." Her voice echoed along the Victorian passageways, and she heard a thump from upstairs. That would have to do, she was too busy to wait until Ben bothered to answer. She whistled for the dogs and went back into the yard.

It was almost two weeks after the funeral, and the new calves were being delivered, thirty of them. They jostled as they ran down the ramp, all bumping shoulders and kicking legs, little black heads with gleaming eyes. Susan whistled again, directing the dogs so they herded the calves towards the barn, where Tom was waiting with the pens. If she wasn't careful, the dogs would follow their natural instinct and chase the calves towards her, their atavistic natures wanting to round up food for the leader of the pack to kill. She didn't want to be stampeded, she wanted to see them safely in the prepared pens, so she could get on with the rest of her day.

With a minimum of shouting and waving, they managed to get the calves into the barn. It was always best to try and keep things calm, too much noise would scare them, and even young calves were big animals to control if they were frightened. The farm had a good routine, with strategically placed barriers, so the animals were directed efficiently into the pens. Tom and Susan separated the calves, four to each pen, and checked the metal fencing was secure. The calves watched with their big eyes.

"Poor little mites," Susan thought, "they were only born a week ago."

Susan reached out, and touched one of the hard black heads. A long grey tongue slid out to find her hand, sliding roughly along her arm.

"Not yet," she said. "You need to settle down a bit first, then we'll get you some milk."

Susan watched the calves, wondering which ones would be the bullies, which would need nurturing. Some of the calves were skittish after their journey, kicking sideways and testing the bars of the fence, which clanged in protest.

The barn was filled with life now, the heavy smell of the calves mixing with the sweet smell from the stored crops and the dry, dusty, smell from the barley crusher. The calves' stamping was muted by layers of straw, their snorts and bellows lost in the cavernous barn; only the rattle of the fences was heard. Above them, secreted in the hay bales, green eyes watched. Susan stared back. The cats were feral, refusing to be touched, even if injured, keeping their distance but often seen, watching. They had knowing eyes, full of hatred and suspicion. Susan fed them, because they kept the rats away, but she didn't like them.

Susan turned back to the calves. She knew they would calm down quickly enough, they were generally placid animals, and it was rare that they had a problem. Tom had bought calves from the supplier before, knowing they'd be decent stock, worth the investment. He liked to buy stock all from the same farm, there was less risk of cross infection, they would all be used to the same environment.

Susan glanced at her watch. She ought to go really. Ben had announced that he "needed to talk", and it was always easier to have heavy discussions outside, in the open air. It helped to take away some of the tension, made whatever "needed to be said" less personal somehow, easier to cope with. Susan didn't know what the latest announcement was, probably a girlfriend, which would be good – he'd taken his time there. But it could easily be something else, some disaster at uni, something stupid he'd done when he was drunk. Susan could tell from Ben's voice that he thought it was serious, even if she probably wouldn't. By the time you got to her age, not much seemed serious in life, there weren't many things that couldn't be sorted out. Ben had waited until now, when he was about to return to university for the remainder of the term, so it couldn't be urgent, whatever it was.

Susan took another look at the calves, with their too long legs, and turned back to the house. She needed to clean out the chickens, and she could do that and listen to whatever it was that Ben wanted to tell her; he could help lug the bale of straw into place for her. It wasn't an activity which required much thought, they could easily discuss whatever was wrong while they worked.

She left Tom in the barn. He would check the ear-tags on each calf, matching it to the corresponding passport, checking everything was correct before he wrote the precious cheque.

The farm had its own rhythm, a steady progression through the seasons. But it was always exciting when the new stock arrived, and Susan was smiling as she walked back to the house.

Chapter Eight

They were in the chicken coop, when he told her. They had chased all the hens into the yard, and Susan was sweeping the floor with a stiff broom, making a pile of dried poo and old husks and dirt. Ben was in one corner, scraping the hard dirt from under the perch into a bucket.

"Mum," he said, "I'm gay."

It was his voice, as much as the words, which caused Susan to stop. Everything stopped. The whole world, for a second, seemed to pause, to hold its breath, to wait until the words made sense. Susan stood there, the broom in one hand, the other groping for the side of the chicken mesh, as if she needed something to steady herself.

She didn't reply. Couldn't, not immediately. Her face was strangely mobile, her mouth working but not speaking, her eyes twitching but not seeing. Then she got her face back under control, managed to speak.

"Oh," she said at last, though it was probably only a second later, a second when her world had rearranged itself and settled back into a position which looked identical but where the foundations had shifted slightly.

"Oh, I didn't know. How long –"

But how long *what*? How long had he known for? How long had he decided for? Did people 'decide' something like this? Susan looked down, aware that her face was still moving, each muscle twitching, betraying her shock. She didn't seem able to control it, and her voice, when she spoke, sounded odd, hollow somehow, as if she had a sore throat. Only the words seemed to be still in her control, and Susan realised she must choose them carefully, that the wrong response, sentences said carelessly, might hurt her child. This conversation, she knew, was significant, would be remembered.

"Well, I think I've always known I liked blokes, not girls," said Ben slowly, as if trying to understand her question. Susan could feel him staring at her, trying to gauge her reaction. He stood next to the perch, trowel in one hand, bucket in the other; watching her. "But I didn't know if you knew, as we've never talked about it. And I've met someone, who I think might be special, so I thought I should tell you. I told people at uni when I first arrived, so a couple of years ago, it seemed silly not to."

"Two years? Gosh, that's a long time. So, all your friends know?"

"At uni? Yes."

"Two years," Susan was thinking, "two years is an age. And other people knew. Other people knew before me, and presumably knew that I didn't know." Susan could imagine the conversations, the whispered questions, the oft repeated: 'Do your parents know yet?' And she didn't, she hadn't. She was, she felt, one of the last to know.

Susan managed to pull herself back, to force the sensible mother back to the front. Did it matter when anyone else knew? This wasn't a competition; she wasn't a rival to his friends. She was his mother, and he was telling her now, and that was what mattered. She wasn't hearing this second hand from a lipsticked gossip in the hairdressers (though she could have done, she realised – he had taken a risk by not telling her sooner. And how that gossip would've loved to tell Susan, would have relished watching her face as the news sunk in. There is little in life as satisfying as seeing other people's children fail at something.)

No, Ben was telling her now, and she must listen. She must quell the bees' nest of emotions that was circling in her chest, silence the myriad of questions hovering in her mind, and listen. Susan owed him that much. Telling her wasn't easy, she could see. His body was stiff, hunched at the shoulders, and his voice was different, she could hear the tension. She knew this boy, he was part of her, and she must be very careful or she would cut him, hurt him in a way that might not heal. There would be time to discuss, to question, to probe – but later. For now, she must listen.

Susan continued to push the broom along the floor of the coop, moving debris to one corner. She could feel Ben's eyes, boring into her, trying to read her thoughts. She coughed, and glanced up, nodded at the heap of mess.

"Can you get rid of that lot too?" she said, managing to sound normal. "Tell me about this boy you've met then – is he a student too?"

Ben moved next to her, and began to scrape her pile into the bucket, talking while he worked. He told her they had met on an online dating app (that was another thorn, another burden to think about later – she didn't like to think of one of her children using such things). He told her the boy's name was Kevin and he was a chemist. Susan heard the pride in her son's voice as he described his friend, told her how clever he was, what a good sense of humour he had, how good he was with animals.

Susan didn't want to listen. She didn't want to accept this new boy, she wanted to blame him. Everything inside of her wanted to scream at her son, to tell him to stop, this wasn't what she wanted for him, he had been led astray by this other boy, it wasn't him. But she didn't. She said very little. Because she had never been here before, she didn't know what the rules were, or even what was right or wrong.

The right or wrong issue bothered her. Susan had been brought up in the church, taught as a child that homosexuality (there, she had said it) was wrong. But recently, she had been unsure, had listened to her more liberal children and their friends, had tried to study what the Bible actually said, test the teaching a little. And she wasn't sure. She didn't know if the context of when the Bible was first written mattered, if perhaps the words shouldn't be taken literally. Or if her son was wrong.

Ben carried the full bucket outside, to the compost heap behind the big barn. Susan used the time to swallow, to take some breaths of air, to try to compose her face into the same lines and expressions it usually sat in.

"I'd like you to meet him," said Ben, as he returned for another load of muck. "I'll bring the hay in now, shall I?" he said, when the ground was clean.

Susan nodded, not sure which question she was agreeing to and glad, for the moment, of the ambiguity.

"Have you told Dad?" she asked. "And the others?"

The boys, Susan knew, would support Ben; young people viewed the gay issue so differently to her generation, where it was still something noteworthy.

Except for Neil. Susan wasn't so sure what Neil would say. Neil and Ben were the only two of her boys who attended church regularly, and Neil was very involved with his house-church, which leant towards traditional views sometimes. Susan wasn't sure if he would take the usual church stance and say that homosexuality was wrong. She hoped not. Susan wasn't sure of her own views, but she didn't want anyone else to think it was wrong – which she knew made no sense, but she would think about that later. She would think about everything later.

"I've already mentioned it to Jack – he said he'd always sort of known. I expect he's told Ed, I'm not sure. I'll tell Dad later; I wanted to tell you first," said Ben, snapping the string around the hay. The dried grass floated outwards, covering the floor of the coop and sticking to Ben's jumper, even rising up, clinging to his hair. He grabbed the pitchfork and began to fling hay through the air, tossing it into every corner, heaping it into the crate that served as a nesting box. It smelt dry and clean.

Susan nodded, and picked up the metal drinker, going to the tap to rinse and refill it. The boys invariably told her their news first, they always had. Perhaps she was easier to tell, served as a practice run before they told their father. Susan noted that he hadn't told Neil yet, perhaps Ben too was wary of his views. She heaved the full drinker back into position on the upturned bowl. It was slightly raised, so when the chickens kicked the hay and dust around, which they always did, the worst of it would stay out of their water pot.

Ben filled the feeder with fresh pellets, hung it back on its string, so the chickens could reach it but not too many mice would be able to share it. Then they opened the door, watched as the hens wandered back inside, keen to explore their cleaned cage, to kick the hay into new drifts, to scratch the earth beneath in search of bugs.

They went back to the house, the dogs joining them, a swirl of fur around their heels. Susan let the dogs into the garden and went into the kitchen.

"Tea?" she said.

"Yeah, thanks Mum," said Ben.

Susan turned on the kettle, then escaped upstairs while it boiled.

Her own feelings were a mess, and she was still on the brink of tears. But she didn't want to dissolve, not yet. She wanted to be strong for her son.

Susan went into her room and closed the door. Sinking to the floor, she searched for God, her anchor. She couldn't pray, her feelings were too muddled. But she could lift that muddle Heavenward, she could seek some support.

"I can't deal with this," she thought, "I don't even know what is right and wrong. I don't know which way to direct Ben, whether to encourage him to leave this relationship, or to support him. God, I need you."

Her feelings settled. A calm, beyond anything she could understand, flooded through her. And Susan knew, with that flood of peace, that knowing what was right didn't matter. Not today. The choice wasn't hers to make, it wasn't her who was choosing a homosexual lifestyle, it was Ben. He was an adult, and she was his mother. What was important, for her, right now, was that she was a good mother. What mattered was that she showed him her love and support, that she kept her muddled emotions under control until it was time to release them. This was not going to be over quickly, they, as a family, had embarked on a journey together. Later, things would become clear. Later, she would understand and know how to behave. But today, she just had to be his mother and love him. And that was easy.

Susan rose from the worn carpet, and went to make the tea.

Chapter Nine

Susan cooked fajitas for dinner. The meat was from their own chickens (a vicious cockerel culled to preserve the peace of the flock) so it didn't need much cooking. Susan sprinkled it with cumin and oregano, added lime juice and olive oil, then pushed a garlic clove through the press. While it marinated she chopped onions and peppers and sliced through mushrooms. It was all fried in a large pan as soon as she heard Tom slam the front door and shout that he was home.

As Susan lit the hob beneath the pan, she heard Ben's heavy steps going into the hall. She couldn't hear what they said, but imagined he asked "for a word" because one of the dogs, Molly, came back into the kitchen. Molly wasn't allowed into the parlour, and the parlour was where family members went "for a word," right back to the days when they were tiny and it was necessary to discover exactly *which* person had thought it was a good idea to push a slipper down the lavatory. Molly slunk over to the cooker, pushing her black nose into Susan's legs.

"I'm cooking, off you go," she said. The dog circled the kitchen before climbing into her basket in the corner. Susan began to prepare salad and to warm up flour tortillas.

When Tom appeared, she could see that he knew. He didn't say anything, not while Ben was there, but the lines were more deeply etched on his face, and his voice was slightly too loud, too forced, as he pretended everything was fine. Tom told her he'd fed the calves, he would check on them after dinner, but they seemed okay, their agent Tony had found him another good herd.

"This is good," said Tom, through a mouthful of chicken, nodding at her. "Can't understand why anyone would refuse to eat something that's clearly intended to be eaten..."

None of them ate much. Susan thought it was like eating sawdust, though she forced some food down. They talked about nothing, the weather, the new road, when the other boys were likely to visit again. She told Tom that the hay bale by the big field needed replacing.

"I'll get Steve to see to it in the morning," he said. "It's worth knowing, because I've heard there are some travellers out by Basset way. Don't want them round here."

They were careful to block all the gates with fat plastic sacks of hay, too heavy to be moved without the strength of lifting gear. It stopped people going into the fields when they shouldn't – kids wanting to race on bikes, joyriders wanting to burn out a stolen car, and travellers.

"Not that I've got anything against travellers," said Tom with a mouth full of chicken, "as long as they keep travelling. It's when they decide to stay that they cause trouble, having bonfires and leaving litter that the animals choke on."

Susan watched as Tom reached for the cheese and added more to his fajita. She noticed that he looked tired, the grey shadows under his eyes more pronounced. Then he began to talk about the travellers, a tirade that both Susan and Ben had heard many times before, but Susan knew it was safer than discussing problems closer to home. It gave them all bit of a break, let things settle; there was something comforting about hearing Tom voice his views on travellers again, something safe about a topic they all knew, all knew where it was going.

"I've always said, each to his own – if they want to live in a van and opt out of society, that's their choice. But they can't dump on the rest of us. They seem to want to live like the nomads in the desert, taking resources as they go and moving on when they need new ones, leaving all their rubbish behind. It just doesn't work in a country as crowded as this one. We don't want their litter blowing around, and why should we pay to clean up after them when they don't pay tax? In fact, why are they even allowed to use our roads if they don't pay tax?

"I don't know, too many people today think they're owed. They think they can live how they like, and someone else will pick up the bill. Well, it doesn't work like that. People need a bit more accountability.

"It's like the deficit," Tom said, moving on to his next oft-repeated subject. "People today think they can improve schools and hospitals, and make some future generation pay for it. All this debt, putting stuff on the never-never, bound to end in tears.

"When I buy something on hire-purchase – which as you know, I have to because the farm doesn't make enough to buy machinery outright when I need it – but when I do, it's set up, right at the start, exactly when I'll finish paying it off. I don't get the machines and plan for the boys to be paying the debt, after I've joined George underground, do I? I don't get a new combine-harvester and leave the bill for my grandchildren to pick up, do I? No," Tom shook his head and reached for another spoonful of chicken. "No," he continued, his speech muffled by a bite of fajita, "if *I* need something, *I* pay for it. Not like the government, who think they can build up debt and leave it for the next generation."

Susan got up to refill the water jug. She kissed the top of Tom's head as she passed. She knew he was struggling, trying to keep everything on an even keel until they were alone. She just hoped he wouldn't start a rant about vegetarians next, she didn't think she could cope with that this evening.

***

They were alone later, after the dishwasher had been loaded, and Susan had escaped to the barn, to look at the calves. She stood next to the pen, watching as they jostled each other, enjoying the simplicity of their lives. They concentrated with their whole being on their physical needs – eating, drinking, pooping, sleeping. That's all that mattered. There was something relaxing about watching living things that were so uncomplicated. No worry, no tangled emotions, no right or wrong. Susan heard the door swing open and looked up. Tom stood there, watching her, his dog Rex by his side.

"Well, this is a pickle, isn't it?" he said.

Susan nodded, feeling the tears prickle again, forcing them down. Not yet. Not while she still had to face Ben.

"I don't like it," she said. "It's not what I want for him."

"No, I know," Tom said, opening his arms. She went to him, snuggled into him, glad they had each other, could carry this together.

"We'll get through it," he said.

Susan felt his rough hand smoothing her hair, pausing to pick out a stalk of hay. When Tom spoke, she could feel the vibrations of his words against her head as she clung tightly to him.

"He's still our boy, and think of all the horrid things we could be having to cope with. At least he's not taking drugs, or telling us he's got cancer – something really bad. This is going to be hard; it'll take a bit of adjusting to, but it's not like one of them things, is it? It's not the end of our world…"

Susan didn't speak, she simply held on, needing him.

"He's still our boy," said Tom, "still our Ben. Nothing's changed really, except our knowing about it. We need to remember that; he hasn't become something new."

Susan nodded. "I want to cry," she whispered, "to let it out. But I know I mustn't, I mustn't make it harder for him."

"No," said Tom, "not yet. Poor kid, I expect it was hard enough telling us anyway.

"Come on," Tom said, giving her one last rough hug, "time to go back inside".

***

The evening passed. They watched television, chatted, behaved like everything was normal. Susan tried to avoid staring at her son, tried not to read his mind, guess his thoughts. He seemed okay now, a bit on edge, but less tense than earlier.

They went to bed early, Tom and Susan at the same time, which almost never happened. When they were in bed, they curled around each other – which was also rare. They didn't speak, but they were both taking comfort from the other, both needed the warmth of another body.

Tom fell asleep first, his arm heavy across Susan's shoulder, his breathing even. Susan slowly, inch by inch, disentangled herself, lifted his arm and slipped from under it. She slid from the bed and went to the bathroom.

Standing by the mirror, her face yellow in the light, Susan stared at her reflection. How had they got to this point? Was it her fault? People said being gay was caused by an over-dominant mother. Had she done something wrong? Was it a punishment?

Susan reached out a hand, turned off the light, and the darkness flooded back. Outside, an owl hooted, and if she strained to listen, she could hear the regular grunts of Tom snoring, but mostly there was only the sound of her own breathing. She took a deep breath, but it came out as a shudder. Then, at last, she let go. The confusion, the disappointment, was immense; and set free, it engulfed her. Consumed by fear for her child, and overwhelmed by a deep sense of something akin to failure, she sank to her knees on the damp bathroom mat, bowed her head, and wept. The emotion swelled inside her and rose up, a deep pain in her chest, hot wet tears from her eyes that flowed unrestrained down her cheeks and dripped from her chin to wet her pyjamas.

Chapter Ten

Susan woke late the following day. She had spent most of the night drifting into light sleep – like stepping briefly into puddles, when she really needed to immerse herself fully in an ocean. Drips of sleep, fragments of dreams, then surfacing again before she was refreshed. She forced herself from the bed feeling rusty, her mind a machine that had been left out in the rain and needed oiling. She scowled at her reflection and cleaned her teeth.

"I feel like someone has died," she whispered to Tom while they got up, as more tears seeped from her red eyes. "I don't want to keep crying, but I don't seem able to stop."

Tom stopped pulling on his socks and came to her, laid his heavy hand on her shoulder.

"Yes, it's all bit of a muddle still," he said. "But early days – it will get better once we're used to the idea I expect."

Susan stared at her face in the mirror, wondering if make-up would cover her red nose and swollen eyes.

"Try to have an easy day love," said Tom, squeezing her shoulder. "You might feel better when you start doing things, don't have so much time for thinking.

"Perhaps in a way, someone *has* died," Tom said, his voice thoughtful. "Perhaps we need time to mourn for the death of who we imagined Ben was. We thought he'd get married, have kids, be like most other blokes. We had our own image of him, of who we thought Ben was. It turns out we were wrong, and we need to adjust to that. He's the nicest of the bunch really, the one who gets on with the whole world. We thought he'd have life easy. Now it seems he won't. Now he's going to have to deal with prejudice and sneering."

"He'll be called 'the gay one'," said Susan, reaching for another tissue. "That's how people will label him. Not 'Ben who's good with animals', or 'the youngest' or 'the one with curly hair' – he'll be known as 'the gay one'. It will define him. And people will say it with a smile, like it's something funny, like he's somehow less of a person."

Tom rubbed her back. "Yeah, I know. I'm not too keen for them all to know at the Farmer's Union. But I'm not ashamed of Ben, Susan. He's a good lad. Try and remember that, don't let yourself get swamped by all this. Remember, he's *still Ben*."

Susan nodded, thinking that it was more easily said than done, that her whole world felt like it had been tipped upside-down. Susan felt Tom pat her shoulder, as if she was one of the dogs, and watched him in the mirror as he left, his solid back walking through the doorway. Then she pulled out her powder compact, and started to dab at her face.

She needed to buy some food, so by 10 o'clock Susan was in the car. As she drove, her mind wandered to Ben, to what his news might mean. She couldn't quite grasp why it had affected her so deeply, what it was that upset her. If she thought about it logically, pretended it was someone else's son she was thinking about, then it was not such a big deal. Apart from the religious angle – which she was still unsure about – there was nothing in modern day Britain that was against homosexuality. Young people went on gay-rights marches, schools were being called on to include gender differences in the syllabus, the law was insisting that everyone should have equal rights.

But it wasn't someone else's son, it was her Ben, and it wasn't what they had hoped for him. "When they're little," Susan thought, indicating left as she turned a corner, "when they're little, it all seems so simple. It's harder physically, coping with no sleep when they're up all night, and having to watch them all day in case they kill themselves, but the decisions are easier. When I forced them to eat vegetables, or made them clean their teeth when they didn't want to, I knew I was right."

A car pulled out in front of her, and Susan braked hard, frowning. "But this is harder," she thought, "how do I protect my son from something like this? I don't know what the rules are anymore."

***

Neil phoned her on Wednesday. Susan was at work, counting the float into the till at the coffee shop, when the mobile in her apron pocket vibrated. Susan had put her phone in there when she arrived, as her coat and bag were safely stowed in the staffroom. Not that it was a staffroom, not really. It was simply a little room at the back of the cafe, which led out to the alleyway that ran behind all the shops. But one of the hygiene rules was that all outdoor bags and coats should be left away from the food, so Mr. Banks had installed a chair and coat pegs, and called it a staffroom. Susan worried that it wasn't particularly secure, opening as it did into the alleyway, so she left her purse at home and put her car keys and phone into her apron pocket. Which weighed it down and made it sag unattractively at the front.

"But after four children, and over fifty years of life, most things are sagging unattractively at the front," she thought with a wry smile.

Susan delved into the pocket and pulled out her phone, noticed that Neil's name was on the screen, so took the call.

She checked nothing was wrong, then told Neil she would have to phone him back later. Susan couldn't count change and talk at the same time, and nor could she delay checking the float in case a customer arrived. She put her phone back in her pocket, looked at the money, and sighed. She would have to start counting again.

Susan tipped the coins from the trays, and began to sort them into piles of £1. It was frustrating to have to recount it, but she couldn't remember where she'd got to, and if the float was wrong at the start of her shift, it wouldn't tally at the end.

"That's the trouble with men," Susan thought, scooping a pile of five pence to one side, "they don't think about the person who they're phoning; if they have something to say, they'll phone when they think about it. Neil knows I work on Wednesdays, but it wouldn't occur to him to wait until later, that I might be busy."

When all the money was counted and back in the till, she phoned him back, carrying a duster to the corner where they kept stock for people to buy: their own brand of tea and coffee, a few mugs bearing the shop's logo, pastries sealed into plastic wrapping which, Susan thought, made the food itself look plastic and unappetising.

"Hi Neil, sorry about that. I can chat now, but if a customer arrives I'll have to cut you off – is that okay or shall I phone this evening?"

"No, talk now," said Neil. "It's about Ben. What are we going to do about him?"

Susan was waving the duster across the shelves of coffee beans, turning tubs so the labels turned outwards, moving stock to the front of the shelf. But at Neil's words, she stopped.

"Do? I'm not sure I know what you mean."

"Ben's told you, hasn't he? About deciding that he's gay?"

"Yes, he told me before he went back to uni," said Susan, frowning, "but I'm not sure we need to 'do' anything."

There was silence for a minute, and Susan wondered if they'd been cut off. Then Neil spoke again, slowly, as if choosing his words carefully.

"No, Mum, I'm not sure you're right. I'm really worried about Ben, I'm scared he's starting on something that could be bad for him – dangerous even, from a Christian view. I'm not sure we should just leave him. We wouldn't if it was something physical, would we? If he had started to drink too much, or snort drugs or something – we'd try and intervene then, wouldn't we? Try to rescue him?"

Susan took her duster to behind the till, and sat on the high stool. She half hoped a customer would appear, so she could delay this conversation. Neil was always like this, he always wanted to protect his siblings, right back from when he was a little boy. Susan remembered how they had laughed at him when he was young, told him he was like one of the collie dogs, always watching out for the flock.

And Neil always came to Susan, never to Tom, when he had a problem. They all did. She supposed it was because it was mostly her who had raised them. Tom loved them, but he was in his own world much of the time, his attention was only ever half there with the family, and half with his cows. When the boys were growing up, Tom enjoyed teaching them things – how to fish, how to drive the tractor, how to repair things – but he didn't want to be bothered by everyday things. The family had had clearly defined roles, and anything to do with children, the dressing of them, listening to them, helping them with homework, had fallen to Susan. Not that she minded. In fact, she would have rather resented his interference if he had tried to help. But sometimes, such as now, Susan wished they would go to their father rather than her.

Susan stared ahead, noticing that one bag of beans had split, and spilled the contents, like smooth brown gravel, across the shelf. Outside, people were hurrying past, some carrying blue cups from the shop in the High Street, drinking as they went, like toddlers sucking on sippy-cups. There was a line of cars waiting for the lights to change, and an elderly man, leaning on a stick, his back bent. Susan looked at the door, wishing it would open to admit customers demanding attention, a distraction. But it stayed firmly closed.

"Neil," Susan said, "I'm not sure this is a conversation for now – I'm at work. But anyway, Ben hasn't 'decided' to be gay, he says that he *is* gay, which I suppose means he always has been, it's just that we didn't know. I'm not sure that there's anything we can 'do' apart from support him and let him know that we're on his side, whatever his preferences."

"No Mum," said Neil, and Susan could imagine him, shaking his head and frowning. "I'm afraid that would be wrong. Homosexuality is a sin, it's against how God created us. We need to remind Ben of that, so he can repent, before he gets in too deep. I'm not sure what's caused this... But it's the wrong choice, and if we love him, we have to help him to see that. We can't just leave him, can we? We can't let him make a decision that will ruin his life, will stop him developing his Christian faith. It's wrong Mum, isn't it?"

Susan closed her eyes. She didn't want to have this conversation. Her own feelings were too muddled, too raw. Instinctively, she felt that Neil was wrong, that the issue wasn't as clear cut as he was saying. But she couldn't explain that, couldn't remember anything in the Bible that did anything other than support what he was saying.

"I'm sorry," Susan said at last, "but I really can't have this conversation now Neil. I'll get upset, and I need to be able to serve customers and make coffee and appear normal. We'll talk later, I'll ring you when I get home. And I will think about what you're saying, I promise I will. But at the moment, I don't think we should do anything other than support Ben in whatever direction he decides to go in. Unless we're sure it's harmful. And I don't know yet whether this is or not..."

"Oh, okay, sorry about that – I forgot about you working on Wednesdays. Sorry.

"But can we talk tonight? Will you have time? I'm really worried about this Mum, it's really upset me to be honest, and I don't think we should sit back and do nothing, not when it's Ben..."

Susan nodded, even though he couldn't see her. Yes, she thought, it's partly because it's Ben. Of all of the boys, Neil has always wanted to protect Ben the most, perhaps because he's the youngest and so is more accepting of help.

"Mum?" said Neil, rousing her from her thoughts. "Mum? Are you still there? Can I phone you this evening?"

Susan thought about her evening, about how tired she would be after work, and then having to feed the animals, and sort the poultry, and cook some dinner.

"Yes, okay," she said – because that is what mothers always say.

Chapter Eleven

Neil phoned and arranged to meet Ben for lunch on Friday. He had tried to discuss things with his mother, but he could tell she was tired after her shift at work, and then she had started to cry, and it was the kind of 'properly upset' crying that Neil knew he couldn't do anything about, especially on a phone call, so he'd changed the conversation until she was calm, and then ended the call. He had talked to Kylie, and discussed things with his church group, and had slept very little. In the end, he decided to meet Ben, so they could discuss things face-to-face.

The brothers met in London. Ben was back at uni, but told Neil he had an afternoon without lectures, so it was easy enough to travel in to London to meet his brother.

Neil managed to clear enough work so he could have a full hour off, and he'd booked a restaurant that served a decent vegetarian option as well as meat. It was quite an expensive place, but he'd discussed it beforehand with Kylie, explained how worried he was, and asked her permission to spend more than usual on the meal. He hoped the gesture would show Ben that this issue was serious and was important. It was therefore, a rather subdued Ben that he found loitering outside the restaurant.

"Hi Ben," Neil said, "thanks for coming, was the journey okay?" Neil found was feeling strangely nervous, and his voice sounded slightly odd. He coughed.

Ben glanced at him, then grinned. "Yes thanks, trains all behaving for once."

Neil saw Ben look into the restaurant and frown. "This looks posh, will it matter that I'm in jeans? I left all my smart clothes at home. I didn't realise we were eating somewhere fancy – didn't get time to look it up online."

Neil wasn't sure, but decided the restaurant was unlikely to turn them away, so shook his head.

"It's fine," he said, "I don't suppose they'll care what we're wearing as long as we pay the bill!"

Neil had never eaten there before, and had booked it on the weight of a recommendation. They went inside, and followed the waiter to their table. As they threaded their way across the white tiled floor, between glass oval tables, Neil began to feel uncomfortable. There were no cloths or curtains, nothing to soften the harsh bright lines, nothing to entice diners to linger. It was clean and modern, serving contemporary food to rich young people, before they hurried back to work or the theatre. There was no comfort, nothing was pretty or warm; it was designed to impress, not to cosset. There were tables of people in suits, having heated discussions over the central potted cactus that was the sole table decoration. Neil felt rather overwhelmed by the atmosphere; by the time the brothers were seated, they were both speaking in whispers.

"I feel like I don't belong here," said Ben, in a low voice, "I might smudge something!"

"Yeah, I know what you mean," said Neil, leaning forwards so he could speak quietly. "It's not quite what I was expecting either. But no one else knows that, I think we can wing it!"

Ben grinned at him, and took the proffered menu from the waiter who was hovering.

Neil stared at his own menu, searching for something to choose. The menu showed food which he could imagine reviewed in a newspaper supplement: *Freshly prepared dishes accompanied by barely cooked vegetables, and unusual fish served with sauces in tiny pots on the side; this eatery is striving to be cutting edge and honest, providing healthy choices with modern ingredients.*

"I'm not sure I actually fancy eating any of it," he thought.

They chose their food, Neil opting for a vegetarian pasta dish and a glass of red wine.

"I don't usually drink during my lunch hour," Neil said, "but considering that we don't have lunch together very often these days, I thought I'd make an exception." He also hoped, though didn't say, that it would help to calm his nerves, which he could feel bubbling in his stomach.

"I think I'll stick with beer," said Ben, "and —" he glanced at Neil, "could I have a steak? Or would that be rude?"

Neil thought it was a bit rude, and also was stretching his budget further than he'd hoped, but he nodded and smiled. "Sure," he said, "whatever you like. I don't expect the whole world to become vegetarian just because I am."

"So, how's that going?" asked Ben, when they had given their order and were pulling warm bread rolls apart and spreading them with butter that had been moulded into curls. "The vegetarian thing, I mean. Don't you miss meat?"

"I did at first," said Neil, deciding to be honest, "especially sausages. You can get veggie substitutes, but they're not the same, they taste more like stuffing. But I'm sort of used to it now. I expect Christmas will be odd, not eating Mum's turkey dinner, but mostly it's okay. And I'm glad I'm doing it, it feels right."

Neil noticed Ben begin to look away, and realised it was the wrong time to launch into a lecture about the wrongs of eating meat. He sat back and held up his glass.

"Cheers," he said. "Thanks for meeting me."

"S'okay," said Ben, sounding doubtful.

"Like I said on the phone, I wanted to have chance to chat with you, about your decision to be gay..."

"Not really a 'decision'," interrupted Ben. "I was made like this, I simply decided to go public with the information."

"Well, can we talk about that for a minute? About whether you were made like that? You see, I think, if we look in the Bible, that it says God made humans to be man and woman – two very distinct genders. And when they joined together, became 'one flesh' as it says in the Bible, had sex..." Neil saw the people at the next table turn when he said sex, so he lowered his voice even more, and leaned forwards. "When they had sex, that constituted marriage, that's what God sanctioned, that's how it's meant to be. Genesis shows how God set things up, right from the beginning. Anything else, any deviation from that, is not what God wants, it's not the best. Do you see? Can you understand Ben, that being gay is not what's best, and therefore it cannot have come from God?" He stopped.

Ben was frowning.

"A deviation," Ben repeated, shaking his head.

"Um, that might have been a bad choice of words," agreed Neil, feeling annoyed with himself. The last thing he wanted was to alienate Ben this early on in the conversation.

The waiter arrived, topped up their water glasses, fussed with the cutlery, and offered more bread. Ben took another roll; Neil sipped his wine. They had both ordered soup as a starter, and it arrived in white china bowls with chives floating on the surface. Neil dipped his spoon in, and took a mouthful. It was too hot, burning his lip, so he reached for his water.

"Okay," he said, "let's start again. Let's look at the New Testament, the stuff that Paul wrote. He wrote letters to the early church, the ones set up right at the beginning, after Jesus had left."

"I know this," said Ben, looking up from his soup.

"Yes, I know you do," said Neil. He leaned forwards again, getting into his stride. Last night, wanting to prepare, he'd spent time going through the relevant parts of the Bible, finding the passages that condemned homosexuality, trying to learn them.

"Anyway, let's think about 1 Corinthians 6 for a minute," Neil said. He hoped it was chapter six, he frowned, maybe it was five. Never mind, it didn't matter. "There it talks about people who cannot inherit the kingdom of God, and it clearly lists 'men who practise homosexuality'. It's in a list that includes being a drunk, or greedy or a gossip – so it isn't like we don't all have things to give up, stuff to avoid. But it seems to be the practising bit that is important Ben." He paused, and took another mouthful of wine.

Ben was silent, slurping his soup and chewing his bread.

"I know it will be hard, I feel for you mate, really I do, but maybe you should decide to be celibate," continued Neil, trying to explain his belief. "Even if you don't think being gay is wrong, would you consider being celibate? If you think about it, if you look at what the Bible says and realise it's right, then surely that is something you might consider? It seems so serious, Ben, not something you should be involved with.

"And then there's 1 Timothy," Neil continued, keen to have his say before they started to bring the main course. He'd done his homework, he wanted to say it all before he got in a muddle; and Ben seemed to be listening – he wasn't interrupting every sentence, as often happened when Neil tried to discuss something with his brothers.

"In 1 Timothy, it talks about sexually immoral men who practise homosexuality – see, it's the 'practise' bit that seems important – and how it's against God's law. It isn't right, because God only wants what is best for us, and this isn't Ben, this isn't what is best for you. So even if we ignore the Old Testament for now, even if we only go to the New Testament as being relevant, it's very clear Ben. It's very clear, this is wrong."

Ben was looking straight at him, but Neil couldn't read his expression. He took another sip of his wine.

"The thing is," said Ben, speaking very slowly, his eyes narrowed, "I don't agree with how you are using those particular verses. I believe that God created me as a gay man, because that's how he wants me to be. I think we look at the Bible in different ways, so when it condemns homosexuality, it also says don't eat prawns – and yet most Christians today think that eating prawns is okay.

Neil waited, while Ben ate some more soup.

"Even the New Testament has to be taken in context. So when it says, very clearly, that women should cover their heads when praying, most Christians today believe that this was a cultural thing, that because only the prostitutes of the day showed their fancy braided hair, the Christian women in those days should cover their heads, so they looked respectful. So, women today should be dressed respectfully – because the Bible is still relevant today; but not necessarily wear hats to church – because that specific thing was cultural."

Ben looked up, and Neil nodded, to show he was listening.

Ben continued: "Now, that piece of theology is relatively new, and a hundred years ago, people said women *should* wear hats to church. Some people still do, but most Christians don't. I think it's the same for the parts that discuss homosexuality. When Paul wrote his letters, there *were* no monogamous, loving, gay relationships. So when he wrote about homosexuality, he *can't* have been referring to them.

"So, yes Neil, I am a Christian, and I do take the Bible seriously. But I am also gay, and I don't believe that is wrong, or something I should be ashamed of. And it would be nice," he said, sitting back in his chair, "if my brothers weren't ashamed of me either."

Neil felt shocked, almost as if Ben had hit him.

"But I'm not," he said, the words rushing from him, "I'm not ashamed of you, of course I'm not." Neil wanted to shout at Ben, to shake him, to tell him that of *course* he wasn't ashamed of him, he only wanted to protect him from something which Neil knew to be wrong. He lifted his wine glass, noticing that his hand wasn't quite steady.

The waiter cleared their plates, and brought their main courses, giving Neil space to recover and arrange his thoughts. The last thing he wanted was for this to disintegrate into an argument, that would achieve nothing. He watched Ben use his knife to saw the end from his steak, blood oozing onto the plate and seeping into the mashed potatoes.

"Your food all right?" he asked.

Ben nodded, his mouth full.

"Look," said Neil, deciding to have one last try. "You need to understand that I'm not ashamed of you, you're my brother, and I will always look out for you. Besides, how *could* I be 'ashamed' of you, when I have enough rubbish in my own life to sort out? That's what being a Christian is, isn't it? God loves us, just as we are, whatever we've done, he loves us. But if we want to please him, if we love him back, then we have to clear out some of the rubbish in our lives, however difficult that seems.

"And I think the Bible is clear on this issue, that if you look at what it says, and don't try and use fancy theology to make it mean what people *want* it to mean, then I think the passages about homosexuality are clear. Being gay goes against what God wants for you, it's not what is best for you." Neil saw Ben open his mouth, and raised his hand.

"No, let me finish, please Ben, and then we can stop talking about this and enjoy our meal. All I ask Ben, is that you read those parts of the Bible again, and read them with an open mind, asking God to show you what he really wants for your life. Will you do that? Will you be honest with yourself and listen to the Bible and to God and to the church?"

"The church?" said Ben through a mouthful of potato, "You want me to listen to the church? That seems a pretty unreliable source of guidance!"

"Not all the church is wrong Ben," said Neil. "I still believe it's the best place to hear what God is saying."

"Okay," said Ben, his voice resigned. "I promise. And will you trust me enough to maybe hear if God speaks to me, and do you trust God to maybe do the talking himself, rather than you having to be the go-between?

"Now, can we change the subject please?"

Neil nodded. He felt miserable. Although he had said everything he'd intended to say, and Ben had been much quieter than he'd expected, Neil felt that he hadn't really argued his case. It was as if Ben had decided to be quiet, to let him have his say, but he hadn't really been listening, he hadn't been open enough to seriously consider any of Neil's points.

Deep inside, Neil felt a lump of pain, a worrying belief that his brother was on a dangerous path, and he hadn't managed to persuade him from it.

"I did my best," he tried to reassure himself, as he tucked into the pasta, blowing on each mouthful and trying to enjoy the slightly over-peppered taste. "I did my best, and tried to say what needed to be said. The rest is up to Ben."

Chapter Twelve

Sunday arrived. It seemed almost strange to Susan that new days kept arriving, that nothing had stopped or slowed down. Her inner world was in turmoil, but outside, everything beyond her own body, was constant, unchanged. Sunday meant church, so she rolled out of bed and sorted the animals, in time to leave the house at 10am.

Susan and Tom attended the small Baptist Chapel in Marksbridge. It was an ugly building, in need of demolishing and rebuilding, but instead added to over the years, so the original chapel – which might have looked quite pleasant originally – was now dwarfed by late seventies brickwork under an over-sized sloping roof.

As Susan sat there, finding Bible references and standing for hymns, her thoughts kept wandering back to Ben. It was like an emotional magnet, sucking all her thoughts and feelings into a whirlwind she couldn't escape from. She looked around the room at her fellow worshippers.

"I wonder what they would say, if they knew," she thought. Some reactions she was fairly confident she knew. Like Mr Baker, who always stood at the door ready to greet newcomers, and who thought of himself as an elder in the church, even though they didn't actually have elders. Mr Baker would be disdainful, keen to say he 'loved the sinner while hating the sin' and then quick to show how much he 'hated the sin' by refusing to acknowledge the 'sinner'. He would avoid physical contact, look disapproving when collecting the offering, be vocal at church meetings about 'upholding Christian morals.' There wouldn't be much in the way of compromise there, not for that particular 'sin'.

Other people wouldn't care, some would even be pleased, view it as some sort of proof that their church was progressive, able to accept people from all persuasions.

"But I don't want my son to be 'the example', the 'token gay,'" thought Susan. "He's not 'gay', he's Ben. Ben who happens to be gay. I don't look at Chris and think of him as 'Chris the straight man', or 'Jack who likes girls'. They're just people, who happen to have certain sexual preferences, but that doesn't define them. So why should being gay? Why will that eclipse everything about Ben?"

Susan felt suddenly suffused by anger, which raged through her, and realised she was glaring across the room at old Mrs Smith. The old lady met her eyes, and looked rather worried by the venom she could see in Susan's expression. Susan forced herself to smile and lowered her head. Rob, the pastor, was talking to the children, but Susan had no idea what he was saying. Her whole world had reduced to the thoughts and worries inside. Tom was next to her, whispering to the person on his right about something. She saw them laugh. They were oblivious to her worries and it made her cross. It seemed unfair for Ben to dump this on her and then clear off back to uni, leaving her to carry it on her own. He seemed unaware of the consequences, how it would change everything.

"Will they let Ben continue working with the children?" Susan thought, thinking of her son's involvement with the Sunday School class once a month during the long summer holidays. "Will he be seen as a bad influence, some kind of sexual deviant who can't be trusted to tell the children Bible stories and talk to them about God? Will people who view homosexuality as a sin, a sexual sin, assume that he is therefore involved in *all* sexual sin? Worry that Ben might abuse a child? Or influence the children towards a gay lifestyle, and therefore he shouldn't have contact with them?"

The service ended, though Susan had heard very little of it, and certainly could not have told anyone what the sermon had been about. She followed Tom into the back hall, and stood in line for a cup of coffee.

"Hello Susan," said Esther, approaching with a smile. "Have you recovered from the family invasion? And how's your mum, now the funeral is over?"

Susan stood for a moment, fighting to control the impulse to tell Esther how she really felt, knowing that if she started to, she would cry.

"I'm fine, thanks," she said, repeating the lie that so easily moved the conversation past anything that might come too close, might prove too awkward.

"Mum seems to be doing okay, I think her and Aunty were relieved really, to get it all over with. How's your week going?"

Esther launched into a funny story, but Susan wasn't really listening, she simply nodded and smiled in all the right places. By the time she left, it felt as though her insides had been through a wringer, and she thought she might actually be physically sick.

***

Susan went to visit her pastor, Rob, the following Friday. She had a free slot in her diary, so she phoned ahead and made an appointment.

When Susan arrived Rob opened the front door himself, and ushered her into his study. Susan's friend, Esther, was Rob's wife, and Susan guessed she was probably in the house, and would be wondering what this was about.

However, for now, Susan didn't want to tell her friend, and she was relieved that Rob himself had let her in. Telling Rob was different, she knew he wouldn't gossip, would listen and advise and then never mention it again. Susan trusted him, trusted his role as the minister, as confidant and spiritual leader – there was something impersonal about his position. Susan wanted his help, to try and sort this out, so it could stop sucking all her thoughts and emotions and whirling them around in a big "Ben is Gay" whirlpool.

Susan sat in one of the two armchairs next to a low table. The room was dim, with bookshelves lining one wall, and a desk laden with two computer screens and three empty mugs next to the window. There was a vase of dead flowers on the windowsill, the petals dry and brown, stamens scattered across the white paint.

After coffee, and the obligatory ten minutes of "How're the family/aren't we having lovely weather at the moment/did you watch the football last night?" Rob sat back and looked at Susan. He smiled at her, and put his coffee back on the tray. She watched his hands, big and dark, with neat nails and a cut on one thumb.

"So Susan," he said, "how can I help you?"

Susan lowered her head, unsure where to start.

"I want some advice," she began, staring at her lap, "you see..." Susan stopped. Something big was pressing on her chest, forcing itself into her throat. "Ben's gay," she said, and burst into tears.

Rob said nothing. He sat very still, and waited. There was a box of tissues on the table, and after a few minutes, Susan blew her nose and wiped her eyes.

"Sorry," she said, trying to grin. "This has all been bit of a shock."

"Yes," said Rob, "I can see that. But don't worry, it probably did you good to let some of that emotion out, it's never a good idea to keep things inside."

Rob leaned forwards, his weight resting on his hands. Susan stared, very intently, at those hands.

"But Susan, why do you think it upsets you so much?"

Susan felt jolted, as if he was being purposefully obtuse. She frowned.

"Well – it's wrong, isn't it?"

Rob sat back and reached for his Bible. It was big and well worn. He didn't open it, but laid one hand across the top, as if taking reassurance from it.

"Some people would say so, yes," he said. "The Bible discusses homosexuality in the old testament, and the new, and it seems pretty condemning if you take the words at face value – which lots of people do. But we'll come to that in a minute. That's not why I asked."

His voice was very deep, full of concern. Susan knew he wanted to help, to make her feel better, and she drew comfort from that. Just being able to talk to someone was a relief, like she was finally letting the problem out. It made it smaller somehow.

"I ask why it has upset you so much because, whether you think it's wrong or not, there are other things that are wrong, aren't there? And you don't get upset about those. So, you have never come to see me because one of the boys has lied, or has been disrespectful, or said something nasty. But I'm sure they have many times. So what is it that upsets you so much Susan? Can you work out what it is that makes this so emotional? Because I think perhaps, once you know that, we can begin to put it into its rightful place, to get some perspective on the issue, and decide where to go next."

Susan was silent. She picked up her coffee again. It was cool now, but she took a couple of sips anyway, for something to do really. Then, very carefully, she replaced the cup on the tray and smoothed her jeans. She understood what Rob was asking, but she wasn't sure that she knew the answer.

"I don't know," she said at last, "it just seems bad." Her voice sounded hoarse, and she coughed, clearing her throat. She could still feel tears, a whole bank of them, waiting to fall if her emotions tipped even slightly. She forced herself to look at Rob, to concentrate on him and what he was saying, to keep her feelings in check. She noticed he had a mark on his tie. And that he was smiling at her.

Rob nodded. "Yes, I can understand that. I expect I might feel the same if it was one of our boys. But I'm not sure that your feelings, that hurt I'm seeing, is from God. And if it's not from God, then we need to help you recover from it, to get things back on track, before you can move forwards."

"I think," said Susan, trying to be honest, "that I'm mainly disappointed and worried. Mostly worried, because of how other people will react. I don't want Ben to be hurt...for them to say nasty things...to laugh at him..."

Rob nodded. "I expect − and I have to admit I don't have much experience here − that unfortunately, that will happen, especially with people of our age; and especially within the church setting. I think that the younger generation have a different viewpoint, they are more accepting, other than a small minority. It's not okay to be prejudiced anymore. In theory." He grinned, "Though of course, real life is a bit different."

Susan met his eyes, understanding what he wasn't saying. Rob was dark skinned. Although he was intelligent, well respected, eloquent, Susan was sure that sometimes Rob still met racism. To some people, Rob would simply be "the black chappy" irrespective of who he really was. Which was not, Susan thought, completely dissimilar to being "the gay one" in terms of titles.

Except that when people talked about gays or poofs, or whatever term they chose to use, it was usually said with a smile.

As though those people were weaker, a joke in some way, people to be ridiculed and not taken seriously. Whereas black people, although stereotyped as less intelligent or lazy, weren't necessarily seen as a joke. Nor did they evoke anger and hatred, just because they were black. At least, she didn't think they did; not now, not in England. Susan realised she was frowning, and made her expression neutral, listened to what Rob was saying.

"I can see similarities with being gay and being black," Rob said. "People use both to define people, to limit what they are capable of, to decide what their character must be. And of course, for some people, it is how they define themselves.

"For me, the colour of my skin is relatively unimportant. I happen to be dark, my wife happens to be white, my children are something in between. But it's not who I am. I am Rob, the pastor, a father and husband and collector of model railway paraphernalia. But some people see me first and foremost as black. I think, if I had had to battle with injustices my whole life, if I'd received a less good education, or been paid less, or faced abuse wherever I went – just because of the colour of my skin – then being black would mean more to me. I would try to readdress the balance, I would 'feel' black. Black Pride would matter. I would define myself mostly as 'black', and less as the other aspects of my life."

Rob was nodding, as if realising the truth of the words as he spoke.

"I think, perhaps, that is how it is for some gay people. They have been taunted since childhood, perhaps attacked physically. Some have kept their sexual preferences a secret, creating problems of loneliness, and fear of rejection. So now, it defines them. They feel that being gay is the most important thing about them. So, when Christians say neat little phrases like 'love the sinner but hate the sin', it really doesn't work."

Susan smiled, remembering how often she had heard those words, feeling they were usually an excuse for someone to be unkind. Like, she thought, when someone says, "I don't mean to be rude" and you know that they are about to say something offensive. There was a clock, ticking on the bookshelf, and Susan realised she was no longer listening to Rob, and that her thoughts had spun away. She forced herself to look back at Rob, who was still speaking:

"…It's how they define themselves. So to 'hate' homosexuality is to hate them. It's a huge problem for the church today."

"But," said Susan, leaning forwards slightly, her voice intense with hope, "don't you think it *is* wrong? Doesn't the Bible say homosexual practices are evil?"

"Ah," said Rob, smiling, "well that's a tricky subject too. I think you have to make up your own mind on that."

He paused, as if thinking.

"I think the Bible is very clear, and any sort of homosexual practise is wrong. Not *being* a homosexual though; I don't think that.

"I think some people are born with tendencies they should not act on. Others have perhaps been bullied into it, they are effeminate males and they can't keep up with the social norm, so they opt out and decide to be gay. And I guess some have drifted into it, perhaps as a teenage rebellion, wanting to make a statement, be different.

"But no, I do believe that some people are born gay, it's just how they are. And for those people, it's not a sin, it is how they were made. However, I think the Bible is very clear that they must remain celibate, they shouldn't act on their impulses, as those impulses are immoral, not what God wants for them. A gay lifestyle isn't what is best for them, and God only ever wants the best for us. Just as someone who is born with a body that runs to fat and a huge appetite, should learn to restrict their eating, to not indulge in lots of sugar and fat, and to exercise – not because their *size* matters but because to indulge without restriction would be unhealthy, would ruin the body they have been given."

Rob paused, not seeming entirely comfortable with his explanation. He ran a hand through his hair, and stretched his back.

"However, I have to be truthful, and say that if you asked Esther, she would give you a completely different answer." Rob grinned. "We have argued about this for many hours. Both of us believe the Bible is God's word, given to instruct us and teach us what is right and wrong. But the way we interpret parts of it is different. We've had to accept we'll never agree, and perhaps that means that it doesn't matter as much as we think it does.

"Certainly Jesus, when he was teaching, never spoke about homosexuality specifically, only about immorality. I worry, in the world today, that the church is spending so much time debating this issue, and it's tearing Christians away from each other, when they need to be concentrating on other issues, like what God wants for their lives."

"But how can it not be clear?" said Susan, frowning. "The bits I remember seem completely clear."

"Yes, but it depends how they're translated and understood," said Rob. "I think the words should be taken at face-value, the Bible says homosexual practice is wrong, and I believe that to be the case.

"But Esther points to the context of when the words were written, and says we should look beyond the words and understand what they are saying. A bit like the passage where it says women should not speak in church. We know that refers to when the women, who were uneducated, were chatting throughout the sermon, and they should have been sitting quietly. So we don't believe we should take the words 'women should not speak in church' literally. And Esther believes the passages about homosexuality are the same – the context of the day, and the translation of key words, matters."

Rob frowned and shuffled slightly in his chair.

"Actually, I'm not sure this is a very helpful conversation. I almost feel you don't need to worry about it – you're not deciding on whether to practice homosexuality, you're deciding how to best mother your son. Whether it's right or wrong, I don't think giving sermons is going to help him at all. That isn't what he needs from you, and it won't make you feel better."

Rob paused.

Outside, Susan could hear cars passing on the main road, the honk of a horn, and the clock, ticking very loudly. She waited for Rob to speak again, wanting him to reassure her, to sort out her muddled feelings.

"The thing is," said Rob at last, "even apparently simple things in the Bible are sometimes not how they seem. We have to take all of it, use it to understand God, what he loves and what he hates. Then act accordingly. And the passages about homosexuality have been discussed, and debated, and argued over, for years. You have Christians taking a viewpoint, and saying that anyone who disagrees with them is clearly not a Bible-believing Christian.

"But I think that's wrong and arrogant. We can only read, and pray, and do our best to hear what God is saying. Because none of us knows the mind of God, not completely. We need to spend more time listening – listening to God, and listening to each other – and reading our Bibles and praying. And less time telling the world what our own views are.

"So, I don't think I can tell you if Ben is right or wrong. I can only tell you what I believe, which is that the Bible tells us homosexual acts are wrong.

"But others have a different view, and you should decide for yourself."

He paused again, as if giving her time to absorb what he was saying.

"I'm not sure that you need to know whether homosexuality practice is a sin Susan," Rob said, reminding her of his opening words. "You are here, not Ben. Ben has his own relationship with God, and sometimes we spend too long deciding what God wants for other people, and not enough time asking what he wants from us.

"I think perhaps, that this is the problem with the whole gay Christian debate. People are busy saying what they think is right or wrong for *other* people. But that is not what we're supposed to be doing. The conversation is about the wrong thing – as perhaps, this one is." Rob looked at Susan, raising an eyebrow.

"Do you know what role God has given *you* in this situation? I think that is what you should be asking – which path should you be taking?"

Susan looked surprised.

"Oh," she said, "I think I know that. I think I just have to be his mother."

Susan told Rob of her prayer, of the feeling of peace (which had now dissolved into a tangle of worry) and the feeling (now lost) that all she had to do was love and support Ben.

"Well," said Rob, "it sounds to me like God has already given you a role. Perhaps you'll discover more later, but for now, I would advise you to do what you feel God said. Be a mother, love your son, and if he asks for advice, give the best and most honest advice that you can. If God is leading you down this path, he'll show you the rest of the way when you need it. We often only see one step at a time – that's what trust is all about."

"But what if Ben asks me?" said Susan, not wanting to let this go. "What then? Do I tell him it's okay, and condone behaviour which is against God's word?"

"Tell him the truth," said Rob. "Do you think it's wrong?"

"I don't know!" said Susan, wanting to shout at him. This wasn't why she had come. She wanted answers, absolutes, not wishy-washy theories.

"Then," said Rob slowly, "that is what you should tell him. That you don't know."

He rubbed the back of his hand under his chin, watching her, but not speaking.

"Listen, Susan, I'm not trying to be evasive or difficult. I simply think that in this case, you need to concentrate on what God is saying to you, not the theology of the situation. So be a mother, love your boy, show him how to live a Christian life. If he asks questions you can't answer, be honest and tell him that, and point him to the Bible, suggest he reads and prays and searches for the answers he's looking for. Because really, Ben and his sexual preferences have to be sorted out by Ben and God – frankly it would be odd if he let his mother decide that one for him."

"And what about this *boyfriend?*" asked Susan, her voice slightly louder than she had intended, trying to force Rob into being definite about at least one thing. "Do I accept him too? Do I invite him round for a meal? Pretend it's all normal?"

"Again, what does the Bible teach?" said Rob, his voice calm. "We are meant to show hospitality, to be kind to people, to show them the nature of God. If this boy comes to you for advice, then tell him what you think. But I don't think he will. I doubt that will be your role. So stick to what you've been called to do. Be generous and accepting and loving. When there is opportunity to witness – to explain what God has done for *you* –

then take it. And trust that God is able to do the convicting of sin if it's necessary."

Rob suggested that they pray, and Susan listened while he spoke to God, asking for his help. She listened to the distant hum of the vacuum cleaner as Esther cleaned, and she wondered if her friend was doing it on purpose, so she wouldn't be tempted to listen, to overhear a private conversation.

At the end Susan said *amen*, made polite noises, and left. She felt slightly deflated, as if Rob had side-stepped the issue and left her back where she started.

***

By the time Susan got home, the calves needed to be fed. Tom had gone to look at a new tractor, and she had agreed to cover the evening feed for him. They couldn't afford a new tractor of course, it would, like all their machinery, be bought on hire-purchase, and they would just about have paid it off by the time it needed replacing. But the old one had been repaired so many times that there was very little now that was reliable, and after the third afternoon in a row spent trying to mend it when he should have been spraying, Tom announced, with a fair smattering of swear words, that he needed to replace it.

Susan pulled on her wellies and went to the little shed where they mixed the milk. As she plunged the measuring scoop into the powder, some clouded up, coating Susan's hand and wrist, settling on the dusty floor. Susan measured powder into the bucket, then took it to the water heater. She added enough hot water to mix, watching the liquid turn white as the powder dissolved, stirring it with an old spoon with a bent handle. The warm sweet smell filled the shed, reminding her of when she had mixed the occasional bottle for her boys when they were young. The dogs smelt it too and arrived from where they'd been sleeping in the yard, pressing against her legs, pushing their noses towards the bucket.

"Get back both of you," she snapped, pushing them away.

Susan heaved the bucket to the cold-water tap, feeling the weight in her arms and her back, and added enough to fill the bucket, checking the temperature with her wrist. The calves might be heavier than her, but they were still babies, and she didn't want to burn them. When both buckets were ready, Susan lifted them from the sink, trying to avoid slopping any, and carried them across the yard. The movement turned the buckets into waves of milk that surged forwards and backwards, as though straining to wash over the rim in a milky tide; the dogs circled, eager to lap up any spills.

The calves heard Susan coming, smelt their milk, began to jostle each other, calling out in their excitement. There were clangs as the calves bumped against the barriers, grunts as they pushed each other. Susan carried the buckets to their feeding containers – Tom had made them from empty water containers, attaching teats bought from a catalogue, each one at the same height as their mother's teats would have been, so the line from nose to stomach when they fed was natural.

Susan smiled, remembering Tom's curses as he made the container, which seemed destined to leak as he fixed the teats; and how enthusiastic he had been when they were finally properly sealed. Susan knew farmers who chose to feed calves from buckets, because it was easier. But when calves lapped, the milk went straight into their rumen – the big stomach full of bacteria where they broke down roughage – and many of the nutrients were lost. It was better to feed them through teats, so they had to suck, which sent the milk directly into their true stomach. And the farm is all about increasing the weight of these little ones, thought Susan, glad to put down her own burden.

There were four teats to each container, with a large opening at the top. Susan poured the milk into the top, careful not to spill any, then let the buckets clatter to the floor as the calves pushed forwards to suck. The biggest ones found a place first, pushing away the smaller ones. Susan leant over the fence and pushed their hard black heads. They were determined to drink, and removing them from where they latched took some effort as she forced their heads to move along to a better space, making room for the smaller calves. When they were all feeding, she picked up the buckets and went back to the shed to mix more milk, the dogs at her ankles. She could hear the calves in the next pen calling out to her, anxious that they had been forgotten, banging against the dividing fence to try and reach the milk.

"Silly animals," Susan thought as she scooped more powder into the buckets. She added water and stirred, pausing to push a dog away. "Get back," she said, "this isn't for you."

Susan heard a car pull into the yard and paused, listening. She couldn't leave the calves, only half of them were fed, and the others would be frantic if left for too long without food. The dogs didn't bark, so Susan knew it was someone familiar. They rushed off, and she heard a door slam shut, and then Tom's voice, telling the dogs to calm down, and his footsteps as he came to the shed. Susan looked up at him, and summoned a smile.

Chapter Thirteen

The first person that Susan told about Ben was Josie. She hadn't meant to. Josie had come round to ask if there was any casual work on the farm, as she was between jobs, and Tom had told her no, sorry, and then sent her into the house for tea with Susan to soften the blow.

Susan was pleased to see her. She was washing the kitchen floor, sliding the mop across muddy footprints, and she was glad for an excuse to stop. The floor would be dirty again within a day, so it seemed a pointless activity anyway.

The radio was playing, rather too loudly, because some of the cows were leaving today, and Susan couldn't bear to hear the mooing and bellowing as they were loaded onto the lorry. Although she knew the point of the farm was to raise cattle for beef, and she never allowed herself to become attached to them – never named them, always knew their stay was temporary – Susan still didn't like to hear them leave. Even Tom, always matter of fact about the animals, ever aware of their intrinsic value, the cost of their feed and the returned value which depended on their weight, rarely talked about the abattoir. Susan knew that when he loaded them onto the lorry, he told them they were going on holiday, rubbed their backs, blocked his emotions.

So when Josie appeared at the door, Susan was glad of the distraction and balanced the mop in the bucket. She poured boiling water into the brown teapot, turned off the radio, and led Josie into the little sitting room.

Josie had been in love with Edward for as long as Susan could remember. Josie had grown up on the adjoining farm, and had attended the same schools, joined the same clubs, and appeared at the kitchen door whenever she could think of an excuse. Edward had ignored her for years, then decided the attention was fun, so had begun to first tease her, and then flirt with her. Susan was never sure how much her son had hurt the girl, as he would never stay and listen to her lectures, but she hoped that over time Josie had realised how hopeless her crush was, and had moved on. Susan had watched the recent rekindling of the friendship with trepidation, and wondered if there was a way to gently warn the girl without overstepping the boundary of what mothers are supposed to say.

"Do you still take sugar?" she asked, pouring the tea into mugs.

"Yes, two please," said Josie, smiling as if to show that she knew she was overweight but didn't care.

"Do you know when the boys will be back?" Josie asked. She sat back in her chair, gazing round the room, looking comfortable.

Susan knew the room was very different to Josie's own home. Josie's mother was an interior designer. On the few occasions that Susan had visited, she had worried about creasing a cushion, and felt rather bombarded by all the bold colours and coordinating fabrics. Susan had no idea how such a house – she couldn't quite bring herself to describe it as a home – fitted with the mud and smells of a farm. She supposed that Trevor, Josie's father, must be considerably tidier than Tom.

"The older boys?" said Susan, knowing that really Josie was only asking about Edward. "I'm not really sure when they'll next be home; I suppose not until Christmas. Though Ben will be back before of course; I think his term ends in a few weeks. It was hardly worth him going back after the funeral.

"Here," she said, passing the tea. "It's nice to see you. What happened with your job at the hairdresser's then?"

"They were cutting back – no pun intended – and I hadn't been there long, so I was one of the first to be pushed. I asked Dad if there was anything on our farm, but he already uses Steve when he needs to, and I can't afford to work for him for free.

"I expect you'll be glad to have Ben around again, it must get a bit lonely here when he's away," Josie said, sipping her tea and settling back into the armchair.

"Does he have a girlfriend yet do you think?" she asked.

Susan put her mug, very carefully, on the edge of the tray, and picked up a magazine, as if she was going to flick through it. She could feel her heart racing, but she decided that she would tell the truth. There was no need not to, not with Josie, who was almost like a niece, she had known her for so long.

"No," Susan said, her voice even but her eyes firmly on the magazine, "he's decided he's gay. He has a boyfriend."

As soon as she'd spoken, she wanted to take back the words and rearrange them. "He didn't 'decide' to be gay," Susan thought, "he *realised* he was gay. Or maybe he'd always known he was gay, but has only just told the rest of us." But the words were out, and she could feel Josie watching her very closely, trying to see into her mind, to gauge how she felt about this, to see if she minded.

There was a pause, which felt to Susan like an eternity, but was probably only a few seconds. The clock on the mantlepiece sounded very loud, and she realised the cattle truck must have left. She stared hard at the magazine, felt she could hear Josie assimilating the information, deciding on a response.

"Oh," said Josie. "Oh! I didn't know – did you?"

"No, not really," said Susan, looking up from an advert for perfume. "But when I think about it, he was always a very tidy little boy, so perhaps I should have guessed. And he never liked being dirty, whereas the others were always covered in mud. And he liked wearing shirts, with all the buttons done up to the collar – why are you laughing?"

Josie was giggling, her mug resting on the arm of the chair so it wouldn't spill.

"You are funny!" Josie said, reaching forwards and placing her mug next to Susan's on the tray. "I don't think those things are a sign of being gay. I have a friend who's gay, and he's the scruffiest person around."

Josie stopped, and Susan knew she was being examined, so looked down, her eyes firmly on the magazine, trying to appear nonchalant.

"I expect," Josie said, speaking slowly as if deciding what to say, "that it's a bit like if you have a baby with Down's Syndrome..."

Susan looked up, surprised. Whatever was Josie talking about?

Josie nodded at her, and continued: "I watched a programme recently, on telly," she said. "It was very interesting, and there were these women, talking about how it felt, when they were told that their baby wasn't what they expected. Anyway, one of them said something which was really good, really explained how it had felt for her, you know, after the baby was born and everything. She said it was like catching a train to Paris, and looking forward to seeing the Eiffel Tower and all that; but when the train arrived, it wasn't in Paris, it was in Amsterdam. And after a while, she realised that Amsterdam was a good city, and it had good things that weren't in Paris, so if she could go back in time, she might even have chosen Amsterdam. But at the time, when she first realised, it was a shock. And finding out her baby was a Downs baby was like that. Like she'd got on the wrong train, and all her hopes were ruined. Is that how it was for you? When you found out Ben was gay?"

Susan began to smile. "I suppose so, a little bit," she said. "I do know what you mean, anyway. But it's still a bit new for me, I'm still finding out what Amsterdam is going to be like, and there's a lot about Paris that I was looking forward to..."

"Do you mind?" Josie asked.

"No," said Susan, and smiled properly. Because right then, at that very moment, she realised that she didn't mind. There was something about the younger woman's acceptance, her openness, that made Ben's news normal, not a problem.

"I've seen that perfume in Boots," said Josie, glancing at the magazine Susan was holding. "It cost a fortune, and smelt awful. I think people must buy it for the pretty bottle. Shall we go and check the cows? I like watching them."

Susan realised that the conversation about Ben was finished, it had been nothing more than temporarily interesting to Josie, of minimal significance. She smiled at the girl, suddenly feeling affectionate. To Josie, Ben was simply Ben, and nothing had changed.

All was quiet outside, and Susan knew it was safe to go and see the cows and calves that remained. Tom would be cleaning out the empty stalls, moving dirty straw and rinsing the concrete with water from the power hose. She nodded at Josie and put her magazine back on the table. They carried the tray back to the kitchen and pulled on wellingtons and coats before going outside.

Chapter Fourteen

As December approached, with all its wet mud and grey skies, Tom announced they would save money by cutting the small pine tree, which he'd spotted in the corner of the north field, hidden amongst tall shrubs, instead of buying a Christmas tree. Susan was busy when he suggested it, rushing to feed the poultry before leaving for the cafe, so she nodded, and said "Good idea!" without really listening. Which was, perhaps, a mistake. Ben knew nothing of this conversation, until a week before Christmas, when he was sitting in the kitchen, chatting to his mother.

The house was beginning to have a festive feel, the kitchen cupboards were crammed with food; wrapping paper and gifts had appeared in odd corners, and there was a lingering smell of mixed spice and cinnamon. Ben was looking forward to Christmas, the old feelings of excitement from childhood stirring in his stomach.

He was sitting with his feet on a chair, because the floor was wet, watching Susan write cards. Suddenly, the door burst open and a fir tree appeared. Long branches protruded into the room, others were jamming it in place, while behind it, he could hear his father, grunting with effort. As Ben watched, the long branches were forced through the too-narrow doorway, whilst mud and dead leaves and pine needles scattered onto the recently washed floor. Some of the mud dissolved on the wet floor, and began to run in rivulets between the tiles.

"Must that come inside now?" said Susan, frowning.

There were sounds of panting, the tree quivered, and then seemed to bounce fully into the room. Tom stood beside it, grinning.

"I reckon this'll do, don't you?" he said, beaming at Ben and Susan. "It's a good size, the others will love it."

"It has two crowns," said Susan, frowning, "and it's too tall for the sitting room. And why isn't it in a bucket?"

Ben saw his father's expression darken, the enthusiasm fading from his eyes.

"But yes," added Susan, "it's a great size, good find."

"I just brought it in to show you," Tom said, "and I thought it could go in the parlour this year, as it's a decent size. You always buy such a tiny one; be nice to have a proper tree this year."

Ben thought his father was in rather dangerous territory, remembering the heated discussions between his parents each year, as to whether having a tree was essential and how much money his mother ought to spend on one. But although he saw his mother open her mouth, as if to remind Tom of this, she simply shook her head, and asked Ben to help move the tree into the parlour. Then she returned to her cards, and Ben saw her write an address, in her neat square writing.

"I think I'll put it into the parlour now, and then decide on the pot once I've seen how much space I've got," said Tom.

Ben watched his father force the tree through the doorway into the parlour. He had been about to eat some breakfast, but he supposed he ought to help, and his mother's face was grim, so he felt their conversation was probably over.

"Did you want me to mop this floor again?" he asked, hoping, desperately, that she would say no.

"No, don't worry," said his mother, "I have a feeling that won't be the end of the mess. I don't know why I bother to wash it anyway, it only gets dirty again." She looked up from her card, and forced a smile.

"Can you go and help Dad? His back's bad again, so he shouldn't be lugging trees around anyway, but it's no good telling him that."

Ben followed his father to the parlour, where he was lifting the tree into a bucket. The carpet was filthy, and Ben knew his mother would have something to say about that. Surrounding the bucket was a small stack of broken bricks.

Tom was holding the tree at arms-length, examining it. He was holding it awkwardly, and frowning.

"Your back hurting again?" asked Ben.

"A bit," said his father, looking rueful, "I'm not in the best line of work for a weak back. I pulled it last week, when I was moving the latest delivery of food pellets. It didn't hurt too much at first, but now I keep feeling it, like a guitar string that's stretched out and is twanging." He shook his head. "Right pain it is."

"Shouldn't you go to the doctor?" asked Ben, crossing the room and taking hold of the tree so his father could let go.

Tom stepped back, and stared at the tree, his head on one side.

"The doctor will tell me to rest it," he said, "and I can't afford to do that, can I? Too much work to do. And I can't afford to pay someone else to do it, unless I claim on the insurance, and I'm not ill enough for that yet.

"Now, this tree – what do you think? Looks pretty good, doesn't it? It's a good size."

"It has two points," said Ben.

Tom stared at the tree, chose the tallest point, and twisted the other one until it snapped off.

"Not anymore."

"Now it's lop-sided," said Ben, "but I suppose it doesn't matter. What are you going to do about all the insects?"

Tom moved forwards and bent down. He groaned, then began to wedge the bricks around the trunk, securing the tree so that Ben could let go.

The tree stood there, leaning slightly to one side.

"The insects Dad?" said Ben, "It's covered in them." He stared at the tree. Each branch, when he looked closely, was crawling. It made him feel itchy, and he shuddered.

The tree had evidently been home to many insects, and now they had come into the house, and felt the warm air, they had woken from their winter slumbers and were uncurling from the holes and crevices where they'd sheltered, beginning to explore.

Tom moved closer too, and peered at the branches.

"Oh yes," he said, "there are a few."

There were dark bodied aphids, adelgids, bark beetles and mites. They were creeping along the branches, as though testing this new environment. Ben watched a small grey spider, almost perfectly round, as it crawled over a branch, then dropped on a silken web to the branch below.

Tom stared harder; Ben watched him, as he squinted to see the smaller insects then sucked in his lips.

"You're right," said Tom, his face gloomy, "This is the sort of thing your mother makes a fuss about. Especially if she spots the psocids, which might decide to breed in her books.

"There's quite a variety," Tom said, glancing at Ben, "pretty interesting really. Do you know them all?"

"No, they're just bugs and spiders," said Ben, having no interest in entomology. "And Mum won't be interested either," he added. "I think we should get rid of them. Before they crawl off the tree. Shall I go and find an insect spray?"

"No, that won't work," said Tom, frowning. "Aerosols are very flammable. We don't want to mix that with the sugary sap of a fir tree – the whole lot might go up in flames if a spark gets near.

"I've read a lot of warnings lately, lots of advice sent out by the Union. Fire is one of the biggest fears on a farm. Electrocution possibly comes a close second. If we spray the tree, and then turn on the lights, who knows what might happen? We'd be combining both of those dangers and then bringing them right into the house! You've seen how fir trees burn, Ben, when we've cut them and had a bonfire."

Ben nodded, remembering the sizzle and whoosh, as the oily branches caught light, emitting heat and sending flames towards the sky.

His father was shaking his head. "No, we'd better take it outside I suppose, give it a good shake."

Tom began to pick up the tree, and groaned again, his face screwed up with discomfort. Ben moved forwards.

"Why don't you let me carry it Dad?" Ben said, "Save your back a bit."

Ben took hold of the sticky trunk and followed his father to the kitchen. It was a struggle to push it through the doorway, and it shed needles and insects as they went. Ben decided to not notice them, there was no way he could move the tree without making a mess, and he was following the trail his father had made earlier, when he brought it into the house.

Susan looked up as they passed through the kitchen. She didn't say a word, but Ben saw her frown, pick up her cards and pen, and leave the room. There was something rather eloquent about her silence, and Ben thought it would be wise to avoid her for a while.

When they got to the yard, Ben held the tree at full stretch, and gave it a good shake. Within seconds, insects were falling out, running along his arm, hurrying along the ground in an attempt to escape. He held the tree still, and he and his father peered at it. At first, it looked clear of wildlife, then gradually things began to move. They were standing next to the big barn, and a line of cows peered at them, straining their necks to see what was happening, their long-lashed eyes interested, as if assessing the success of the tree shaking.

"There's still a ton of bugs on there," said Ben. "Maybe we should just burn this and buy a proper one."

"This is a *proper* one," said Tom, "and I'm not wasting the money. We've got most of them off, I think that'll do."

"Dad, it won't. Mum'll hate it," said Ben, thinking that he too would hate it. He wasn't very keen on bugs, and the tree was crawling with them. "What about the hose?" He nodded towards the power hose, which lay on the yard floor, next to the cage used for holding the cows still while their fur was cut when they were moved into the barn.

They carried the tree over to the hose, and Tom held the tree steady, while Ben squirted the water over the branches. Tom shouted every time the icy water splashed him, and they were both laughing, as the spray shot up, soaking both of them and drenching the tree. When it was done, they stood there, dripping, examining the tree. Nothing moved. Quite a few of the pine needles had been washed away with the water, so it looked slightly bare, rather forlorn, as if recovering from a nasty illness. They both looked down at the puddle of dirty water and pine needles.

"Those would've fallen off in a couple of days anyway," said Tom, "so we've saved your mother some housework by washing them away. Come on, let's get it back inside."

Ben gave it a last shake, to remove most of the water, and then carried it back into the house, kicking his wet boots off in the boot-room, through the kitchen, along the hallway, into the parlour. Tom held it in the bucket, drips of water falling onto his collar, while Ben jammed bricks around the trunk until it was secure. Ben tried to do all the bending and heavy lifting, hoping to save his father's back.

"We need to give it some water," said Tom. "If we treat it like any other cut plant, top up the water in the bucket regularly, it won't lose any pine needles."

"Any *more* pine needles," corrected Ben, under his breath.

They stepped back, surveying their work.

"Pretty good, I reckon, pretty good," said Tom. "We'll leave it while the branches dry, then your mother can decorate it. She's good at that."

"Right, better get those cows fed," said Tom, heading back towards the boot-room.

Ben went to the kitchen and busied himself with packets of cereal, looking fully occupied, hoping his father wouldn't suggest he went to help.

***

The tree was undoubtedly lop-sided. Jack sat looking at it after Christmas lunch. He felt pleasantly full, and the whole family was sprawled on chairs in the parlour, belching loudly and feeling satisfied. He stared up at the plastic star that his mother put on the tree every year. It leaned drunkly to one side. At least, he thought it did. It was very possible that both the drunkenness and the leaning were on his own part.

The same decorations were brought out every year. From his position next to the fire, Jack could see the pendant with his photograph on, that he'd made with Miss Mott in the reception class; it was faded now, but some of the glitter remained, and it shone as it swayed gently in a draught. There was the bauble with a dent, that Ed had used as hockey practice one year, and the fancy glass dome that Neil and Kylie had brought back from a trip to New York. Towards the back, where Susan had tried to hide them, were the clay angels that Aunty Elsie had made one year. They too appeared slightly drunk, and more resembled ghosts than angels; but Elsie would notice, and be hurt, if they didn't appear each year.

Thinking of his great aunt and grandmother, reminded Jack of the funeral, and he shuddered, the memory eclipsing the contentment of Christmas. Although most of the funeral day had been fine – good even – and he had for the most part managed to forget his problems and revert back to being with his brothers and laughing with them, there had been that one, terrible moment, when he went to collect the coats.

Susan had asked Jack if he could be coat monitor, and there had been no problems when people arrived, and he took their damp coats, carrying them upstairs to throw them across the bed, then hurrying to return so he could help Josie pass around plates of cake. It was later, when he had gone to collect them so people could leave, that he had begun to consider what might be in the pockets. As he lifted each coat, slinging them across his arm, he could tell by the weight that some had purses and wallets in the pockets. The thought of being so close to all that available money, money which he could easily take without anyone noticing, was almost too much. He was so desperate, and he doubted the owners needed it as much as he did, would probably not even notice it had gone, if he was careful. So, he had stood there, thinking, listening to the sounds of conversation floating up from the parlour, while he considered.

He had heard Edward laughing, still teasing Neil and calling him Peter; there were snatches of conversation about the music at the funeral: "Why would George have chosen those songs?" and "I do think Neil spoke well, don't you? Shame about that one little slip at the end..." A door banged as someone went to the washroom, a car revved outside. And Jack stood there, considering, thinking about the money.

But the very thought had made him feel sick. Even thinking about it now made his stomach turn; a fat grey worm of self-loathing slid through him. What was he becoming, that he would start thinking about stealing from mourners at a funeral? The worm turned, grimy and damp, polluting his insides, pushing through his arteries, squeezing his heart into something tight and mean. He sighed, trying to dismiss the feeling, reminding himself that he wasn't that person, he hadn't sunk that low. He was feeling guilty about something that he hadn't actually done.

"Though you thought about it," said a voice inside, "and it's bad enough that you thought about it...what kind of a person are you...?"

Jack took a deep breath, trying to clear the memory. Then exhaled quickly. The air smelt putrid, of old drains. He wasn't sure if it was the effect of too many Brussels sprouts, or if his parents needed to repair the plumbing. He sniffed again, more tentatively. Yes, something was definitely off. He wouldn't mention it just yet, Mum was looking tired, and there was nothing she could do today. His attention was caught by a small brown beetle. He watched as it climbed the wall, keeping to the corner, all the way to the top. It disappeared behind a crack in the wallpaper.

Beneath the tree, only the gifts for Gran and Elsie remained. The elderly sisters had gone to Aunty Cassie for Christmas this year, so would have to open their gifts later in the week, when Mum took them round. Thinking of gifts made Jack squirm again. He'd done his best, borrowed some cash from a couple of friends, but he'd bought pretty paltry gifts in comparison to his brothers. None of them had said anything, but Jack could see in their eyes that they'd noticed, been a bit surprised. Even Ben had bought better gifts – mainly bottles of alcohol – and he was still managing on the grant that Tom gave him. But Jack thought it was okay, they'd forget soon enough, there were so many gifts going around.

The worm in his gut slithered again, making him feel wretched. He pushed down the feeling, concentrated on the fuzziness that alcohol induced, tried to summon that contented fullness that followed a big meal.

At his feet was a heap of gifts that Jack had received. Whiskey from Ben, a hoodie from Neil and Kylie, a bigger bottle of whiskey from Ed, and several bits from his parents. If they'd asked, Jack would have tried to find a way to ask for money. But they never did, his family tended to think a gift was only a gift if it was a surprise, so now he had a lot of very nice items that he didn't need, and which did nothing to off-set the deficit in his bank account. Jack leaned forwards and peered down at them. He wondered if he could take a couple back to the shops, ask for a refund. But probably not, as he didn't have the receipts. Unless he had a quiet word with Kylie later, said the hoodie was a bit tight, did she have the receipt so he could change it? Yes, that might work, she wouldn't guess, would give him the receipt if she still had it. It might be worth a few quid. Might help a little bit.

Jack looked up when his mother came into the room and asked if anyone wanted coffee.

"Why don't you sit down Mum," said Neil, scrambling to his feet, "I can make coffee if anyone wants one." Jack shook his head in unison with the others, and Neil sat back down.

Susan came and sat next to Jack. She sniffed.

"What's that smell?" she said, "It smells like old drains."

Jack shook his head again.

"Oh! It must be the tree," she said, leaning towards Jack. "I bet the water Dad put in there has gone stagnant. Can you smell it?"

"A bit," said Jack, not wanting to worry her. "Perhaps you could add some bleach or something, to kill the bacteria."

"Maybe," said Susan, her voice doubtful.

"What did Aunty Elsie give you?" asked Jack.

"Oh, I don't know yet, I went to boil vegetables earlier, and forgot to open it," said Susan.

Jack watched as she leant forwards and took the slim package from under the tree. It was wrapped in red and gold paper, slightly crumpled, and Jack wondered if it had been saved from the previous year.

"I'll open it now," Susan said, "it can be my after-dinner treat."

She read the label aloud: *"Dear Susan, Happy Christmas, Much love, Aunty Elsie."*

His mother always opened gifts carefully, often folding the paper as she went. Jack had found it frustrating when he was young, wanting her to rip open the wrapping and see what was inside. He watched now, as she lifted the small package, and slid her finger under a flap, and moved it, breaking the seal of tape, then gradually unfolded the wrapping paper. Jack glimpsed pale pink material, folded into a rectangle. Susan lifted it out, and began to unfold it, then shook it out and held it up, so everyone could see.

It was a tee-shirt, short-sleeved and round-necked, made of pink jersey. Across the chest, in bold black lettering, were the initials: "WTF".

"Oh!" said Susan, "That's a surprise!"

Jack chuckled. "Does Aunty Elsie know what W-T-F means?" he said.

"I'm guessing not," said Susan. "The bigger question is, should I tell her?"

As if on cue, the house telephone shrilled in the hall.

"That'll be your mother," said Tom, struggling to his feet, "no one else rings the normal phone except for sales calls, and surely they won't phone today."

Tom left the door open when he left, and Jack felt a draught of cold air. It diluted the stagnant smell a little.

"Hello Dot!" Jack heard his father yell, "Happy Christmas! Yes, we've finished dinner, I'll go and get her. Say hello to Elsie for me."

Tom stepped back into the room. "Susan, it's your mother."

"I thought it might be," she said to Jack, heaving herself up from the chair and going to the hall.

"Hello Mum, happy Christmas," Jack heard.

"Yes, yes, that's right. No, the turkey was a bit dry – it usually is. And of course, I had to cook something else for Neil and Kylie this year..."

Jack flinched, hoping his mother knew that they could all hear her, wondering if he should get up and close the door.

"No, no," she continued, "it wasn't too much bother after all. I found some veggie steaks, looked like rubber, but they seemed to eat them. Of course, they wouldn't eat my gravy. No, well it's made from meat juices, isn't it. Yes Mum, they don't eat any meat, not even things that have come from animals. It was fine, I made some of that packet gravy you can buy.

"Anyway, thank you for the candles and gloves – they're lovely. Can I have a quick word with Elsie? And I'll see you on Wednesday, when you're both home.

"Yes, bye Mum...

"Oh, hello Aunty. I just wanted to say happy Christmas, and thank you for the tee-shirt. It's a lovely colour, I've just opened it.

"Well, yes Aunty, I do know what the letters stand for – do you though? I wasn't sure if you...oh you do? Edward told you, did he? Ah, 'where's the fun' – that's what he was, it was? No...yes...well it was a lovely thought, thank you."

Jack glanced at Edward, who was grinning broadly.

"She saw a text on my phone," Edward said, spreading his hands wide in a gesture of innocence. "When she asked what the letters meant what was I supposed to say? I could hardly tell her the truth, could I? I didn't know she was going to go and buy Mum a tee-shirt, did I?"

Jack shook his head. He could hear his mother as she ended her call, then the click as she replaced the receiver.

"Edward," she said, coming into the room, "I need to have a word with you..."

However, Edward was leaving, walking quickly to the kitchen, pulling his phone from his pocket as it buzzed.

"Hi Emm, how's it going?" Jack heard, watching his brother march from the room, the door banging behind him. Jack shook his head, and stared once more at his gifts before leaning back in the chair and closing his eyes. He dozed off for a few minutes, then was woken abruptly. Edward was kicking his foot.

"Hey, Jack!"

Jack looked up.

"I see me and Ben both bought you whiskey. How about I buy one off you, so you can get something different?"

Jack sat up straighter. "Sure, great, sounds good," he said, picking up the larger bottle.

"Not that one, the little one," Edward said. "I'll give you ten quid for it."

"Ten quid? It cost more than that," said Jack. "Fifteen."

"Twelve, and you have a deal," said Edward.

Jack grinned. "Done," he said, and lifted the bottle. "Don't tell Ben."

They both glanced across the room. Ben was stretched out on the sofa, a magazine on his lap, his eyes closed. "Not a word," promised Edward.

Chapter Fifteen

Boxing day morning, Jack was waiting in the kitchen when Edward opened the door. He was reading a magazine, but put it on the table when the door opened, and moved to the kettle.

"You making coffee?" said Edward, easing out of his jacket and putting it on the back of a chair.

"Where've you been then?" said Jack, frowning. "You been to Trevor's farm? Seeing Josie *again*?"

Edward glanced at him, surprised by his tone.

"What if I have?" He shrugged.

Jack thumped the kettle onto the surface, water splashing out of the spout. "Can't you just leave her alone? You know you're not serious, you're still with Emily aren't you?"

There was a pause, Edward seemed to be considering how to answer for a moment.

"Hey, calm down a bit mate, I thought we'd already sorted this – I'm getting a feeling of 'déjà vu' here..." Edward said with a grin, as if hoping to deflect the question. "If I want to see Big Jose, I'm not sure that I need to explain anything to you anyway. Josie knows the score, she knows I'm with Emily. But it's Christmas, and we've always been friends, you know that. I just popped over to see her, as a friend, to say hello, took her a little gift, like mature people do. It doesn't mean anything, Josie knows that."

"Does she? I'm not so sure she does. Seems to me like you're stringing her along, taking what you can get. But she's not a toy, she's a person. You shouldn't treat her like that."

Jack pulled a mug from the cupboard, unscrewed the jar of coffee and spooned the granules into his cup, pausing to wipe away the spilt ones with his sleeve. He reached up for a second mug, then changed his mind. Let Ed make his own coffee, he thought.

Edward came and stood next to him. There was a tiny spider climbing the wall. Edward reached across and squashed it under his thumb. Jack watched him, shaking his head.

"Well, you seem very concerned all of a sudden," said Edward, grinning, trying to change track. "You got your eye on her yourself or something? Go for it mate! I certainly wouldn't want to stand in your way, it's not like it's anything serious."

"Not to you maybe," said Jack, "but Emily might see things differently, if I should mention it."

"Yeah, but you won't," said Edward, scowling. "Now, let's change the subject to something more interesting. When can I come and see this fancy flat of yours I keep hearing about?"

Jack stared at his brother, wondering what he knew. The grey worm in his gut slithered, and he felt slightly sick.

"Kettle's hot, if you want a drink," he said, and carried his coffee to the safety of his room.

***

Susan was preparing Boxing Day lunch when Neil approached her for another discussion. She was wiping the table, and Neil appeared, looking serious, and asking if she wanted any help.

"You could set the table," said Susan, wondering why he had really come. His expression was sombre, and she guessed he had something on his mind. Neil took a handful of knives and forks from the drawer, and began to scatter them across the damp table. Susan threw the cloth into the sink and moved back to the oven.

"Have you thought any more about Ben?" said Neil, taking the spoons from the drawer. There was a small beetle making its way along the edge of the table, and Susan watched as Neil flicked it onto his hand and went to the window.

"In what way?" asked Susan, opening the oven door. A wave of heat rushed into her face, making her eyes sting, and she moved away while it passed, then reached inside for the tray of potatoes.

"About what we can do to help him stop being gay. And this other boy."

Susan heard him close the window.

She frowned, staring at the potatoes in the oven. The ones on the top shelf were brown, the ones beneath still looked pale. The 'other boy' was a problem she had been ignoring. Usually, when her boys had been in relationships, they brought their girlfriends to the farm as a matter of course, wanting to introduce them to the family. But Ben hadn't yet suggested that Kevin should visit, and Susan hadn't mentioned it either, not quite knowing how she would feel about meeting him. She didn't know how she felt about anything really, and whenever she tried to think about it, a knot of tension rose up in her stomach, and she felt cross. She rather resented that Neil had raised the topic, especially while she was trying to cook dinner for everyone. However, now that Neil had raised the subject, she felt bound to defend Ben, even though her own views were still unsure.

"His name is Kevin," Susan said, her voice more curt than she intended, "and if Ben wants him to meet the family, then we'll all be polite and welcoming, because that's the right way to behave." She lifted the potato tray from the oven, the heat piercing the worn oven gloves, burning her hand. She put the tin rather too quickly onto the hob, and it clattered down, splashing hot fat.

"Is that oil or goose fat?" asked Neil, peering over her shoulder.

"Oil, of course," said Susan, her hand smarting, adding to her irritation, and making her want to lash out. "Because Neil, although I do not understand, in the least, why you are convinced we're cruel to cattle, I respect your decision. I will therefore try to cook an alternative, even though it's extra work, and a right pain in the backside. Which is," she said, lifting her head to meet Neil's eyes, "my point."

Susan tried to make her voice calm, to explain rationally to Neil, how she was feeling and the point she had currently reached through her maze of indecision.

"Whatever our own views, this boy is special to Ben, and so we have to welcome him to the family. Otherwise, we'll just lose Ben. If he has to choose between someone he's fond of and his family, he won't choose us. We'll see him less and less – and it's hard enough for a family to stay close when everyone starts moving away as it is.

"If you value your brother's company, you'll do your best to be friendly to this Kevin. Out of respect for Ben."

Susan turned back to the cooker, and began to turn the potatoes, covering each side in the hot oil so they would brown evenly. They glistened as the light caught them, sizzling as they touched the spitting oil. The smell was not, thought Susan, as satisfying as roasts cooked in goose fat, they didn't have that rich warm aroma. In fact, she thought, lifting the tray to return it to the oven, the smell mainly reminded her of a chip shop, which was not at all what she was hoping to create.

"No, Mum, no," said Neil behind her. "I really feel that is exactly what we *mustn't* do. Don't you see, if we welcome this boy, we are condoning the relationship, in effect saying that it's okay, we accept it. And we should never do that, because it's wrong. We can show Ben that we still care about him – obviously – but we shouldn't do anything that affirms the relationship."

Susan turned and glanced at Neil. He was leaning against the work surface, cutlery in his hand, his expression serious. She guessed he may have prepared a speech for her – "affirm" was not a word Neil would normally use. Susan sighed. Neil had always been thorough, she thought, always the one she didn't need to nag to do his homework. She went to the pantry and pulled out the carrots.

"I'm not sure you're right," Susan said, her voice echoing in the dark cupboard as she delved into the vegetable sack. "I mean about 'affirming' the relationship. Surely it's just a matter of being hospitable?"

Neil was shaking his head. "No Mum, no. I've been reading about it, online. I've joined some forums, to see what other Christians say, and it's pretty clear that anything which could be construed as affirmation, would be wrong. So people talk about what to do if they're invited to a gay wedding, things like that, and there's got to be a clear line drawn, an absolute decision to do what is right, what God wants, and not compromise our faith. We shouldn't do anything which appears accepting of this decision, this immoral lifestyle. We need to help Ben, don't we? Before it's too late."

Susan picked up a carrot and ran the peeler along its length, a fine orange ribbon falling onto the work surface. She thought about what Neil was saying, testing it against her own views, feeling that somehow such an intransigent statement was harmful, condemning. She thought back, to what Rob had advised her. There was something pressing on her chest, a lump of emotion and anger, a primeval need to defend her child from attack, albeit the attack was from another of her children.

Susan felt there was something hard about what Neil was repeating, something that sounded smug and self-righteous; she heard nothing loving in those views, nothing humble, nothing that sounded like Neil was trying to reach out to his brother, walk by his side and support him. Susan wondered who these people were, who so easily spread their views across the internet, preaching a theology that was detached from real people, people who would be hurt. People who Susan loved.

"There is," Susan thought, "only a priggish determination to defend a theology. They are all unwilling to consider that other people hold a different opinion. Neil has found people online who share his views, and he's using their words to express how he feels. He seems to think that because other people have the same views as himself, it's proof that he is right. He's not even questioning it."

Susan had noticed this in people before, any view that complimented what someone thought, was from God; anything which challenged that was deceptive, and should be shunned. She had no patience with it, this belief that God would honour certain people with complete understanding of what his Bible meant, and others, who were searching as diligently, were left floundering in a mire of self-deception.

"So, how does that view apply to your other brothers? I shouldn't meet Emily, who Edward is shacked-up with, because I would be condoning that?" Her voice sounded harsh, even to her own ears, and Susan saw Neil draw back, surprised.

Susan moved the pile of carrot peelings to one side, and pulled out a drawer, looking for a knife. She found a small pink one, her favourite, but as she closed the drawer, it caught on her finger, pinching her. The pain fuelled her anger, and she began to slice the carrots, chopping rapidly, her anger coming in short sharp raps of the knife as it dissected the carrot, orange disks spinning across the surface.

"It seems to me," Susan said, her voice sharp and clipped, keeping time with her knife, "that you interpret the Bible in a way that suits how you want to live, and how you think others ought to live." She continued, "But I think –" Susan glanced

"That would be my job then," thought Susan, and began to thump them into place.

***

Lunch was a subdued affair. Neil was curt, hardly speaking to anyone and impeccably polite when forced to answer. Even when Edward asked him to: "Pass the potatoes, Jason," he simply muttered "I thought that joke would be old by now" and handed his brother the dish of roasts. His mood cast a damper over the rest of the family, no one other than Susan knew what was wrong, and they were wary, not wanting to make things worse.

Susan felt her son's mood keenly. She knew Neil was angry with her, knew he believed she was wrong, and wondered if he blamed her for the choices that Ben was making. Her own anger had dissipated, leaving her with a core of hurt and sadness, and she wasn't sure what to do. Tom was giving her constant looks, trying to find out what was wrong, but she avoided his eyes, not wanting to share the hurt.

The other boys were trying to behave normally. Ben told her that something was wrong in the parlour, and it smelt like a public lavatory; which Susan guessed was because she'd added bleach to the Christmas tree water. But she didn't say anything, and gradually the conversation fizzled out, each of them influenced by the atmosphere. The silence became heavy, oppressive, stifling appetites and making everyone tense.

When Susan carried the fat gooseberry pie to the table and asked Jack to get the steaming jug of custard, Neil stood.

"Thank you for lunch, and Christmas, Mum and Dad. But I won't have any pudding thanks. I'm going to pack, and then Kylie and I are leaving."

"But, I thought you were staying for tea..." began Susan. Her voice sounded hollow, and she stopped. She didn't know what was happening. Her family didn't do this; they argued – shouted at each other sometimes, slammed doors perhaps. Then they calmed down, either sorted it out or let it simmer, but they carried on. They didn't leave. They did not leave hurts and arguments half finished; they didn't build barriers that might never be broken down. They were a unit, a family, tied together. Neil couldn't leave. If he walked out, that was too big a statement, too great a chasm; one which might never be bridged.

Susan looked at Neil, seeing his face was carved marble, pale with suppressed emotion; and she knew his words, though polite, were intended to hurt. She felt he was full of righteous anger, sure that the time had come to make a stance, to stand up for morality and truth; Neil could no longer compromise his beliefs for the sake of unity within the family. Susan wasn't sure if he was reacting to what she had said, or the anger with which she had said it, and she knew that the anger was only partly directed at him. Mostly she was angry – or rather, *had* been angry – because she was worried and confused.

Neil pushed back his chair, and left the room. The family heard his footsteps as he climbed the stairs, and the bang of his bedroom door. No one spoke, not even Edward.

As soon as dinner was finished, Susan escaped to the barn. She found a corner, where the feed was stacked, and sat on a pile of pellet sacks. The cows moved, aware of her presence but unperturbed, and something was scratching in the rafters. Susan sat, head in hands, trying to make sense of her mood. She felt that everything was slipping from her grasp, that she had been holding sand for too long, trying to pretend that all was normal, the family was still on kilter; when actually all was disintegrating around her. Tom wasn't managing to keep up with the heavy lifting on the farm because of his back, and nor could they afford to employ someone to help. Ben had announced he was gay, and she still wasn't sure of her own views, but Neil it seemed, was unable to compromise his own beliefs and was determined to try and save Ben, whether he wanted 'saving' or not. Edward was still messing about with Josie whilst living with Emily; and Jack – well, she didn't know what was wrong with Jack, but something was making him thin and pale and unable to meet her eyes.

Susan felt the burden of carrying the family as keenly as she had when the boys were small; and when she sighed the air left her in a shudder, as if she would break in two. Something hard was pressing on her chest, and her head felt constricted, as if her skull had shrunk and was pressing her brain into a knot. The thoughts were circling her head, like so many birds circling a pond but refusing to land.

As her despair grew, Susan felt a hand placed, tentatively, on her shoulder, and raised her head, expecting to see Tom, or Ben. It was Kylie.

"I came to see how you were."

Susan stared at her, then looked at the hand on her shoulder, the long red nails, the rings on each finger. The view misted as teardrops filled her eyes and hung there, balanced, waiting to fall.

"I – don't know. I'm not sure what to do any more," Susan said.

Kylie sat down next to her, her body pressing against Susan as she squashed onto the pile of sacks. Kylie put an arm around Susan and pulled her close, took hold of her hand with the other hand.

"It'll be all right," Kylie said, "Neil just needs a bit of time. He's only being like this because he's worried about his brother, and he wants to do what he believes is right."

"But he seems so angry about this," said Susan. "Angry with Ben for being gay; angry with me for not stopping it – or causing it, which is what he more or less accused me of today. And he seems to think that any compromise, any sort of acceptance, is a rejection of his beliefs, is somehow going against God. He thinks he has to choose between God and his family – and I'm sure that's not right..."

Susan stopped. The lump in her chest had moved to her throat, and the tears pricked her eyes, threatening to fall, and if they fell more would follow, so that she would dissolve into sobbing, all control gone. She felt like a small child again, lost and frightened; she didn't know what to do. And the person who had come to help her, the person who seemed to care, was the one person who Susan didn't want to see. Susan had nothing in common with Kylie, yet here she was, an arm firmly clamped to Susan's shoulders, black fingers entwined with Susan's white ones.

"It'll be all right," said Kylie again, "I'll talk him round," and she squeezed Susan, pulling her closer in an awkward hug.

"But you don't like me," blurted Susan, unable to hide her feelings, the tangle of emotions forcing her to be blunt, honest, rude even.

Kylie was silent for a moment. She didn't move, didn't speak. Susan wondered if she had offended her daughter-in-law too. She could feel the arm, heavy across her shoulders, and Kylie's thumb was stroking Susan's hand.

"It's not that exactly," said Kylie at last. "It's just that we don't have much in common, do we?"

Susan felt her move slightly, and knew that Kylie was staring at her. She tried to smile, very aware that whilst Kylie had perfect make-up and smelt faintly of perfume, she herself hadn't yet looked in a mirror today and probably smelt of roast dinner.

"You see, my upbringing was very different to Neil's," said Kylie, her voice slow, as if deciding how to explain. "We lived on a pretty rough council estate. Dad wasn't there much because he was always off driving lorries to the continent, and Mum worked as a dinner lady at the nearby school, and then cleaned houses for a dozen rich people; so they were both busy."

Susan nodded, she knew most of this, wasn't sure how it was relevant, but decided to listen. Listening was easy, and this was nothing to do with her, which gave a rest from all those uncertainties that threatened to overwhelm her.

"We grew up with shop-bought cakes, and worn out carpets, and lots of telly. It wasn't a bad place to grow up, there were always loads of other kids around to play with, but we didn't get much time from Mum and Dad, because they were just too busy. And it was pretty messy; I guess after Mum had cleaned other people's houses, she didn't have the energy to clean her own. I always promised myself that when I grew up, I would have a clean house, full of shiny white surfaces. I like things that are pretty, and clean; and I like being with other people, going out at night, things like that.

"Then I met Neil, and everything about him was different. It seemed like he'd grown up here on the farm, surrounded by his family but not really mixing with other people. He had school friends of course, but he didn't seem to *need* them, not like I needed my friends. He had his brothers, and that was enough really. All he needed was the farm and his family. There was something very secure about him, he's comfortable with himself, isn't he? And the way he tried to look after everyone, making sure everyone was all right all the time, taking the lead. Well, I liked that, I wanted him to look after me too, I suppose." She gave a half laugh, as if embarrassed, and Susan found she was hugging her back, wanting Kylie to continue.

"Everything about Neil seemed better than me. He's very clever, isn't he? And you're all a bit posher than me. You've got a big house, and expensive cars, and everything."

Susan wanted to point out that they didn't own any of that, the farm was drowning in debt with everything bought on hire-purchase and they only had a Land Rover because it was a machine, necessary for crossing muddy fields. But she remained silent, knowing that she shouldn't interrupt, she should listen for once, try to understand. Kylie was still talking about Neil.

"He seemed so much better than me, and I was gob-struck when he noticed me, asked me out. I still think he's impressive – and he seems to like me back. We respect each other. Which I suppose is why we get on so well. And like I said, he's kind, and he stands up for what he believes is right, even when it's difficult for him."

Susan nodded, but didn't speak.

"But he does listen," Kylie continued, "and he does change his mind. It just takes him a bit longer than most people. It's part of his strength, which I admire – but it's also the bit of him that drives me bananas sometimes! I know you're worried about all this."

Kylie gave Susan another rough hug, pulling Susan close, squeezing the air from her before releasing her, keeping hold of Susan's hand.

"But it will be all right. Give him some time. And I'll talk to him. I know you don't rate me much," Kylie looked down, her expression rueful, "but I know how important you all are to Neil, how he wouldn't be who he is without you all. So I will help, I'll make him see that he has to accept a few changes, that things aren't as certain as he thinks. He will see that accepting Ben's situation doesn't have to mean rejecting his God. But it will take time – you'll have to be patient."

Susan looked up, surprised. "But don't you agree with Neil? Don't you think Ben is wrong?"

Kylie shook her head. "No, we've never agreed on this. We disagree on what the Bible says about being gay. I do believe the Bible is from God," she said, meeting Susan's eye.

Susan nodded.

"But I don't think it's a good idea to take little snippets and make a whole rule about them. You might be right, but there's a good chance you might be wrong. We should look at the whole message, you know, understand what's important. And if you take an individual word, well, it might be misleading, you might not have understood it how the author intended. So does the word, the English word, "homosexual" mean to us today, the same as it meant to the bloke who first wrote it? Paul wrote a Greek word, and he was writing at a time when people didn't have same-sex monogamous relationships. So does the word we use even mean what Paul was writing about? It might, but it might not. So I figure to create a whole lot of rules around that, a whole lot of definite rights and wrongs, is a bit dodgy. You can look at what the whole passage teaches – about not treating people like sex objects, making sure that God comes first, stuff like that that – but to place too much emphasis on one word feels a bit...I don't know...conceited I suppose. Why should one person claim they absolutely know God's view over another person?

"I expect, that for some people, they shouldn't practise same-sex relationships. But then, I think some people shouldn't marry either. It says that too, you know, Paul wrote that it would be better to remain single, but we don't talk about that much in church, do we?

"And some people probably shouldn't have children."

Susan glanced at Kylie when she said that, trying to detect if she was referring to herself, but there was no flicker in her expression, nothing that suggested she didn't want children.

"But I don't think," said Kylie, "that we should make up rules for other people. It's too difficult. Like the "Do not kill" commandment. I expect, during the war, that caused all sorts of trouble. Some people translated that as meaning murder, so being in the army and fighting a common enemy was okay, didn't go against God's wishes. But for pacifists, that went against everything they believed. They didn't think they had the right to end life, any life, only God should do that. I'm sure both sides prayed about it, sought God's will and all that; but they landed on different sides, didn't they? And I suppose they both believed, very honourably and sincerely, that the other people were misinterpreting something that was very clearly written.

"I think each person should read, and pray, and ask God what he wants for their own life. That's not to say there aren't rules, because there are, but they're not for us to apply to other people, they're for us to apply to ourselves. For what God wants for me and for you."

"So," said Susan, frowning, not quite sure if she understood, "are you saying that you think being gay is okay? That God doesn't think it's wrong?"

"Yeah, I think I am," said Kylie. She grinned. "I will talk to Neil again, in time, but I think all this has been too big a shock to him. Because he's always felt hugely protective towards his brothers. He does think being gay is wrong, he always has, and he's never had to challenge that belief before. It was just something he knew, so when this happened, he jumped straight onto the 'I have to save Ben from this' bandwagon, without really thinking it through again. He hasn't had time to have doubts, to question something that he simply accepted, because it seemed so clear. But he will. In time. He's a good man, isn't he?"

Susan nodded, the tears hanging in her eyes again, balanced on her lashes, ready to run in streams down her cheeks. She couldn't answer. She could feel the warmth of Kylie pressing into her side, her hand with the red tipped nails and multiple rings, was still holding her own, the dark warm skin pressing into her own flesh, comforting, safe.

"Do you know what I think? I think that God made Ben gay, because God wanted Ben to be gay. I don't believe it was a punishment or a mistake, or something that Ben has chosen for himself. I don't think being gay is wrong."

There was silence.

Susan sat, thinking about what Kylie had said, absorbing the words, letting them comfort her and seep into her mind, changing how she understood things. It made sense; the argument sounded right. And she wanted, oh so very much she wanted, to believe it.

"It does make sense," Susan thought, reasoning to herself, "it doesn't contradict what I know about God. He is always fair, always loving and always holy – so although there's stuff about the gay lifestyle he must hate, in the same way that he hates the things that are wrong with the way some straight people choose to live – it might not mean that *being* gay is wrong. Having a loving, monogamous relationship with someone of the same gender, that *might* be okay – not wrong. Different, and hard for me to get my head round, but maybe, maybe, *not* wrong."

Sounds from outside the barn began to filter through the walls, breaking the spell of the two women, moulded together. They heard Tom's engine, as he drove through the yard, the calling of the cows as they became aware of people who might be going to feed them, the chickens fighting over a kernel of corn. Kylie let go of her hand, and moved away slightly, and Susan felt herself being examined again.

"You a bit better now?" she asked.

Susan nodded. "Yes. Thank you." She leaned over, and very gently, kissed Kylie's cheek. It was soft and perfumed and very smooth.

Kylie grinned.

Susan felt a rush of affection for Kylie, a bond of unity. They were still very different, they would never completely understand each other; but they had made a start. Susan felt that, at long last, her and Kylie were on the same side. They were, finally, in the same family.

Chapter Sixteen

Winter passed, with mornings of frost and mist, which hung on the lower fields so that they looked like the paintings in a storybook. There were days when Susan needed to break the ice on the top of the water bowls and drinkers, watched by rows of grumpy-faced chickens who refused to leave their perch. The farm seemed to slow, time was spent cutting hedges and ploughing earth, ready for when the weather would turn warm enough to start the next cycle of sowing. The fields which were left fallow began to turn green as grass became established, waiting for the cattle to be released into the open. Some days it was so cold, that Tom couldn't feel his fingers all day, and struggled to open the padlocks that secured some of the more remote gates. When he walked across the fields, the mud, which in the autumn had clung to his boots, was now hard and unyielding, standing in uneven lumps where earlier the cows had walked, their footprints preserved as though in concrete.

As spring approached, Tom sat in the kitchen, Susan was placing eggs into the incubator. He knew she had bought the eggs on eBay, and they had arrived in special polystyrene boxes with the morning's post. It was always bit of a gamble, buying hatching eggs online, as there was no guarantee they would be fertile, or that their journey through the British postal service wouldn't have shaken them to pieces. But they'd had some luck in previous years, and it was a cheap and convenient way to obtain them. Cheap was especially important at the moment. It was good to introduce new blood into the flock from time to time, and not to allow too much inbreeding of the ducks they kept.

Susan had rinsed a couple that had arrived covered in muck, complaining to Tom that they should never have been sent out in that state. Now the eggs all lay in the incubator, moist warm air surrounding them, the machine whirring every hour when the plate at the bottom slid sideways, rolling the eggs to a new position. All Susan needed to do was glance at the thermometer again at Neil, her eyes very black, a sign she was angry, "that Ben has that right too. If you can follow your conscience, and live how you think you should, why can't Ben be afforded the same rights? Why are you so convinced that Ben is ignoring God? Don't you think that perhaps, if God wanted to tell Ben he was wrong, then God would do it? When did *people* become responsible for convicting of sin? Where in the Bible does it tell us to go round pointing out what everyone else is doing wrong?

"In fact," Susan said, as the thought occurred to her, "doesn't it say the opposite? Doesn't it warn against noticing the 'speck in your neighbour's eye and ignoring the plank in your own'?"

Susan scooped up the carrots and thrust them into a saucepan, splashing water over them and dumping them onto the hob.

"Right, so we never preach the Bible, is that it?" said Neil. His voice was getting louder, and Susan realised Neil too was now angry. "We never stand up for what is right, we never try and save other people when they go astray. We never say what's wrong."

Susan stared across the kitchen at her son, all the worry of the last few months combining in a fury that she wanted to release. For the moment, Neil represented the views that Susan was afraid of, a hard, unyielding view that condemned Ben.

"Not if preaching the Bible is only so we can condemn other people," Susan said. "It's not meant to be used as a weapon that we judge others with. We're not meant to quote little snippets and use them to support our own views on things. So yes, if you're asking me if I think you should stay out of the Ben situation, my answer is yes. I don't think you should be getting involved, and I certainly don't think you should be wasting time looking online for people who say what you want them to say so you can use it as proof that you are right. Where's the humility in that?"

"Well, if that's your attitude, no wonder things have gone wrong," said Neil. "I'm going to find Kylie."

Susan watched him go. She waited for the door to slam behind him. There was a pile of spoons on a corner of the table, but Neil hadn't distributed them.

occasionally, to check the machine was working, and top up the water reservoir when the level got low.

Tom was at the table, watching Susan and half listening to her, papers spread across the table, laptop open beside him. He was reading through the latest news from the Farmer's Union, trying to assimilate advice about avoiding accidents. He should really have been out on the tractor, working the fields. But, although he didn't like to say anything to Susan, his back was playing up again, the pain was worse than ever, and he didn't think he could cope with several hours being juddered across a bumpy field. Not today.

It was nice being inside, having some company for once. Susan was busy with her poultry, getting the little barn ready, checking the incubator. He liked watching her as she moved around, liked the company. Usually he spent the day entirely on his own, only seeing people when he popped into the house or if he went to the pub before dinner. It was better now, of course, now that they all had mobile phones. At least he could speak to Susan if he needed to, could send the odd text while he was on the tractor. And it was safer, there was a way to call for help from the isolation of a barn or a field, if there was an emergency. Not that they'd had any, not on his farm. But accidents happened, hay bales toppled, or power lines were touched, or animals turned nasty when you weren't expecting it. Which was why he needed to read what the Union had sent, he thought, looking back at the papers. It seemed unnecessary, but you could never be too sure. It was boring though, and he felt restless, knowing that really he should have been in the field.

Tom screwed up his eyes and stared out of the window. He could see a bird, looking for berries on the tree outside. He sighed, not quite sure what the solution was. Really, he needed to employ someone, who could take some of the heavy work from him. But they didn't have the money, the farm was only just ticking over as it was, and finding enough for someone else – bearing in mind they'd need enough to pay rent somewhere – wasn't possible. He toyed with the idea of suggesting they housed a labourer, gave them lodgings so the wage could be lower. But Tom knew Susan would hate that, having to change one of the boys' rooms into a rental. He didn't feel he could even suggest it.

Not yet. If things got worse, if the weather let them down so they had to buy in winter feed this year, then he'd have a rethink. But so far everything was on track, they were having a decent amount of rain, and everything was growing well. No, he thought, hopefully it wouldn't be necessary, but they had four empty rooms if it came to it, they could always fill one with a lodger.

***

Several miles away, in a London suburb, Jack arrived home from work to find two men waiting for him. They moved from the shadow of the hedge as he approached the front door, and something about the size of them, and the way they moved so quietly, made him look up. He knew at once who they were. He glanced towards the front door, which he shared with the flats above and below his, and considered running. But there was little point, he couldn't run for ever. That worm of self-loathing turned in his guts and, shoulders hunched, he turned to face them.

"Jack Compton?" said the taller man, coming towards him.

They arranged themselves, either side of him. One was older, about fifty Jack thought, with very short white hair and a wart on the side of his nose. The other man was shorter, about Jack's height, but broader. They both looked as if they knew how to handle themselves, hard muscles that they weren't afraid to use, and hard eyes to go with them. Those eyes were assessing Jack now, deciding whether he was likely to give them any trouble. It was clear that they knew who he was, even though they had asked, so Jack nodded, waited for what would come next.

"We're enforcement agents, here on behalf of the Richmond Collection Agency," the older man was saying, level with Jack now, standing right next to him on the doorstep. "We've come to repossess items to the value of one thousand pounds in lieu of non-payment of debt. You will have received a Notice of Enforcement last week."

Jack nodded, there was no point in denying it.

The man continued, "Here's my identification. You'll see everything is in order. Here's the paperwork—" he handed Jack some papers. "Shall we go inside?"

Jack opened the door, and they all stepped into the hallway. The men didn't exactly push him – there was no physical contact – but Jack felt crowded, they stayed very close to him. Jack led the way up the first flight of stairs, used his other key to open the door to his own flat. The men followed him inside. One of them shut the door.

As soon as they were inside, there was a tangible difference in attitude. The men turned from Jack, he was no longer necessary, and they walked quickly away from him, into different rooms.

"Wait," said Jack, moving towards his bedroom, after the older man. "Where are you going? I'll show you where things are. There's nothing in here, this is my bedroom, what are you looking for?"

The man was opening drawers, tipping papers from his bedside table. He glanced up. "Better if you go and sit somewhere," the man said, "we know what we're doing. Don't worry, we'll give you a receipt for what we take."

In the lounge, the younger man had collected Jack's laptop and speakers, and was making a pile on the table. He looked up when Jack entered, held out his hand, "I'll have your phone too."

Jack slid it from his pocket, stared at the screen for a second.

The man took it, frowned, passed it back.

"I'll need you to open it, so I can access the settings," he said, "nothing I can do with a locked phone."

Jack used the face-ID option to open the mobile, deleted his emails and contacts and internet history; handed it back to the man, who went back to the table and started to change the settings. The man noticed the recharger, sitting on top of the bookcase, and added that to his pile.

The older man came in from the bedroom, carrying Jack's iPad, and added it to the pile. "This might be enough," he said, and pulling out a chair, sat at the table with a calculator.

Jack sat in a chair, his head in his hands. Next to him, in the wastepaper basket, waiting to be recycled, was the letter he'd received two weeks ago. He could see the blue and white paper, the black writing at the top of each form: Claim Form, Response Pack, Defence. He'd barely glanced at them when he pulled them out of the fat envelope, only stared at them for a moment, registered what they were, then tossed them in with the rubbish.

He could see the corner of one, the "N9" stamped clearly on the bottom right corner, an accusation of his non-response, his inability to face what was happening.

The grey worm slithered around his guts, filling his insides, forcing its way into his head; while something black, something full of despair, pressed his skull from the outside.

Jack had known, for over a year now, he had known that things were beginning to slide. He was spending so much more than he could earn, his rent and travel expenses absorbing all of his wage. But he'd thought it was temporary, and the need to spend was still there; he was young, it was the wrong time to be denying himself, and he was 'in IT', so he needed to have the latest laptop, some decent equipment. And he needed to socialise, to buy the odd round of drinks, plus the clothes, so he looked reasonable. Jack maxed out on his cards, which would have been fine, everyone did it after all; but then there had been the cut backs at work. So the bonus he was relying on never came, and his rent went up again, and even though he hardly used any heating, the bills started flowing faster than he could pay them.

He'd tried to sort it out, at first, of course he had. He found an agency who would lend him the money, spoken to a girl who'd understood. She told Jack that no one could manage in society today without bit of a loan occasionally, he'd be surprised how many people had them, and he wasn't to worry, how much did he need? Jack filled out the forms, barely reading the small print because what was the point? He knew he needed the cash to tide him over anyway. He received a nice fat cheque, used it to pay off his over-draft, paid the interest on his cards, had even gone out for a curry with his mates to celebrate.

But then the tone of the emails changed, the interest they were charging was even higher than the amount he'd been paying to the credit card companies. And Jack hadn't known what to do; so he'd done nothing. He stopped reading letters, deleted emails before he read them, tried to think about other things. He wasn't stupid, he'd known it would catch up with him one day, especially when they started talking about court dates and legal proceedings, but there was nothing he could do by then. He was in quicksand, and he felt that any move might make things worse. So Jack did nothing. Which he knew, deep down, was stupid; and that was when the grey worm took hold, that feeling of utter despair and self-loathing that slithered around his insides, and never let him completely forget what was happening.

The older man was approaching him, handing Jack another form.

"This is the bill for our fees," he said, passing it to Jack.

"*I* have to pay for you to come?" said Jack, not quite believing that things could actually have just got worse.

"Yes, that's right. You can check with Citizen's Advice, it's all legit," said the man, the wart on his nose obscuring his cheek, distorting his face when he spoke. "It's all written here for you: £235 for this visit, a further £110 for the cost of the sale of items. There'll be a further cost if we have to come back, but I think this should cover it." The man nodded towards the pile of electrical items and Jack's leather jacket and a suitcase, which his parents had given him for Christmas last year. The shorter man was loading everything into the case, folding the jacket and laying it on top. Jack watched. It seemed unnecessary to say anything.

The men turned to leave. Jack half stood, politeness prompting him to see them out, his mouth almost forming the words of thanks that usually accompanied visitors when they left. The words died in his throat, choking him, rising up to form a single sob. He heard the door slam shut, and sank back into his chair.

For a moment Jack simply sat there, trying to assimilate what had just happened; the shame of it. He felt violated, powerless, dirty; a complete failure. He could feel the grey worm in his throat, threatening to choke him, the despair swelling, the blackness pushing at him from all sides. His head dropped into his hands, Jack covered his face, and he cried, as he hadn't cried since he was a child.

Two hours later, after he'd swallowed two paracetamol and eaten a packet of crisps and half a packet of ginger biscuits, Jack decided to go out. He couldn't stay in the flat any longer, it felt violated somehow – and with no computer or phone, and too wound up to read, and too broke to get drunk – he knew he needed to do something. Jack knew he needed help. He had known for some time, but there was no way he could ignore it any longer. So he stood in the shower until the water ran cold, then dressed in his jeans and a smart top.

Jack leaned forwards, staring into the bathroom mirror. His nose was a bit red, his eyes a bit puffy, but he didn't think it was too obvious. He looked like he was short of sleep, which was true enough, but he didn't think anyone would guess he'd been crying like a baby. He straightened up and pulled a comb through his hair, felt marginally better. The grey worm was still in his stomach, but had curled back up again, was easy to ignore. Perhaps, Jack thought, trying to be positive, he was on the way to getting rid of it completely.

Jack delved in the back of his cupboard for an old jacket, checked pockets for enough money for a ticket, and set off for Neil and Kylie's house. He couldn't phone ahead, as his mobile was gone, and without it he had no idea of anyone's contact details.

By the time he arrived at Neil's station, it was dark. Jack walked from the platform up the hill towards their house, his feet heavy. If there was a way he could turn around, go back home, delay facing the situation, he would have done. But he knew that he couldn't leave it to fester any longer, knew that he needed help to stop things getting even worse. The weather was mild, a light rain falling but more damp than wet; so fine that Jack hardly felt it on his face, though when he put up a hand to wipe the hair from his forehead, it came away wet. He turned up the collar of his jacket and trudged up the hill, past the little grocers that was open all hours, past the blank fronts of dark cafes and closed hairdressers. There was a bus stop, Jack knew the number 20 would take him practically to Neil's door, but he may as well save the money. He walked on, ignoring the enticing smell of beer that flooded out of the pub when the door swung open, spilling light and snatches of laughter into the street. He passed houses, their lights flickering on as the evening developed, glimpsed people pulling curtains, closing doors; the blue flicker of televisions. Jack turned the corner by the chip shop, and began to walk along Neil's road. He wasn't sure if he hoped they'd be at home, which would be terrible because he'd have to explain why he was there; or hoped they'd be out, which would be a disaster as he had no money for the fare back and wasn't sure if his cards would still work.

The houses were fairly small, sold as 'starter homes' and occupied mainly by young couples. They had square windows and a tiny patch of grass at the front. The road was lined with cars, because no one had a garage.

Jack arrived at Neil's house, walked up the path towards the front door. The lights were on downstairs, he could see them through the glass-panelled door, and guessed Neil and Kylie were in the kitchen. He stood for a minute, not knocking, just standing there, feeling wretched. Then a car turned into the road, and he didn't want to be seen standing there, so he lifted his hand and pressed the bell, listened to the single shrill peal echo through the house. More light, as the kitchen door was opened, then Neil's shape, fuzzy through the glass, but still clearly Neil, coming closer, shouting something back to Kylie, reaching the door, opening it, staring down at Jack.

"Jack! Hello, this is a surprise. Come on in." Neil turned, shouted down the short hallway towards the kitchen: "Kylie, it's Jack!" Then Neil shut the door behind his brother, looked at him properly, and stopped. "Is something wrong?"

Jack opened his mouth to say no, then closed it. He was worried he might cry again. Something about being with his brother made him feel like a child again, brought back memories of school, when he'd needed Neil to sort out a bully, or to help him find his rugby boots because Mum would kill him if he told her he'd lost another pair. Jack felt young and vulnerable. But he was a grownup now, so he squared his shoulders and nodded.

"Yeah, it is actually. No one died or anything," Jack said, seeing the worry leap into Neil's eyes, "but I've got a problem. Things are bit of a mess – and, well – I don't know what to do. So I came here." He stopped. He wasn't completely sure why he'd come, didn't know what he expected Neil to do. But he had always looked to Neil for help, they all did; like they looked to Ed for a laugh, and Ben for company.

Kylie emerged from the kitchen, wiping her hands on a red chequered tea-towel. "Why are you standing out here?" she asked. "Hello Jack, nice to see you. Come into the kitchen, I'm just making some tea – unless you want something stronger?"

"Oh, well, a beer would be great, if you've got one," said Jack, not sure if he'd be able to swallow. He followed her into the kitchen, put his damp jacket over the back of a chair. The kitchen was very clean, lots of white plastic. There were the foil dishes of two ready-meals on plates, waiting to be reheated. Jack nodded towards them, "Sorry, I'm getting in the way of your dinner, aren't I?"

"No worries," said Neil. "Have you eaten?"

"No, actually," said Jack, deciding that half a packet of biscuits didn't count.

Jack saw Kylie look at the two ready meals and then at Neil, but she didn't say anything, just turned and pulled a beer from the fridge.

"Right," said Neil. "We'll have a drink, and you can tell me what's wrong. Then I'll walk up to the chippy and get some chips to go with the dinner, that will stretch it, won't it Kylie?"

Kylie nodded, looking uncertain. Jack watched as she poured tea into a mug for Neil, and made a ginger tea for herself. Then she excused herself, saying she needed to sort some stuff upstairs, they could call her when they were ready to eat.

The brothers looked at each other. Jack busied himself with the bottle opener, and took a long swallow, wishing Neil was drinking beer too. It made him feel a bit desperate, to be drinking on his own. As if reading Jack's thoughts, Neil stood, and got another beer from the fridge, flipped off the top and held it out.

"Cheers," Neil said, clinking bottles. "What's the problem then? Girls, job, health or money – or did you murder someone?"

"Money..." said Jack, "Money. In a big way. And I don't know what to do."

Jack told his brother. He explained how it had all started when he'd found the flat, which was too good to pass up with its great position and being fully furnished and there not being anything else on the market. He'd known it would be tight for a bit, but if the promised bonus had arrived, it would've been fine. And if the rent hadn't risen unexpectedly, and if they hadn't lied about how much the bills would cost each quarter.

Neil listened. He didn't say much, just the odd question to clarify things sometimes. When Jack told him about the bailiffs,

Neil made an odd noise in his throat, but he still didn't really say anything, mainly looked shocked, and cross. But Jack couldn't tell if he was cross with him, Jack, for messing up, or with the loan sharks who'd gone to court. Jack struggled on to the end, trying to be honest, but also trying to show how in many ways, it wasn't actually his fault, he'd had a lot of bad luck. When he got to the end they sat there, neither of them saying anything, drinking their beers.

"I don't know much about bailiffs," said Neil at last, "but I think what they did was legal. I also seem to remember that after a first visit, they can come back, at any time, and go into a property even if you're not there. So if you don't want to see them again, you need to pay off any debt you still have. Apart from the loan sharks – which I can't believe you used, by the way, I wish you'd asked me about them first – but apart from them, who else do you owe?"

Jack thought. He didn't really want to get into this, didn't want to start going through actual numbers with Neil. Jack had wanted Neil to listen, and help him sort it out, but now he was here, talking about it, it felt private, like Neil shouldn't be asking questions, prying into Jack's personal life. It was, Jack thought suddenly, more difficult than talking about sex even. There was something about your money, how much you earned and what you chose to spend it on, that should be kept secret. Jack didn't want his brother to know; which made no sense, because how could Neil help if he didn't know the situation?

Neil was watching him, and he held up his hand, as if to stop him. Neil stood up.

"Look, I think that might be enough for now, nothing can happen tonight anyway. You've been having a horrid time, haven't you?" Neil paused, staring down at him, and Jack saw concern in his eyes, knew that his brother cared, and would help.

"Let's go and get some chips – I'll pay – and eat some dinner. We've both got work tomorrow – do you want to stay here or go back to your flat?"

"My flat, I guess," said Jack, not wanting to, but knowing it was easier to get to work from there.

"Right, well I'll drive you back after we've eaten. Then tomorrow, I'll come round after work, and we'll go through everything, and make a plan. You'll need to show me all your bills, and all your income, and I'll help you to sort it out. We can make a plan. It'll only get worse if you ignore it – you know that, right?"

Jack nodded. Something inside of him had shifted slightly. He didn't feel better, he felt trapped, which was, he thought, what debt did to you. It took away your choices and left you locked in a prison where you couldn't make your own decisions about things anymore. But at least now it was Neil who would be controlling things, telling Jack what to do, helping him to make sense of things. At least now, Jack thought, as they walked through the fine rain to the chip shop, there was a bit of hope. The rolling snowball of despair that had been carrying him along had been stopped, even if it hadn't yet melted.

Then Jack stopped thinking, and looked up at the menu board in the yellow-lighted chip shop, breathing in the oily steam and deciding, for himself, what he wanted to eat.

Chapter Seventeen

When Jack moved back to the farm in May, Susan was hatching the eggs. For the last two days, the machine had been silent, the eggs no longer turned. Susan had added more water, as the humidity was increased, and had started to check, every time she passed the corner of the boot-room, to see if anything was happening. This morning, when Susan had come downstairs, one of the eggs had a tiny chip missing. Now, ten hours later, there were cracks in six of the eggs, and one duckling was half out of the shell.

Susan bent towards the lid – she could hear the ducklings, all still inside their shells, cheeping to each other. There was something about the shrill noise, the announcement of life eager to escape, that was always exciting. The duckling that was almost hatched lay on the floor of the incubator, looking dead. The yellow down was damp, sticking to its body, and it lay completely still, only the slightest rise of the stomach showing it was still breathing.

Susan left the duckling where it was. If the duckling died, she would remove it instantly, so the bacteria couldn't grow and infect the other eggs. But for now, Susan knew it should be left undisturbed, that although it looked barely alive, it was simply tired from the effort of breaking the shell and wriggling out. Unseen, there was a strand of umbilical cord attaching the duckling to the yolk, the hatchling must finish absorbing the remainder of the yolk, to have sufficient food to survive for the next few hours. Ducklings often didn't survive the struggle of hatching, but this one stood a good chance, it was almost completely free. Susan went to prepare a brooder, somewhere soft and warm where she could put the duckling once it had dried out.

Susan went into the little barn, next to the house. She reached up, and felt for the lamp on the top shelf. Spiders scuttled away, and her hand closed around the box. Susan slid the lamp from the box, and carried it to the beam, attaching it to the wire that had been left hanging from last year, pushing a large crate beneath it, before going to find some hay. It was good to have something other than Jack to worry about, and hatching new ducklings always lifted her spirits, gave her hope. There was something about the new life, the simple concentration on survival, that somehow put the rest of life into perspective.

Neil had phoned her a few weeks ago, and told her about Jack. From what Susan could gather, Neil had spent several evenings with Jack, helping to sort through old bills, and working out a budget. Neil had phoned Susan – while she was at the cafe of course, he always seemed to phone when she was at the cafe – and warned her that Jack might need to move back to the farm. Susan had been surprised when Neil called her – at first, she thought it was about Ben again. But he didn't mention Ben, simply launched into: "Have you heard about Jack?" and then, when Susan told him that she hadn't, with her heart in her throat because she thought Jack might have been in an accident, Neil explained.

Susan wasn't sure that Jack knew Neil was phoning her, so when, a couple of days later, Jack also called, she hadn't mentioned it, and had listened as though surprised, when he asked if he could move back to the farm. Jack said that there was no way he could continue to live in London and stay solvent, never mind trying to eat as well, so the only option, for now, was to move back home with his parents. The commute to his job was too far and too expensive, so he would work his one month notice, and then leave. And was that all right?

Which was more than all right, actually, thought Susan, as she switched on the lamp. The lamp shone red, lending a rosy hue to everything in the barn, softening shadows, warming the air. Susan placed her hand on the pink-tinged hay, under the light, testing how hot it was.

Susan would, of course, have welcomed any of her boys home if they needed to return, but right now, with Tom's back hurting more than he would admit, it had all worked out rather well. Not that she could say that, she thought, going back to the incubator. Tom would deny it, and Jack was so down, so deflated, that she hadn't liked to say much about anything.

Susan peered into the incubator. The duckling was up now, moving around, shedding specks of yellow fluff as it staggered around the hard plastic surface. It knocked into other eggs, moving them, and it looked healthy and dry, so Susan decided to move it to the brooder. She didn't like putting one hatchling there on its own, it would be lonely. But it was so active, she worried it might upset the other eggs. She opened the incubator, grabbing the duckling, shutting the lid immediately so the temperature would stay constant. Then Susan carried it, out to the barn, trying to keep it warm by enclosing it in both hands. It had no weight, but Susan could feel it tickling her palms as its beak searched her hand, a steady flicker of life.

Jack had moved back into his old bedroom, and Susan could see in his eyes that it felt as if he was going backwards, returning to where he'd started, no longer a grown-up. They hadn't said much when Jack told them, they could see that he had hit rock bottom already, so there wasn't much point in giving him more lectures. Tom said the farm couldn't afford to pay him a proper wage, not at the moment, but if Jack worked there, he could have some spending money, and food and rent would be free.

The first thing Jack did was throw out all his old things, all the toys and posters that he hadn't let Susan throw out before. Previously, Jack had said he still wanted them, had been horrified when Susan suggested taking them to the charity shop, or even putting them in the loft; Jack had wanted his room left, as a shrine to his childhood. It was as if, when he came back to the farm on visits, the childhood memories had been welcome, familiar, something to cling on to.

But now Jack had come back to live – now living at the farm spoke of failure, of going backwards – he didn't want mementoes. He needed to throw them out, as if, thought Susan, he needed to prove that he was living at the farm in a new way, as an adult, not returning to his adolescence.

Susan placed the duck under the lamp, watched it totter around. She filled the plastic drinker with water, then lifted the duckling, submerging its beak in the water, placing it back on the hay, waiting to see if it had learnt, would bend by itself to the water and drink. It moved away, and Susan left it. After the yolk was absorbed, ducklings didn't need any food or water for several hours. She would check it later. As Susan walked away, she could hear it cheeping, calling to her with its high-pitched cry, not wanting to be left alone. Poor little thing, it needed some company, but until some more hatched, there wasn't much she could do.

Susan went into the kitchen. Tom was there, having a coffee.

"Look at that," Tom said when he saw her, "that boy's left his phone on the table, after all I told him. I reminded him when he got home, taking a phone with you isn't a luxury, it's a safety net. While he's out there in the field, if he needs help, he's got no way to get anyone. I suppose he thinks he's immune to accidents, too young for something to happen to him." Tom picked up the phone and slipped it into his overall's pocket. "Now I'll have to waste time taking it to him," he said, whistling for the dog, and going back to his tractor.

Susan made herself a coffee. She knew why Jack had left the phone: it epitomised all that had happened. There had been a row – Susan wasn't sure of the details – but on the first evening that Neil had gone to help Jack, he saw a phone in Jack's flat. Susan didn't know what kind, but it had obviously been expensive because it had caught Neil's eye, and he asked about it, wanting to know why Jack, in all his debt, owned such a fancy phone. Apparently, unable to cope without a phone, Jack had bought it on his way to work that morning. There had been some sort of a row, and Neil had insisted the phone should be returned to the shop, before cutting up all Jack's credit cards. In return, Neil bought Jack a cheap mobile, which Jack had to keep topping up at the supermarket. Susan knew Jack hated it, he complained about the buttons, said it was from the last century, he'd rather not have one at all.

But a mobile phone was pretty essential now on the farm, as Tom said, it was often the only way to contact people when you were in the middle of several acres of crops. Farmers had wasted lots of time in the past, running to the nearest house if there was an emergency, sometimes even dying simply because they couldn't call for help. It was, Susan thought, carrying her coffee back to the incubator for another look, a very isolated life, and mobiles made things a tiny bit easier. She sipped her coffee, watching four more ducklings as they struggled from their shells.

Tom mentioned the phone again when he met Jack at the dinner table. Tom arrived with a stash of papers, which he spread across the table, pushing knives and forks to one side with a clatter, telling Susan this wouldn't take long, she could dish up while they talked.

"I've got the farm risk assessments," Tom told Jack. "If you're going to work here, properly, we should probably have a real meeting, like you were any other employee. Just so we can tick it off, so's I know I've done it all properly."

Jack looked at his father, then turned and stared at the mess of papers on the table.

"This is the farm plan," Tom was saying, pointing to various points. "These lines show our vehicular routes, where we drive, and where we walk. I need to get them marked up really, put up some signs so visitors know where they're likely to meet a tractor when it turns the corner; but I don't have the funds at the moment..." Tom stopped, not sure if Jack would take that the wrong way, think he was having a dig at Jack's situation, which he wasn't, he was just talking about the farm. And talking about the farm invariably meant bemoaning the lack of money.

They were careful with where they parked and drove around the yard. Tom was very strict about it, and although they hadn't marked out routes, everyone who came onto the farm knew exactly where the vehicles went. They managed to avoid machinery rounding corners and finding a parked car or pedestrian in the way. Avoiding accidents was important, too many farm workers were killed, just because they hadn't taken the right precautions. Tom shuffled the papers and spread out another one.

"This is the OHPL map," Tom said, "the overhead power lines. Look, they go over a couple of fields, and their heights are marked. You need to keep an eye on this one," he said, flapping the map towards Jack, "it's in the third drawer down of my unit, if you ever need it. You should have a look before you take out any of the taller machines, because some exceed the height of the lines. We can always apply to have the power disconnected for a period of time, but it's easier to just be careful. Eventually, I hope to get them relocated, ask for the DNO to move them to somewhere that isn't in the middle of a field we need to plough —" Tom stopped again. He'd been about to add that at the moment they couldn't afford that. But he managed to stop in time, left the sentence hanging there, unfinished. Tom began to roll up the map.

"Always remember – 'Look Out, Look Up!' – that's the ENA safety slogan. Not very original, but they're trying. And of course," Tom said, remembering something to add, and unrolling the plan again, "the summer height of the power lines is lower, because they sag in the heat."

Tom sat back in his chair, trying to think of the other points he ought to make, things he would mention to any other new worker. His back hurt and he moved slightly, trying to find an angle that was comfortable.

"The bull we reared is in the west field," Tom said. His face darkened. The calf had grown into a strong enough bull, but one horn was wonky, it wouldn't be winning any prizes in the early show. Maybe later, in a different category. He hoped so, unless it won something he couldn't charge as much for people wanting to breed from it.

"You'd best not go in there, unless you need to," Tom said. "I've put up signs so we don't get walkers wandering through the field, and we need to remember to check them each week, make sure they haven't blown down or been removed by an idiot."

"The bull seems fairly quiet though?" said Jack.

"Yes, but you know the rule," said Tom.

"*Never trust a quiet bull or an unloaded shotgun,*" recited Jack.

Tom grinned, he'd taught the boys that when they were small.

Tom began to repeat other safety procedures, to remind Jack of rules and practices they had followed his whole life, but in the few years he'd been away Jack may have forgotten. Tom glanced at his son. Jack was staring straight ahead, his eyes blank. Tom wasn't sure if he was even listening. With a sigh, he rolled away the final paper, and went to put them all back in the bureau. It probably wasn't important, Tom thought, the boy had known all the rules from the day he was born. Jack was unlikely to get anything major wrong.

Chapter Eighteen

Towards the middle of June, the hay was ready to be cut. Tom had scrutinised the weather forecasts, trying to predict which would be the most accurate, considering the percentage chances of rainfall. When Tom was as sure as he could be that they would have a few dry days, he cut the tall grass. Afterwards, as he drove the tractor away from the fields, the long grass mown in drifts behind him, he prayed the night would be dry. He'd had enough bad luck lately, he thought, he needed the forecasts to be right.

The following day, he got up early, soon after dawn. Susan groaned at him.

"You were very restless last night," she muttered, hoping he would take the hint and go away.

"I was worrying about the weather," Tom said, going to the window. He moved a curtain, allowing an inch of light to streak into the room, ending the night. Susan groaned again, and pulled her pillow over her head. But Tom was nodding, satisfied. It was dry, which meant they had a good chance of harvesting the hay without problem.

By 7am, Tom was driving across the biggest field with the tedder. The rotating forks behind him were turning the hay, adding air and encouraging it to dry out. The sharp prongs glinted in the early sunlight, sharp and spiteful as they raked through the cut grass, tossing it into the air, scattering it into heaps. As he bumped across the field, smelling the clean sharp smell of drying grass, feeling the itch of dust on his face, he felt in tune with nature, part of the landscape around him. The tractor was noisy, and sometimes Tom wondered what life would have been like for his ancestors, who would have turned the hay with pitch forks. The fields were smaller then, and the risks were greater because everything took so long, was such an investment of back-breaking effort before the rain came.

But perhaps, he thought, as he turned the tractor at the end of a furrow, perhaps there would be more company. When men's wages were cheaper, and the farm relied on labour not machinery, there would have been some comradery, a sense of shared purpose. It would have been less lonely. Even though Jack was back at the farm, he was often working in another field, so although there were two of them now, there was still no company. No opportunity to chat, or pass the odd comment. Tom spoke more to his cows than he did to people. He sighed, wiping his face where the grass was tickling. He would be covered in tiny bits of grass and dust by the time he was finished, though he wore a cap to keep the worst of it off. He'd need to remember to shake off as much as he could before he went into the house, or Susan would moan at him. Tom turned the tractor again, and headed back through the hay.

Jack was feeding the cows. He heaved the top bag of crushed grain from the pile, and carried it to where the cows were waiting, their heads pushed through the bars, waiting for the trough to be filled. Jack poured the grain into the trough, smelling the malty dust as it rose up, watching the grey noses reaching for it. Some of the more stupid cows were trying to squeeze into the same space as the cows that were eating, and needing to be directed back, to where there was a space for their own head to push through the bars. Jack watched them eat, their great heads filling the space, their jaws moving, big eyes watching him, even while they ate. He liked cows, always had. He sort of understood Neil's reluctance to eat them, but thought it was natural, how things were meant to be. Plus, Jack thought, as he folded the empty sack ready to be refilled, if no one ate beef, there'd be no need to raise cattle. Farms would be purely arable, there wouldn't be the money to keep animals, not just as pets. England wouldn't be England, he thought, without cows and sheep in the fields. It was how things were meant to be. Even if it was hard to balance the books. His stomach clenched at the thought of money, and he coughed, aware once more of that blackness that followed him around. He might not be adding to his debt, he might be making ends meet now, but he was still a failure, having to live with his parents. He hated it. He pretty much hated himself.

By the end of July, Susan was ready for a break.

The farm had its own rhythm, moving from sowing to spraying to harvest, never stopping, a relentless cycle that dictated Tom's days and filled his thoughts. He spent much of the time on his own, caring for the animals or driving the tractor or mixing feed. Susan thought that Tom didn't really mind, his brain was attuned to the heartbeat of the farm, and he never felt the need for constant human interaction. A drink at the local pub with his neighbours, and the odd event organised by the Farmer's Union seemed to be sufficient.

But for Susan, it was different. She wasn't consumed by the farm, not like Tom was, and she missed the boys now they were grownup. Her once-a-week job at the cafe helped with both finances and social contact, but it wasn't enough – for either. Even though Jack was living here, he was out of the house for as long as Tom was. Ben's university course had finished in June and he was supposed to be applying for jobs, but Susan had seen very little evidence of anything other than 'resting'. Although Ben was now at home for the summer, he spent most of his days either asleep because he'd been out until the early hours the night before, or in a virtual world on the internet.

Therefore, when Dot and Elsie suggested they go to the sea for a day, Susan found herself surprisingly keen to accompany them, and offered to drive. Unexpectedly, Ben announced that he would come too; so they set off together to collect the elderly ladies and drive to Camber, which was the nearest beach that didn't involve driving through a confusing one-way system in a busy town.

When they arrived at the house, Susan found the front door wide open, and a variety of bags blocking the hall. She rang the bell, and Dot appeared at the top of the stairs.

"We're all ready," Dot said, "can you give me a hand with the bags?"

"Are all these coming with us?" said Susan, wondering how long they had packed for.

Dot came downstairs and started to explain, pointing at various bags. "That big one's in case it rains, it has our coats and boots, and an umbrella in case it's not windy."

"It's always windy," thought Susan, but she didn't interrupt.

"That's got my knitting, and Elsie's book, and a jigsaw puzzle," Dot said, pointing at a large reusable bag with *Morrisons* printed on the side.

"You're taking a jigsaw to the beach?" said Susan, not sure she had heard correctly.

"And a tray, of course, to do it on," said Elsie, appearing from the lounge. "We're there all day, and we don't want to be bored, do we?"

"That's our swimming things and towels," said Dot, "in case it's hot."

"But only if there's somewhere to change," said Elsie. "At our age, we can't be coping with hiding under towels on the beach to change, can we? And if the towel should slip...well, we don't want to scare the locals!"

"And those two are our packed lunch," said Dot, pointing to two large yellow bags, bulging at the sides, ice-cream containers balanced on top.

"Are you wearing your *'Where's the Fun'* tee-shirt?" asked Elsie.

Susan looked to where Elsie stood in the centre of the hall and saw her pull back her brown cardigan to reveal a pink tee-shirt with WTF in bold print across the bust. Or at least, across where the bust used to be.

"I bought one for myself, too," said Elsie, "are you wearing yours?"

"Not today, no," said Susan.

"Goodness," Susan thought, "it's worse than taking teenagers out for the day." She looked again at the bags, wondering what the packed lunch would be. Susan very much hoped that the ice-cream containers were full of sandwiches, and not ice-cream, but knowing Elsie, anything was possible. She decided not to ask, and began to carry the bags to the car; returning for folding chairs, and a windbreak folded round pine legs, and a parasol with a pointed stem that could be plunged into the sand. Susan knew it would be much too windy for anything other than the windbreak, but it was, she decided, easier to load them into the car and leave them in the boot, than to try and discuss whether they were necessary. As she picked up the food bags, something chinked.

"Did you pack plastic plates?" Susan asked, frowning.

"Don't you worry about the lunch," said Elsie, with a smile, "I know how to do a picnic properly."

When the car was loaded, Susan sat in the driver's seat next to Ben, and waited. Dot locked the front door, and then Elsie decided she needed to use the washroom again, just to be safe, and then the door was relocked, and the two sisters joined her in the car. Susan could sense their excitement, their pleasure at a day by the sea, and it felt like a mini holiday, something significant. With a smile at Ben, Susan started the engine.

It took two and a half hours to drive to Camber. It would have been faster, but they had to stop twice to visit toilets and stretch their legs. They stopped for the first time at a petrol station, and Susan browsed the packaged sandwiches in the shop and wondered what Elsie had prepared, while the old ladies collected the toilet key from the attendant and used the facilities. When they reappeared, Elsie was drinking a bottle of juice and Dot had bought a newspaper. Susan wasn't sure there would be time to read a newspaper. The second stop was more hurried, when Elsie announced she was desperate, and could Susan pull over next to that pub? Susan wasn't sure that the pub would welcome an elderly lady who simply wanted to use their facilities, but she stopped the car, and Elsie sprinted inside. She was gone for a long time, and Dot and Susan were discussing which of them should go and check on her, when Elsie reappeared, smiling and waving at the people inside.

"Such a lovely couple in there," Elsie said, lowering herself onto the back seat.

"Jane and Daniel, they're called," she added, shutting the door and reaching for her seatbelt. "They've been living there since Christmas, and they've never owned a pub before,"

Susan moved back into the flow of traffic heading towards the coast.

"You had quite a chat then, while we were waiting," said Dot.

"Yes, I did," said Elsie, "I like meeting new people." She then told them how long Jane had been married, that they'd been trying for a baby for six years, and that they used to live in Norwich. Susan was too stunned by the amount of information gleaned during one short toilet stop to comment. Her mother sat behind her, her mouth in a grim line, her silence a weight of disapproval that her sister seemed oblivious to.

They wound their way past Rye, and the old ladies stared at the stone turrets and commented on the width of the river and the sheep on the moors. When they arrived in Camber, Susan drove to the car park next to the beach. She had been here often when the boys were small, usually during the winter months, when the dogs could run free on the beach, chasing seagulls and foraging for old shells.

Today the car park was crowded, and Susan parked on the far side, near the sand dunes. As soon as she had parked, Elsie opened her door, and headed towards the concrete toilet block. The others pulled bags from the boot, and headed towards the sand. Elsie joined them, and they began to walk towards the sea. Ben left, saying he was going to look around a bit, and would find them in a few minutes.

"Where shall we stop?" said Susan, thinking they couldn't walk far with so many bags.

"Well, we don't want to be too near that," said her mother, nodding towards the smattering of buildings which included a cafe and amusements.

"But not too far from the toilets," said Elsie.

Susan led the way, past a couple of holiday cottages, their gardens filled with piles of sand, towards an area of beach empty of people. She stopped, lowering the heavy bags, feeling the ache in her muscles even after a short distance – whatever had Elsie packed? Susan took the rug that was balanced on top, and shook it into the wind, spreading it over the sand. Then she picked up the windbreak and found a large pebble to use as a mallet, bashing the legs into the ground until it was stable. The two elderly ladies huddled behind it, kneeling on the rug.

"We'll wait here and guard the things while you go back to the car for the chairs," said Elsie.

"I wonder if we want to move further away from the amusements," said Dot, looking back towards the carpark, "it's nice to have our own space..."

"Not when you're the person doing all the carrying," said Susan, and stomped across the sand back towards the car park.

She didn't really mind doing all the lifting, she was strong enough and the two ladies were elderly and needed help. But she sometimes wished they would notice what other people did for them, to not treat it as their right. Ben met her in the car park, and they walked back to the beach together.

The morning passed pleasantly enough. Ben had brought a book he wanted to read, so he moved his beach chair slightly away from the group, nearer to the dunes. Then he sat, his long legs stretched out across the sand, and read, at regular intervals raising his head, his eyes shut, his face towards the sun.

Dot sat on her chair next to the rug, the legs deep in the soft sand so she was at a slight angle, a tray precariously balanced on her knee while she sorted jigsaw pieces. Every so often a gust of wind would sprinkle her tray with fine sand, lifting her skirt and causing the windbreak to ripple. Susan watched her, wishing she would keep her knees together. For as long as she could remember, her mother had worn thick tan-coloured tights.

"They must," Susan thought, "be very uncomfortable now, where the sand has seeped into her sandals."

Gulls swirled overhead, searching for picnickers, their plaintive cries piercing the air as they floated on the warm currents. Susan watched them glide, longed for their freedom, the simplicity of their lives. Elsie also turned towards them, frowning.

"Nasty creatures..." Susan heard her muttering under her breath.

At 11:30, Elsie announced she was going to "have a little swim" before lunch. Her sister said she was too warm and comfortable, and the sea looked cold. Susan promised she would paddle, but said she didn't much like swimming and she agreed with her mother that the water would be too cold. Undeterred, Elsie removed her bathing suit from one of the bags, and crossed the sand back to the toilet block. Half an hour later, when Susan was beginning to wonder if she was all right, Elsie reappeared. A towel was now wrapped around her waist, her thin arms clamped to her sides, her eyes excited. She grinned at Susan, showing long teeth, and dropped the towel, revealing a red striped swimsuit with very thin arms and legs protruding from the edges. Susan noticed the breasts that reached her waist, the stomach that drooped, the skin that sagged from her bones where her muscles had wasted. And yet, Elsie had an aura of excitement, an air of anticipation which somehow gave her the appearance of a little girl, a child happy to be alive, enjoying the treat of being at the seaside. The wind played with her hair, pulling it across her eyes then away from her forehead.

"Come on then," said Elsie, walking towards the sea. It was nearly high tide, and the sea was only a few yards away. Susan knew that at low tide they would hardly be able to see the waves and the flat wet sand would stretch out into the distance.

"Have you checked for red flags?" warned Dot. "This coast can be dangerous with rip tides you know."

"It's fine here," said Elsie over her shoulder, not to be dissuaded.

Susan heaved herself to her feet, and followed her aunt to the water. They slowed when they reached a wide line of stones across the sand.

"I wish I'd kept my shoes on now," said Elsie, reaching out and clinging on to Susan's arm for support. Susan walked with her to the wet sand, then stopped to remove her shoes while her aunt carried on, squealing as the water rushed over her ankles.

"Is it too cold?" asked Susan, concerned. "It might be best to not swim today, if it's not warm enough. It's not a very hot day, and the wind is quite strong..."

Elsie shook her head. "This might be the only chance I get this year," she called over her shoulder, the wind catching her words and carrying them away, so Susan barely heard them.

Elsie walked forwards, into the water. The waves rose about her, "Oh! It tickles," she squealed, as the water reached her thighs.

Susan watched her, saw Elsie lift her thin arms as the water reached her waist, and for a moment Elsie stood there, as if frozen, arms outstretched, head held high, the occasional gasp drifting across the water to Susan as the waves lapped higher. Then suddenly, Elsie plunged forwards, disappearing from view in a circle of white bubbles.

Susan stared hard at the bubbles, not breathing until, after what seemed like an age, her aunt reappeared, coughing and laughing, and pushing back her hair. Susan waved, and Elsie lifted an arm in reply, then turned, and swam a few strokes parallel to the beach. Susan walked beside her in the shallow water, feeling the waves as they tickled her skin, the sand soft beneath her feet.

Elsie stood again, the water no more than waist height, and began to walk towards Susan. As she reached the shallow water, and the waves rushed at her more strongly, she staggered, and Susan reached out, and took her elbow, wetting the bottom of her rolled up jeans. Elsie was laughing, exuding happiness, and Susan found she was laughing too.

"Oh, I feel *alive* after a swim," said Elsie, pushing back her hair as water dripped onto her face. "I try to swim every year, but it's getting harder and harder to find the opportunity," she told Susan, clinging on to her arm. "But you have to, when you get to my age, you have to keep trying, or else suddenly you'll be old, and not able to anymore, and wouldn't that be a shame?"

They walked back up the beach, the sand clinging to their wet feet. Susan thought she could almost *feel* her aunt's joy, as if it was a tangible thing, something contagious and precious.

"That was quick," said Dot, moving her puzzle slightly so it didn't get dripped on.

"You should have come," said Elsie, breathless with enthusiasm. "It's lovely once you're in." She picked up her towel and went back to change.

"Where are her clothes?" asked Susan, watching as the elderly lady tottered over the sand towards the concrete toilet block.

"Probably left them in there," said Dot, frowning. "Not very hygienic I'd have thought. But hygiene never was one of Elsie's strong points."

"I hope they haven't been stolen," said Susan. Then she suddenly giggled, the thought of a naked Elsie wrapped in towels striking her as funny. Dot would be outraged by the offence, and would rant about it for hours, whereas Elsie would be completely unaffected, would wrap herself in towels and carry on as if normal. In fact, knowing Elsie, they would have trouble keeping her out of shops and the amusements, even if she was completely naked.

"I can't imagine," said Dot, laughing too, "that anyone would want to steal those clothes. Though it would serve her right if they did. She'll have to wear her coat and wrap a towel round her legs. Goodness, what a sight that will be. I hope she's not long, I'm hungry now."

When Elsie arrived, she was fully dressed, her curly grey hair wild around her face.

"Did you bring a comb?" asked Dot, looking at her.

"No, I forgot," said Elsie, placing her swimsuit, rolled in the towel, next to the bags.

"Your hair is a mess" said Dot.

"It's happy hair," said Elsie, unperturbed. She began to remove items from the food bag, placing them on the cloth.

"They'll get sandy," said Dot, watching her. "You'd better just pass us things one at a time."

"I want a cup of tea first," said Elsie, "to warm me up a bit."

Ben moved back to join the group, and Susan saw him watch, fascinated, as Elsie removed first two teabags from a small plastic bag, then a flask from the bag, and finally, after rummaging for a few seconds, she pulled out a brown china teapot. Elsie balanced the teapot on the rug, put the teabags inside, then unscrewed the flask lid and poured in hot water. The lid chinked into place on top. She delved into the bag once more and brought out four china mugs, which she passed to Ben.

"Hold these for me will you?" Elsie said, "they might topple over if I put them down."

Ben took them, looking surprised. "You brought a teapot?" he said, holding the mugs by the handles.

"Well, what else is she going to make tea in?" asked Dot, who was obviously used to this.

Susan laughed. "We always took a teapot and a bread knife on picnics when we were young. It wasn't until I met your father and he told me to make the sandwiches at home, that I considered doing it any differently."

Dot wrinkled her nose. "Squashed sandwiches where the filling has leaked into the bread," she said, and shuddered. "I like my food freshly made."

"We need to let it brew," said Elsie, removing a lid from a plastic beaker and pouring a little milk into each mug. "Do you take sugar?" she asked Ben, "I can never remember."

Ben was shaking his head, as Elsie pulled out a small bag of sugar and a teaspoon, and piled two spoonfuls into two of the mugs. Then she removed the teapot lid and stirred the tea. "I can't wait any longer," she said, "I need a warm drink." She held the teapot lid with one hand, and poured the dark liquid into the cups. Elsie passed one mug to her sister, and took one herself, stirring it before passing the spoon to Dot. She slurped the tea. It was, thought Susan, a very satisfied slurp. Then Elsie wiped her mouth and smiled. "Ooh, that's good."

Ben passed a mug to Susan and she sipped the tea. It was not, she thought, good at all. It was barely hot, and had the faint taste of something else, something old. Perhaps the flask had been used for coffee previously. She put her cup next to her, and decided to pour it into the sand when no one was looking.

Next from the bag came a wooden bread board, a large knife, and a loaf of bread. Elsie passed Susan a packet of butter and a knife.

"I'll slice, you butter," she directed.

Smiling, Susan did as she was told. As Elsie carved great slabs of bread, Susan buttered them. When four were ready, they all took one. The old women bit into them with their long yellow teeth, savouring the food, chewing noisily. Susan ate quietly, thinking that next time, she would bring the picnic. Though she couldn't deny the freshness of the bread, or how good it tasted outside in the salty air, listening to waves crash onto the beach. The seagulls had noticed the food and were closer now, wheeling overhead, crying to each other. Elsie glared at them and waved her hand.

"You shoo," she shouted, her mouth full of bread, "there's nothing for you lot."

The birds saw the wave and swooped low, thinking she might be throwing food.

"Just ignore them," said Dot, "they'll move on if we don't feed them."

An ice-cream container held tiny tomatoes, that burst when they bit into them, spurting seeds onto their shirts and fingers.

The second container had slices of apple, cut at home, now soft and brown. "I like to prepare what I can at home," said Elsie, offering the container to Susan, who shook her head and reached instead for another tomato.

Ben was eating a chunk of bread and butter, his eyes blank, when Elsie turned to him.

"Now Ben," Elsie said, "I've been meaning to ask – do you have a young lady yet?"

Before Ben could answer, Dot spoke.

"No," said Dot, "he's part of the BLT group, we told you this already, don't you remember?"

Ben laughed. "Actually Gran, that's a sandwich. I think you mean LGBT community. But you can just tell people I'm gay."

"That doesn't work so well with my age group dear, they'll all think you're happy."

"Isn't Ben happy?" said Elsie, "Aren't you happy dear?" She paused, a tomato poised in her hand, her eyes concerned.

"Yes, Elsie, don't you worry. Ben seems very happy. Haven't you been listening? He's become a homosexual."

"Oh, like Oscar Wilde? Does he write? He doesn't look any different to me." Elsie turned back to Ben and stared at him, as though trying to find a trace of something in his face, or the way he did his hair, some clue she had missed that betrayed his sexual preference.

Susan decided this conversation was too much for her, and was concentrating on her food.

"Not all homosexuals write, silly," said Dot, her voice scathing, her expression superior. "Some are artists – or dancers."

"Oh," said Elsie. She looked at the tea in her hand, and slowly lowered it to the rug. "Oh, I didn't know..."

Susan glanced at Ben, and he looked back at her, his eyes dancing, his mouth twitching.

The picnic concluded with fruit cake, cut from the whole cake with the bread knife. "Silly to carry a whole extra knife when you're out," explained Elsie, "you don't want to carry that extra weight."

There was so much that Susan could have said, but she just smiled and finished her lunch. They packed the remains back into the bag, and Elsie left her chair, and stretched out on the sand, using her damp towel as a pillow.

"I think I'll read the paper and have a little nap," Elsie said, unfolding the newspaper. The wind tugged at it, so she sat up, spreading it over her lap, holding the edges with her hands. Elsie looked very happy. The sun was warm, and although small gusts of wind found their way under the windbreak, it wasn't cold, and Susan thought it would probably be good for her aunt to rest, after her swim. The gulls had mostly moved on now, and were wheeling above a family further down the beach who were eating. The father kept throwing crusts into the air, and the great white birds would swoop, catching the food in their sharp beaks, rising again with their prize.

"I'm going for a walk," said Susan. She lifted the picnic bags. "I'll put these back in the car on my way," she said. "Anyone else want to come?"

"I'm all right thanks," said Ben. He picked up his chair and went back to his spot near the dunes, where he could read undisturbed.

"I want to finish this," said her mother, staring at her puzzle, "and then I'll come and meet you. Which way are you going?"

"I'll go back to the car first," said Susan, thinking she might pop into the cafe for a decent cup of tea. "Then I'll walk back past here because I want to walk in the sand dunes, towards Rye. I'll walk back along the water's edge, so I can paddle."

"Right," said Dot, who didn't appear to be really listening, "don't get lost."

Susan dumped the bags in the boot of the car, slammed the lid shut, and looked around the car park. People were still arriving, driving over the sand that had blown from the beach, looking for spaces. There were families and couples, but no animals. She knew that in the winter months, the car park was very different, with people unloading horses ready to gallop along the beach, dog walkers setting out for a trek. But in the summer, this section was reserved for people, the sand kept clean for sandcastles and picnics. A few businesses had set up shop along the beach front. Kiosks selling ice-creams, inflatables, and a cafe. It was the cafe that attracted Susan, and she strolled towards it.

There was a wooden veranda surrounding the cafe, and she walked around it, careful not to slip on the sand. There was sand everywhere, blown into drifts on the veranda, seeping under the doorway of the cafe, the fine grains chasing each other in a continuous flow whenever the wind blew. It stung her ankles, and when there was a bigger gust of wind, it blew up, scratching her eyes.

She went to the window at the front, and ordered a tea, then stood, sipping it, looking towards the sea. It wasn't, she thought, very good tea, but at least it was hot and didn't taste of mouldy coffee. Her standards had dropped recently.

Susan then set out, striding along the beach. She passed the windbreak where her mother and aunt were resting, lifting her hand as she went. Dot raised an arm in reply. Elsie seemed to be lying down, holding the newspaper above her head like a sail. Susan wondered if Elsie was actually managing to read anything as the wind was tugging at the pages; then they were behind her, and she was marching towards the dunes.

Susan looked out to sea as she walked. There was a fishing boat heading towards the harbour in Rye. She could see its masts, surrounded by a cloud of white dots that she took to be seagulls, following the scent of fish. There were white capped waves, rushing towards the beach, hissing on the sand as they drew back, pulled by the tide. More wet sand was exposed now, and children were settling with buckets and spades to build castles and collect shells. As she neared the river from Rye, the dunes were higher, and Susan detoured from the beach, wanting to climb the soft mounds. The sand was warm underfoot, and the dunes were steep, so she slid backwards with each step and had to take big strides to climb them. They were tufted with clumps of grass which hissed in the wind, their blond heads waving on long thin stalks; and gorse, stark and prickly and dry. The air smelt warm, of dry plants and salt.

Susan found a spot, sheltered from the wind, and sat down, hidden from view. It was warm, the sun caressed her head, and the sand was soft. She couldn't see the sea, but she could hear it, swooshing and hissing; and voices, carried on the wind, disjointed, fragments of sound. For a moment, she just sat, absorbing the warmth, the peace, the space of the moment.

But Susan didn't reply. She was thinking about the elderly lady, shivering after her swim, settling down on the towels to read. She remembered the childlike joy in her eyes in the sea, her sense of fun, the pure enjoyment of simply being there. And her aged body, her fragility.

Susan began to walk faster.

Her mother, sensing her mood, kept step beside her. Still those pages kept appearing, raised by the wind, set free. They almost seemed alive, the way they moved so freely, flying off, dancing in the air, as if imitating the seagulls, floating on the warm air. Page after twisting page. Rising, suspended, then racing away down the beach.

They were almost trotting now, still not speaking, but both thinking, wondering, a sense of dread. Over the dry sand that clung to their wet feet and sucked them down, slowing them, making them lift their feet higher. The sun, less hot than earlier, but still there, casting shadows, warm on their hair. The waves behind them, crashing, calling, hissing, as if sending a message. Then, after the dry sand, the patch of shingle, sharp stones that pricked and stung – but Susan barely noticed, so focussed was she on those sheets of paper rising, falling, twisting, as they danced away. The stretch of beach between them seemed to have grown, her legs moving in slow motion, as she moved forwards. Her throat was dry, and she could feel her heart beating.

She reached the windbreak, holding her breath, hardly daring to look.

"Aunty?" Susan said, as she rounded the side and saw the heaps of shoes and bags, the mound of towels, with a grey head above it, silent and not moving, the mouth open slightly.

She paused, suspended, unsure for a second if she should move, not wanting to find out.

The mound of towels began to move. The mouth closed. The eyes opened, squinted at the sky, closed again.

"I fell asleep," Elsie said, her shoulders rising. Her hair was tousled and sand had stuck to the ends. Her face had red lines where she had lain on a folded coat, and there was dribble on her chin, which she wiped away. She had pulled all the towels over her, in an attempt to stay warm, and covered them with the newspaper, which as she slept, and her arms had moved, had become unanchored and blown away. Elsie yawned, and struggled to sit up.

"I thought you had died," said Dot, reaching the windbreak and peering over, "and what have you done to my newspaper?"

"Oh," said Elsie, "oh dear."

She began to scramble from her cocoon of towels but Susan stopped her.

"Don't worry," Susan shouted, as she chased the sheets of paper, collecting as many as she could, crumpling them under her arm, running across the sand. Ben joined her, and they ran together, snatching at the pages, grabbing any that came within reach. They managed to rescue a few sheets, the others escaped, dancing away too quickly, too far for them to run. They watched them, twirling, rising and falling and rolling. They would fall eventually, Susan knew, and spoil the dunes, littering them. But she wasn't fast enough to catch them all, and she didn't know what she could do. She hoped they wouldn't be fined for littering. She felt bad, didn't want to spoil the beach, but knew she would never catch them. I'll walk back that way when we go, she decided, see if I can pick up more when they've fallen. Susan walked back to the windbreak with Ben.

"Time for another cup of tea," said Elsie, unscrewing the lid of the flask.

***

Later, when Susan was feeding the poultry, she remembered that feeling of dread as she watched the newspaper pages rise from behind the windbreak. Susan was in the barn, scooping layers pellets into a bucket. They were small and grey, and as she dipped the scoop into the container, the hard pellets rattled into the metal bucket. Something about the noise made her think about the day, the noise of the surf on the beach, and Elsie.

Susan thought about her aunt's face as she prepared to swim. That childlike excitement, wrapped up in an old body.

"We're all fragile really," she thought, heaving the now full buckets, one in each hand, and walking to the duck feeder next to the pond. "Elsie looked so happy, so pleased to be there," she thought, lifting the lid of the feeder and tipping the bucket to fill it. The pellets hissed inside, some falling at the edges and rolling across the dry mud. The ducks saw her, and started to swim across the pond towards her, the females quacking loudly, as if shouting at her, the males quieter, but still excited, all pleased to be fed.

Susan stood for a moment and watched them. They hauled themselves from the water and waddled over to the feeder, the dominant females pecking at the younger ducks, making them scoot away. Each duck ate, first scooping the pellets into their beaks, then walking back to the pond to drink. They stayed by the water, dipping their heads, raising them to swallow, repeating until they were done. There was a low murmur of noise, contented grunts and quacks, as if they were women, chatting at the school gate, thought Susan. They seemed so happy, secure and contented. Yet she knew that one visit from the fox, and they would have no defence. One bought of bird flu, and she could lose the whole flock.

"What's inside," she thought, watching a particularly cross female chase a male back onto the pond, "doesn't really reflect the whole situation. These birds look secure and happy, but one stroke of bad luck and they'll be defenceless. Aunty Elsie was like a little girl at the beach, she was so happy, so pleased to be there. But her body is wearing out. I'm not sure how much longer we'll have her."

Without warning, the precariousness of life struck her, and her stomach twisted. Nothing really was stable or secure, nothing lasted. She'd grown used to the farm animals arriving, growing, leaving; the general cycle of life as she hatched eggs, raised poultry, knew that the fox might get some, disease the others. But humans had seemed different, less fragile, more reliable. "But none of us really knows how long we've got," thought Susan, "none of us knows what's waiting round the corner."

As if gripped by some terrible premonition, tears pricked her eyes, and her heart beat faster. I don't want things to change, she thought, I don't want to get old, lose people who I love.

Susan realised she didn't want her boys to make decisions she thought were damaging, didn't want Tom to sink into a mire of over-work and depression, didn't want her mother and aunt to become more frail.

"I want to stop things changing," she thought, sighing and picking up the empty buckets. "But I can't. All I can do is grab life as it passes, try to consume as much of the good bits as I can before they flutter away, like paper carried on the wind. Nothing lasts forever, everything is transient. We have to make something worthwhile of the little piece we're given, but even that, eventually, will pass."

Susan carried the buckets back to the barn, and hung them on the rusty nails hammered into the wall next to the door.

However, Susan had no inkling that it was neither her mother, nor her aunt, who would be dying unexpectedly.

Chapter Nineteen

The summer had been a dry one – too dry to be helpful. By early August, the wheat was ready to be cut, the heads small and shrivelled, the stalks brittle. Jack met his father by the big barn. Tom was staring at the stores of food, and rubbing his head. He looked up as Jack approached.

"Just checking the feed," said Tom, nodding towards the stacks of hay and straw. "I hope we've got enough for the winter. I've already had to start it, all the grass in the big field is brown, there's nothing there for the cows to eat. I've used up four bales already, trying to supplement what's growing. I just hope it rains soon, so the grass picks up again. Then if we get a dry autumn, they can all stay outside until late, so we won't have to start the winter feed proper until later..."

Jack nodded, pulling his overall over his tee shirt as he listened. He knew that the whole point of the farm was to grow beef cattle, so it was imperative to keep the cattle well fed, and if the weather wasn't right, it was difficult to keep the weight on them. Lighter cows would bring less money. "You can't control the weather, Dad," he said with a shrug, moving away, towards where the machines stood. "No one can. All the other farms are the same."

"Yes, which means the price of feed, if we have to buy in more, will be even higher," muttered Tom, joining him by the tractor. Then he smiled. "At least I'm not having to pay an extra worker – that's a saving on last year."

He sounded cheerful, which Jack thought was a bit tactless of him. Like it was a good thing that Jack's whole life had been a disaster and all he could do was go home and help his dad.

"Right lad, you can drive the woman today," Tom said, laughing. "Get it? It's called a 'combine harvester' because it *combines* lots of different jobs – we could call it a '*multitasker* harvester' – or a *woman*, for short!"

Jack forced a smile, though his eyes were hooded. He'd heard his father's joke every year for as long as he could remember, and it hadn't been funny the first time. Jack climbed up into the cab and started the engine. Molly jumped up next to him, wanting to have a ride. He pushed her down. He didn't want company, not today, not even from a dog.

Jack saw his father watching with concerned eyes. Tom whistled to the dog, who joined him on the tractor, sitting where she often did, partly sharing his seat and partly balanced on the wide mudguard of the right wheel. Tom fondled her ears, and Jack knew he was being scrutinised. But he didn't care, he had no enthusiasm for anything, and certainly none to spare for an animal.

Jack knew he was being churlish, not caring about either the finances of the farm, or the animals that lived there. But he couldn't bring himself to care about anything, not anymore. The grey worm of loathing had shrivelled since his debts had been sorted, the tension dissipating with the relinquishing of each possession. No more phone contract, no more house contract, no more credit cards; and most importantly, no more loan sharks waiting to catch him.

But as the worm reduced, nothing grew to take its place. Jack was left with an emptiness, a pointlessness, which he couldn't shake. It was as if he had been under such tremendous pressure, trying to appear normal, to ignore everything, that when that pressure lifted, he found he was as empty as an overstretched balloon that has spun out of control and whizzed around in all directions, and is now deflated, empty, useless. He looked the same, his shape was unaltered, but everything inside had shrunk away to nothing. Jack was gone, and the shell that had been Jack was acting the part, going through the motions. He felt completely worthless, not because his financial value had dropped, but because he had failed, utterly, at being an adult.

Jack steered the combine harvester out of the yard, and headed towards the wheat field. He felt the power of the machine surrounding him, and hoped he wouldn't meet another vehicle in the narrow lane. It was easy enough, in a tractor, to pull onto the verge and let motorists pass, but this machine was something else, and he was keen to get to the field with no obstacles.

When Jack arrived at the field, the hay bale blocking the entrance had already been moved and the gate swung wide. The harvester lumbered across the dry earth, and Jack moved to position. The field was big, he had been told that in his grandfather's day it was three fields, but the hedges had long since been removed, to allow for the larger machines. Jack looked at the control panel in front of him, and lowered the cutter bar to the correct height. The teeth, unseen below the cab, would open and shut like pincers, cutting the wheat at the base. Jack clicked on the conveyor, felt the spinning augurs send vibrations up into his seat, which were joined by the deep throb of the threshing drum when he set it in motion. The threshing drum would shake the wheat as it passed beneath it, shaking the grains so they would fall through the sieves into the collecting tank below; the stalks would be discarded. The vibrations passed up, into Jack's head, and he knew he would have a headache before the field was harvested. His foot pressed the accelerator, and he began to harvest the field.

The sun was bright above him, glaring into the cab. It had been such a hot summer, long and stuffy, with no rain, and Jack missed the cool computer room of the bank. He missed the camaraderie of his work mates, the steady income (albeit not enough) and the routine of getting up, commuting to work, operating the computers, going home. The farm had its own rhythm, but it changed day to day.

"And, I don't feel part of it," thought Jack, turning the harvester at the end of the field. "Mum and Dad say they're glad to have me, that Dad needs the extra help; but they could as easily employ someone else. And once the harvest is in, once we're back to the more mundane stuff, Dad'll be hard put to find things for me to do. I feel like I'm a teenager again, with Dad trying to create jobs to occupy me so I can feel like I'm earning what they'd have given me anyhow."

Jack sighed, the shudder joining the general vibrations and noise of the machine. He could smell the wheat, dry and dusty. The straw chaff was spurting from the back, ready to be baled later and used with the cows. In the corner of his eye, Jack saw his father, driving the old tractor towards him – it was the only one big enough to pull the trailer. Jack swung the auger round, the long unloading bar high above the ground, waiting for the trailer to move underneath. When the trailer was in place, he expelled the grain, emptying the tank at the base of the harvester. The noise and dust and vibrations juddered up. It was hot and uncomfortable work.

As Jack waited for the tank to empty, he undid the buttons of his blue overalls. He had worn them to protect his clothes, from habit as much as anything. But it was too hot, he could feel his tee-shirt clinging to him like a damp second skin, sweat trickling down his back. Dust was finding gaps in the glass cab, was billowing inside, sticking to his damp forehead, itching his neck. He wriggled out of the top half of the overall, it was only a bib and braces, but it was too hot for the extra fabric; he hooked the braces back, over the seat. He'd have to leave the trousers on, he couldn't be bothered to stop the machine and jump down to remove them, but it felt slightly better now. His father signalled that the trailer was ready – the full extent of conversation when working the fields – and began to drive away. Jack turned off the unloader, and began to harvest more of the field while Tom drove the trailer, heavy and swaying, across the field, back to the grain store.

The harvester growled over the field, feasting on the dry wheat. Something was wrong with the balance of the machine, and Jack frowned, peering through the window, squinting through the dust. The harvester was moving forwards, chomping the wheat in front, spurting out the straw at the back. But the sound was wrong, and there was a lag on the steering, as if driving on a road where the camber was set the wrong way. Jack changed the steering a fraction, first one way, then the other, trying to work out what was wrong.

He saw it, at the exact same time that the engine died.

There was a pop. Everything stopped.

The auger, which he'd forgotten to secure when the trailer was full, had been swinging, and as he moved, unaware, underneath the overhead power lines, it had made contact. The harvester was now conducting a deadly amount of voltage.

Jack sat; for a long moment, he just sat. He had forgotten to look up. In front of him, stuck to the steering wheel was the sticker his father had placed there: *Look Out! Look Up!* But he hadn't. His body, moving as an automaton had mindlessly worked the machine without thinking. Without caring.

Below the slogan, was the number provided by the distribution network operator, to be phoned in an emergency. It was there, bold black numbers on a round dusty sticker – DNO, and the number.

But Jack's phone was where he'd left it, in the kitchen. He hadn't wanted it with him. He still wasn't sure he wanted it with him.

Jack knew he had a few seconds, and those seconds would decide everything. He knew the drill, had been trained since a child. While he was in the cab, suspended above the ground, he was relatively safe – unless something caught fire. But getting from the cab to the ground, making that connection between live and earth, could be deadly. He should open the door, and leap, with both feet, away from the cab, then bunny-hop, double-footed, until he was a safe distance. If he was lucky – and there wasn't much in his recent life that made him feel lucky – then he would be clear, there would be no join between the live electricity and the earth, his body wouldn't make the fatal connection; he would survive.

Still Jack paused. The problem, and until now he hadn't even considered it, but the problem was, Jack was not sure that he *wanted* to survive. He knew, deep inside, that he could never take his own life, could never be selfish enough to leave his parents and brothers with the horrible knowledge that he had decided to end everything. But this? This wouldn't be suicide. This would be a tragic accident. This would be a stupid forgetfulness due to being under so much pressure. This would be one of those not-so-rare accidents that happened on farms.

He was pretty sure it would be quick, painless. The power surge would stop his heart, that would be it. A second of agony, at most. All he had to do, was open the cab door, and climb down. One foot, just one foot, on the sunbaked crop would do it.

What, he asked, would he be leaving behind? A failed life, that's what. No steady girlfriend, no job, no flat, nothing. Sure, his family would be upset, they'd cry for a bit. But they would recover, people did. They would move on. And Jack? Jack would be no more. No more struggle, no more grey worms crawling

Susan felt suspended, all her worries about Ben and Jack put on hold, all the tensions seeping away, so that there was only this moment, this present, a tangle of sounds and warmth.

She was disturbed by a dog, nosing its way through the dunes. It stopped and stared at her, its eyes very round, ears up, mouth open so it looked as if it was smiling. Then the owner called, and it turned, kicking up sand as it ran back to the path. Susan stood, and walked back to the beach, sliding down the steep hill, seeing the expanse of sea in front of her. As she walked, her thoughts and worries returned.

"Should I do something about Ben? Will Tom manage to keep working the farm on his own when Jack gets another job? Is there enough money to employ someone full-time?" The thoughts chased each other round her mind, like the sand being chased by the wind. Round and round in a futile loop, never going anywhere but never still, working its way into places where it was unwelcome, an uncomfortable nuisance.

She came to the water's edge, and let the waves run over her feet, cold and persistent. Susan turned, walking back towards her family, the water around her ankles, splashing her legs as she walked, the sand underneath firm and smooth. When she was about half way back, her mother appeared at her side, and they walked together, enjoying the sensations of wind and sun and water, chatting about nothing, their words snatched by the wind and mixed with the crash of the waves, so they didn't hear every word, and were more nodding at the gist of what the other was saying. Then her mother pointed and said something, which Susan assumed meant they had walked far enough, as she could see the windbreak on the beach level with them.

They began to walk up the beach. Susan could see the windbreak, pushed concave by the wind. She couldn't see Elsie, but as she watched, a white sheet of newspaper rose into the air, twisting and turning, floating away. It was followed by another page, and another, until there was a line of them, white and tangled, chasing each other along the sand, away from the windbreak.

"That's my newspaper!" said Dot, frowning. "Elsie hasn't held onto it and it's littering the beach."

round his insides, no more bleak emptiness, no more blackness pressing on his mind. No more failure. It would end it all, and it was so easy.

He reached for the door handle, clicked it open and pushed. The cab door swung open, away from him, across the dry wheat, which looked so innocent, so harmless, waiting for him to touch it. The dull gold stalks reaching towards him, silent, looking no different to every other day. Behind him were the cut stalks, a soft bed in rows, like golden waves on an ocean. He could hear crows, wheeling above, waiting to come and investigate the harvested field; bees were busy in the hedgerow. Wisps of cloud were scudding across the blue sky; the sun glared down searing into the cab, willing him on, forwards, down to sudden oblivion. The air was warm, the dust settling now, leaving a warm caress on his skin; all was soft and golden and still. It was, he thought, a good day to die. A good place to end; so much better than a hospital ward full of tubes and beige and clinical smells. He was part of this land, had grown up here, laughed and cried and learned here; it was the right place, he thought, making his decision, soon he would be at peace.

He began to move, to lean forwards. Then stopped; stared; horrified.

Turning into the field was Tom and the trailer. Jack watched as the tractor slammed to a stop, saw his father wave his arms, heard the shout as it carried in the air towards him.

No, no, not yet, not now; too soon.

Tom was off the tractor, running towards his son, arms waving, yelling instructions that were lost by the distance between them.

Jack knew that the area around the cab would be live, that if Tom came too close he could be electrocuted. Jack could see the wild panic in his father's gestures, the lurching run as he charged towards his son, intent on saving Jack, perhaps forgetting in his panic that he too would be in danger, the electricity might arc, the power might surge through both of them.

Jack had to get out, had to warn his father, stop him coming nearer. All thoughts of his own demise flown, his one thought was for his father's safety. The second of insanity had passed, only living and ensuring his father's life mattered. Jack could feel his heart, hammering in his chest, his breath was shallow, short puffs, his brain distorting everything, so he felt as though he had been spun round, was dizzy, the world not quite steady. He began to climb from his seat, moving his feet, lifting his bottom, leaning forwards; stopped, was held fast, couldn't move. He thumped back down.

A flash of black and white caught his eye. No! It was Molly, slinking from the tractor, following Tom, racing towards Jack and the harvester and the deadly power. She overtook Tom, was running ever nearer.

The braces from Jack's bib, looped across the back of his seat, had caught on a nail, were stuck. Jack wriggled round, trying to see what was holding him. He couldn't turn, was stuck fast. He tried to pull away, to rip the fabric, to force the trapped braces to give way. But they were too well made, stuck too securely, he couldn't escape.

Jack watched in horror as the dog drew nearer, images of her gentle head pushing against him, her wet nose comforting him as a boy, the feel of her body when he hugged her. They'd had her since she was a puppy, tumbled with her fat waddling body as boys, seen her grow into a trained worker. Molly was more gentle than Rex, always keen to be with them, would lean her warm body against their legs in sympathy, an innocent giver of comfort. No, not Molly, surely no. She wouldn't know it was dangerous, she wouldn't stop in time, would race straight to where Jack was. And he couldn't move, couldn't escape, couldn't stop either of them running into danger.

He pulled again, using all his strength, heard stitches rip, felt something give; but not enough, he was still held fast. He couldn't force his way out.

An acrid smell crept into his nose. He glanced down. One of the front tyres was smoking. A thin black wisp, floating up towards the sun. In seconds it could be aflame, the smoke would reach him first, the flames would spread across the dry field in minutes. He was trapped, needed to escape. The dog was still advancing, intent on reaching him first.

He twisted, tried again to turn, moved his arm behind him. He pushed his hand back, behind the seat, felt with unsteady fingers, forced himself to slow down, to follow the line of the braces down, past the seat cushion, down the hard plastic backrest, along the metal strut.

Tom too was getting nearer, he staggered as his ankle turned on a furrow, then righted himself, continued his run; arms waving, still shouting, pointing up at the auger, desperate to warn his son of the danger but perhaps forgetting his own vulnerability. Closer Tom came, his words now reaching Jack. Then Tom fell, arms up, his feet slipping from under him as a clod of hard mud tripped him. Molly noticed, heard his yell, stopped her forwards trajectory, turned towards her master. She saw he was down, curved back to investigate, looping behind him.

Jack moved his hand lower, his fingers squeezed against the back of the chair, too fat to go much lower. At last, his forefinger found the nail, worked its way around the material, unhooked the braces, scooped them up over the back of the seat. He was free.

Tom was up again, man and dog continuing their race towards Jack. The dog moved ahead, enjoying the game, intent on reaching the harvester first, a streak of black and white.

Jack was moving, used a hand to push the door wide, measured the gap from the cab to where he would land.

Tom was still advancing, his shout coming in snatches: "Power lines," "Electricity" "Auger". Arms waving, leaping across furrows, almost falling, staggering forwards.

Jack took a breath, used his arms to propel his body forwards, leaped. He left the cab, landed two-footed a distance from it. Bent his legs, swung his arms, leaped again; then again.

Tom and Jack met. In the final leap, Jack felt his father grasp his arms, pull him forwards, they both fell over. The wheat was dry, spiky, the mud beneath hard and lumpy. They fell, Jack squashing his father, thumping all the air out of him, bruising him with his weight, then rolling away from him. They both sat up.

"The power lines," said Tom, gasping, as if the words had stuck in his mind, and he was unable to say anything else.

Jack nodded. "Yeah, I know." Then, because he couldn't think of anything else to say: "Sorry."

Sorry for what? Sorry for not listening and remembering to look up? Sorry for wanting to end it all? Sorry for yet again failing? Sorry for landing on his father and hurting him? Jack didn't know. He was crumbling inside, and there was nothing he could do to stop it.

Tom was shaking his head. Jack saw the lines on his father's face, and guessed the run and fall would have further damaged his back. He could hear their breath, as they both struggled to recover. They sat for a while, waiting for their breath to steady. Tom was panting, his arm was looped around Molly, keeping her close. Suddenly he grinned.

"Maybe we won't mention this one to your mother," he said between breaths. "I suppose your phone's in the house?"

Jack nodded, not quite trusting himself to speak. "Sorry," he said again.

Tom pulled out his phone, scrolled through his contacts. "Better ring the network people," he said, "tell them they've got a combine harvester conducting their power. I put their number in here ages ago, at the last Union talk we had. Didn't think I'd ever need it mind..."

Jack listened, as Tom looked away, started to speak, to explain what had happened, to say that no, there wasn't any fire as yet, but it was all very dry, they needed to disconnect the power asap. Or phone the fire brigade and explain why they hadn't.

Jack sat beside him, feeling the dry crop beneath him, noticing that one elbow was sore where he'd fallen on it. Now he was safe, had nearly been trapped and managed to escape, he felt better; more alive perhaps. The world had shifted, was back on kilter. Perhaps it was the burst of adrenaline, the sudden realisation that although he'd mucked up, there were still people, things, he valued, loved, cared about. He still had a place in the world, even if his role was a bit uncertain at the moment. Jack sat, next to his father, Molly going from one to the other, not sure of why they were there but sensing something important. The sun shone down. They waited.

***

When they finally got home that evening, they were exhausted. The power had been disconnected almost immediately, so there hadn't been a fire. But the harvester had needed more expertise and tools than Tom had, and when the engineer had arrived with jacks and tools and knowledge, some of the wheat had been ruined.

Eventually the machine was working again, moved to a safe place away from the power lines, and the power switched back on. Jack had found he was shaking when he first stood up, his arms and legs quaking as if he'd run for miles. Tom noticed, tried to send him home: told Jack to take the trailer and send Ben back in his place. But Jack refused. He could see his father was hurting, the fall had made his back worse; Tom didn't say anything, but there were new lines on his face, and he held himself awkwardly. So although everything inside Jack wanted to run away, to go home and forget that this was all his fault, he didn't. He stayed and helped the engineer, then eventually climbed back into the cab of the harvester, and began to cut the remaining crop.

They worked until the light was gone, until they were forced to abandon the final few rows because they couldn't see what they were doing, and they'd had enough accidents for one day. Every bone ached, and his head was thumping, and he felt he could sleep for a week, but Jack realised it was a 'good' tired. It was a tiredness born of hard work and physical expenditure, not from stress and worry.

They ate in the kitchen, not saying much, half listening while Susan told them about her day, that Elsie had a nasty cold and the fox was back and had got another chicken. Ben was out, and it was easy for Tom and Jack to eat without speaking, to let the strains of the day seep away.

Molly sidled under the table while they ate, and rested her head on Jack's knee. He reached down, fondling her soft ears, thinking that he was glad to be here, glad to be alive.

Chapter Twenty

On a cloudy morning in September, Susan was feeding the ducks. She watched as they heaved themselves onto the bank of the pond, and stood there, a couple of feet away from her, as if talking. The males made soft raspy noises, their heads on one side, as if trying to hurry her. The females were louder, more insistent, quaking impatiently while she tipped the bucket of pellets into the feeder. As they stood, surrounding her, it was exactly as if they were a crowd of people, all talking at her at once, each one having their own discussion, listening was unimportant, it was a time to talk.

Susan stood for a moment, watching them, looking to see if her favourites were there: the black East India duck that always managed to avoid being caught, the hybrid with the green head, the one with a blue patch on his wing. As soon as the food was in the feeder and she stepped back, only one step because they knew her, they rushed forwards, busy with the serious business of eating and drinking and pushing each other out of the way so they could be first.

"I don't know," she said, watching as they waddled around, "you think when the children are small that it will all be easier when they're grownup, that being a mother will finish at some point. But I feel as much their mother now as I did when I could pick them up, I still worry about them. Being a mother seems to go on and on for a very long time..."

There was a footstep behind her.

"Are you talking to the ducks?" said Ben.

"Ah. I guess – yes...sort of...to be fair, they listen better than people do," said Susan, smiling. "And they never contradict me, or gossip about what I've said."

Ben laughed. "Great! I have one parent who talks to cows all day, and another who chats to ducks."

He joined her on the bank, watching the ducks while Susan went to check the nesting boxes. There were only a few eggs;

ducks were moody layers, as soon as the weather began to get cool they stopped giving her eggs. Chickens were more reliable, and unless they went broody, would supply an egg most days, even through the winter. Susan felt Ben turn to watch her as she put the eggs into her bucket.

"I was wondering," he said, as if choosing his words with care, "if Kevin could come for your birthday? It would be a chance for everyone to meet him."

Susan picked up the last egg and closed the nesting box, keeping her face hidden because she wasn't sure if she could control the expression. Ben had mentioned the possibility of Kevin visiting several times, but never a specific date, so it had been easy to side-step, to sound willing without actually issuing an invitation. She wasn't sure if this was because she didn't want to meet him herself, or if it was easier to manage the Neil situation.

Her own feelings were still a muddle. Although she was gradually accepting the situation, understanding that Ben was still Ben, he hadn't become 'camp' or effeminate, and other people were mostly completely accepting of the situation, barely interested in fact, which had helped. However, part of her still struggled with this other person, this unknown boy, who – in an irrational part of her mind – she sort of blamed for her son's gayness. Susan wasn't sure how she would feel if she saw them together, especially if they showed any affection towards each other. This other boy was Gay. She didn't know him as anything other than Gay. A faceless personification of homosexuality; not someone who she wanted to meet. But she knew that this was a temporary solution – more of a delaying tactic than a solution – and that at some point she would have to meet Kevin, or one of Kevin's replacements if the relationship didn't last. So when the nesting box was bolted, and safe against foxes, Susan stood up and faced Ben.

"Yes, okay, good idea."

"And do you think Neil will make a fuss?" said Ben. "I don't want to ruin your birthday."

"Well, it's not a special birthday, I was surprised when Ed and Neil said they were coming back for the day, so it doesn't really matter if he does make a fuss. But I don't think he will.

Gran and Elsie will be here too, and Ed said he might bring Emily for once." She gave Ben a wry look, "You all tend to behave yourselves when strangers are present."

"Really? That doesn't happen very often – seeing Emily I mean, I haven't seen her for ages," said Ben, sounding surprised. "Do you think Josie knows she'll be there?"

"I have no idea," said Susan, carrying the empty buckets back to the shed.

She reached for the broom, and began to sweep the floor, where pellets and odd bits of straw had fallen. She noticed a hole in the side of the shed and sighed; rats must have found the food sacks. She'd have to ask Tom to repair that, and as the rats would find another way in, she would have to start keeping the pellets in the big barn, where the cats lived, which was inconvenient. Susan went to the shelf where she kept the bait boxes, and filled one with poison, setting it on the floor near to the hole, where she thought the rats would be used to running. Rats were a nuisance, they were hard to get rid of, and caused a lot of damage, killing hatchlings and contaminating food stores.

"I hope," she said, moving a couple of boxes to secure the bait box, watching spiders scurry away, "that there is nothing to tell. Ed always tells me that Josie is just a friend, and she knows all about Emily." Susan straightened. "I hope that's right, she's a nice girl. I wouldn't want to see her hurt.

"Now, will you help me move these sacks of pellets while you're here?"

***

The family all descended for the birthday. They had decided to come to the farm for tea on the Sunday nearest Susan's birthday, so she didn't need to start cooking dinners or making beds. It would take Neil and Kylie over an hour, but was near enough to be possible. Ed and Emily could do the journey in 40 minutes, if the traffic was clear.

Susan was preparing lunch, when Ben came to ask if he could borrow her car. They had decided that Kevin would arrive early, for lunch, so that he could meet a few people and see the farm before everyone arrived en masse.

"What time is his train?" asked Susan, glancing at the clock, and thinking that dinner wouldn't be ready for nearly an hour.

"Ten past," said Ben, moving to steal a piece of the carrot she was cutting and putting it into his mouth. "I thought I'd drive home the long way, via Becksville. It's so pretty, with all the thatched worker's cottages and windy lanes and everything. Sort of chocolate-box-countryside. I want Kevin to think we live in a nice place."

"Yes, it is pretty," agreed Susan, moving from carrots to parsnips, thinking about the hamlets between their farm and Marksbridge station. "Prettier than Jameston anyway, which is bit of a scruffy place, I always think..."

Ben waved and left, and she was left with saucepans of bubbling vegetables and a nervous flutter in her stomach. She had, until now, worried only about whether she could cope with meeting this boy, this Gay boy. But she now realised that actually, it was more important, in terms of her relationship with Ben, that *the boy* liked her. If this boy, this Kevin, decided he didn't like the farm, or Tom, or Susan, then he would never want to visit again. Which meant that when Ben found a job and moved out, he too would rarely visit. Susan added salt to the saucepans, frowning.

***

Susan was carrying plates into the parlour when they arrived.

"Mum, this is Kevin," said Ben.

Susan stopped, and turned. She saw a short – shorter even than Ben – stocky young man with a mass of curly ginger hair. No feather boa or lipstick, simply a confident stride and a wide smile.

"Hello Mrs Compton and happy birthday," he said, marching into the room and holding out a card and a present wrapped in pink spotted paper with a yellow bow. "It's very kind of you to invite me, I've been hoping to meet you soon. Have you had a nice birthday? I hope we're not late, I think Ben drove me the scenic route, and it certainly was very pretty. All those little cottages, and flowers in window boxes and things...Here, let me take those plates from you so you can open your gift." He took the plates from her hand. "Where shall I put them?"

Susan closed her mouth. Looked at the gift, led the way to the parlour.

"In here," she said, "thank you. Just put the plates on the table, I thought we could have tea in the parlour, as it's a special event. But we'll eat lunch in the kitchen."

Kevin placed the plates on the cloth, next to a pile of paper napkins.

"Shall I put these between the plates – or is there something I can do to help with lunch? I'm good at peeling veg, or I could set the table?

"This is a nice room, isn't it. I've heard Ben talk about the parlour before, but I always imagined somewhere dark and foreboding, like from a gothic novel. This is lovely, very light and comfortable. Have you changed it much? Ben told me that the farm used to belong to his grandparents. I think that's really cool. One of my grandfathers was a butcher, so sort of linked to farming. He had a shop in the high street where they lived, but I don't remember it of course. He's dead now, he died when I was seven, so I don't really remember him.

"His wife, Grandma Joan, still lives in the same town. She talks about him all the time, almost as if he's still alive, even after all this time – oh, do you like it?"

Susan had stood for a moment, waiting for the flow of words to end. When she realised that it would possibly never end, she decided to open her gift, and peeled away the paper to reveal what looked like a china plate, decorated with china flowers, and a tiny bottle of room perfume.

"You sprinkle the scent over the flowers, I think they absorb it, makes the room smell nice," said Kevin, as if not sure whether Susan realised what it was.

"Thank you, it's lovely, very pretty," said Susan. "It was kind of you to bring a present, you didn't have to."

"I'm glad you like it," said Kevin, beaming.

Susan smiled back. There was something completely unthreatening about the boy, he seemed to be a bubble of smiles, and very chatty. Her first impression was a good one, and she was relieved. "He's just normal," she thought. "And he certainly talks a lot. Perhaps it's nerves."

Kevin was talking again, a flow of consciousness about room deodorants, and how when he was little his mother used to spray a smelly deodorant around the toilet, and it stank, and once she'd got it muddled up with the fly-killer spray – did Susan remember those? – he wasn't sure if they still made them, probably they did, but he hadn't seen one for years, they smelt so awful that you almost felt sorry for the flies didn't you?

Susan went back into the kitchen, kissing Ben's cheek on the way, followed by Kevin and the steady stream of words.

Jack and Tom arrived for dinner as Susan was putting it onto the table. Kevin stood when they entered the kitchen, and walked round to shake their hands. Jack looked surprised, but Susan could see that Tom was pleased, liked the politeness of the gesture.

"Hello, I'm Kevin, it's very nice to meet you, Ben talks so much about the farm I almost feel like I know you. I'm dying to see the cows later, if that would be okay? I've always liked cows, though growing up in the city we didn't get to see them very often. When I was little, my mum used to take me to one of those pretend farms, where they had all the animals, and a big barn full of toy tractors and things. You could pet the animals and play, and have a picnic there and things. And one day..."

Susan coughed. They were all sitting at the table, waiting for the words to stop so they could say grace. Tom always said grace on a Sunday. She wasn't sure why they didn't say it on other days, because she was sure remembering the food came from God and being thankful was important, but somehow it never happened on other days.

"Let's say grace," said Tom, before Kevin started to speak again. The family bowed their heads.

"Thank you Father for this food, and for Susan who has prepared it. Amen."

They all said *amen*. Kevin said a particularly loud *amen*, as if keen to show he was in agreement with the prayer.

"We don't say grace at home much," Kevin said, as Susan passed him dishes of potatoes and bowls of peas and Tom sliced the roast beef and served it onto the plates. "We go to church every week, of course, that's one of the things I like about Ben." He turned, and smiled at Ben, a big grin, eyes shining.

Susan paused in reaching for the Yorkshire puddings. She had thought she would mind that sort of gesture, that sudden show of affection. But she found that she didn't. It seemed natural, and she realised that she liked seeing the look, was pleased to see that Kevin valued her son, thought Ben was special.

"Our church is very modern," continued Kevin, "we tend to only sing choruses, and all the old people complain that we never sing the traditional hymns. Even at Christmas, sometimes we barely sing a Christmas Carol, just lots of modern songs. But I suppose that's right really, don't you think? To sing songs that actually mean something, not just hymns about it snowing in Bethlehem, where I doubt it ever snowed in real life.

"Though I can't be sure, as I've never been there. One of my aunties has, and she said it was really scary, what with the war and everything. Well, not actually a war, but you know what I mean, all the bad feeling between the two parties and bombs and things. She said she went to the Gaza Strip, on a sort of tour, not sure what I think about that really, I wouldn't want to go somewhere like that on a holiday, would you? I mean..."

The family ate, while Kevin talked. Tom looked up, caught Susan's eye and grinned. The boy was certainly unexpected, she thought. At least they weren't having awkward silences. There was no need for anyone else to speak at all.

When they finished eating, Susan loaded the dishwasher and Kevin offered to wash up the meat tins. He stood at the sink, his arms covered in bubbles and grease, telling her about all the pets he'd owned as a child, and the car he wanted to buy, and how the met office had the ability to predict weather exactly, but the computers took longer to calculate the forecast than the time they had, so they could tell you exactly but not until after it had actually happened, which was a bit daft wasn't it?

Susan finished wiping surfaces, and began to pull out bread, cheese, butter, whatever she could think of to make sandwiches. Ben and Kevin offered to help, and as she cut thin slices of bread, Ben buttered them and Kevin cut the remains of the beef into slices. It was relaxed, companionable, their hands busy while they chatted.

"Whatever can I make for Neil and Kylie?" said Susan, "They won't eat meat, and I don't think Kylie will even eat cheese."

"Cucumber?" said Kevin.

"Isn't that what vicars eat?"

"No idea. But my mum likes cucumber sandwiches, with ham in."

"I don't think that counts," said Susan. "Oh dear, I should've thought about this before. Do you think I could give them jam sandwiches? Or marmalade?"

"Marmalade," said Kevin. "It sounds more grown-up than jam. Though there was that bear, wasn't there, who ate marmalade sandwiches. Did you read the books when you were little?

"My favourite books were those *Revolting Science* ones, I loved those. Perhaps that's where my love of science comes from. Either there or Uncle Sam, he works in research. Did you know..."

Ben offered to show Kevin the farm, and Susan was grateful for the break in conversation, not that it really was a conversation, more of a monologue. She took a cup of tea upstairs, and read a novel until her guests arrived.

Chapter Twenty-One

Neil and Kylie arrived at the same time as Ed and Emily. Susan heard the first car drive into the yard, and went to meet them. She had spoken to Kylie a few times on the phone recently, mostly just chatting, but also trying to gauge how Neil would react to meeting Kevin. Kylie assured her that although Neil was unlikely to be friendly, he would be polite. He would, she said, treat Kevin as any other person who he was introduced to, and wouldn't embarrass Susan by launching into a heated discussion. Neil was worried that Susan was wrong to invite Kevin into the house, but he realised they would never agree on that.

Susan was rather unsure when Neil and Kylie arrived, watching her son's face to see how he was feeling. But Neil hugged and kissed her as warmly as usual, whispering that he hoped she was having a nice birthday. Her heart lifted, but before she could reply, another car swept into the yard. Ed and Emily climbed out of Emily's Mazda MX5, the tiny sports car looking out of place in the muddy yard. Emily had driven down, and she opened her door to change into high stiletto heels before going across to say hello. She was small and blonde, and wore a neat suit with the very high heels.

Susan noticed Kylie's glance of approval and sighed. Her boys were attracted to very different women to herself.

Emily put her scented cheek next to Susan's and kissed the air, then passed her a gift.

"Hello Susan, lovely to see you again after so long," Emily said, managing to somehow convey that she would have seen Susan more recently, had Emily been invited, as she should have been, to the various family gatherings that had happened in the interim.

Susan decided to ignore the insinuation, as it was her son's decision, not hers, and she didn't want to get involved. She thanked Emily for the gift, admired her car, and led the way into the house, hoping the dogs wouldn't jump up and spoil Emily's suit.

"Is there anything I can do to help?" asked Emily, as they walked through the kitchen and she saw the food, covered in clingfilm, sitting on the table.

"No, I don't think so," said Susan, noticing that Kylie kept her head facing forwards, and was walking quickly. Susan smiled, and followed the family into the parlour, where Ben was waiting.

"Hi Neil, Kylie, Ed, Emily – this is Kevin," said Ben, as they walked into the parlour. He stood by the fireplace, obviously keen that his brothers should like Kevin. He glanced towards Neil, looking nervous.

Susan saw Neil walk forwards, shake the proffered hand, nod his head in greeting, then withdraw to the bookcase in the corner. Edward filled the gap, by shaking Kevin's hand and introducing Emily and Kylie again. Edward knew how to be charming, and Susan knew he would rather enjoy that Neil was being reticent, giving Edward the opportunity to show what a sociable person he was.

"Hello, pleased to meet you," said Kevin, giving them one of his wide smiles. "We've just been round the farm, looking at the cows. I don't know much about cows, so Ben was explaining the differences, how the steers and heifers can all be mixed together because the males are neutered – I never knew that, I always assumed only males were used for beef, and that all females were kept separate. They're big animals, aren't they? I guess you must be used to the size, growing up with them, but I was a bit scared, to be honest."

He laughed – a sudden snort that took them unawares, so they laughed too, even Neil, shocked by the noise.

"What do you do?" asked Emily, moving to sit on the sofa. Susan noticed her slip off one shoe, and reach down to rub her ankle. Kevin was talking, and everyone was nodding, and pretending to listen, and Susan knew they were all wondering if there would be a break in the conversation. Kevin talked for a long time, about studying chemistry, and what he planned to do next and what his father and mother did.

While Kevin talked, Susan looked around the room. Her children were all sitting, though not slumped into sofas as they usually were, but upright, polite smiles frozen on their faces. Emily was looking bored, and kept shooting glances towards Edward, who was ignoring her. Kylie appeared to be listening, and kept opening and closing her mouth, as if about to join in, but not managing to find a gap in the flow of words. Ben was looking anxious, and Susan noticed him look towards Neil, who forced a smile and nodded, as if to reassure his brother, whilst everything in his stance seemed uneasy.

There was a pause in conversation when Susan heard her mother and Aunty Elsie arrive in the kitchen. Ben took Kevin through to meet them. When they left the parlour, Edward looked round at the others,

"Well? What do you think?" he said.

"He certainly talks a lot," said Neil, slumping onto the sofa next to Emily.

"Yes, but I think he's rather sweet," said Kylie, "and I like that he smiles a lot. He wants to be liked by us doesn't he, wants to be part of the family."

Edward shot her a glance, but didn't say anything.

"How's work going Emily?" said Neil, as if trying to change the subject, "Ed told me you'd been promoted recently."

Susan didn't hear Emily's reply, as she decided to leave at that point, and join the others in the kitchen. She thought that Neil had seemed okay – or at least near enough to 'okay' for her to not need to worry.

In the kitchen, Elsie and Dot had arrived in a bubble of excitement.

"I do love birthday parties," said Elsie, giving Susan a big hug and a tiny gift wrapped in crumpled Christmas paper. "I've been looking forward to coming for tea all week! Do you like my dress? It's new, I went shopping with June from Bingo, and she persuaded me to buy it."

Susan looked at her aunt, dressed in a flowery dress with a small collar and a belt, which was exactly like all her other dresses, and smiled.

"Gran, Aunty Elsie, meet Kevin," said Ben, walking over to the sink where Elsie was getting a glass of water.

"Oh!" said Elsie, putting her glass in the sink. "You must be Ben's LBGT friend, hello, I'm his Aunty Elsie."

"You can just call him Kevin," said Ben.

Susan wished Ben had never used the 'LGBT' phrase with his grandmother; it had just confused them. She found it difficult herself to remember the order of the initials.

Kevin walked forward, his hand outstretched. Elsie looked at it, took a breath, then reached out her own hand and shook it.

Kevin then went to shake hands with Dot.

Tom and Jack appeared in the boot-room, stripping off muddy overalls, going to join the family. Jack gave his great aunt a big hug, and kissed his grandmother. Susan watched, thinking that he looked less pale these days, less tense about the eyes. She hoped that he'd find time to talk to Neil while he was there, to thank him for his help. Susan wasn't quite sure of the situation, but knew enough to realise that Jack had been sinking fast and Neil had saved him.

"Let's go into the parlour with the others," she said.

"Is there a cake?" asked Elsie, "I've been looking forward to the cake."

"Would you like a more comfy chair, Aunty?" said Neil, starting to stand.

"No, thank you dear, I like it here," said Elsie, taking an upright seat in the corner.

Susan began to remove foil and clingfilm from the plates of food, to place knives and cake forks in convenient places. She saw Jack lean towards Emily.

"So, Emily, we haven't seen you for a while. I was wondering, has Ed shown you his sports injury yet?"

"Really?" said Edward, sounding dismissive, "Is this really what we're going to discuss?"

"Oh yes, I think we should," said Ben, laughing and crossing the room so he was standing next to Kevin. "He got it playing rugby," Ben explained. Then, turning back to his brother asked, "How many times were you on the team Ed? Just the once wasn't it?"

Susan stopped moving things around and glanced at Emily. She was sitting very upright on the sofa, and she looked confused. Susan smiled to herself. The boys were always like this when someone new was introduced, they liked to try and embarrass each other, bringing up inappropriate stories from their past. She was simply glad it wasn't poo-related this time. Four boys, growing up on a farm, could be exceptionally vulgar when they got started. Susan looked across to Neil. He was also smiling, and was more part of the group. Susan knew this was familiar territory: all the boys teasing one person. She was interested that it was Ed they had started on, and not Ben – maybe they too found the relationship too new, were unsure of the rules. But Edward was fair game.

Edward was trying to turn the conversation, was saying how Ben had always fluffed catching, so had never made it to the cricket team, but his brothers were not to be distracted.

"Go on Ed, show her your scar," said Ben, grinning broadly.

"You have a scar?" said Emily.

Edward shook his head, and raised the hair on his forehead. There, right under the hairline, was a faint pink line.

"Oh," said Emily, "I've never noticed that before. And you got it playing rugby?"

She sounded confused, and Susan knew she wasn't keeping up, hadn't realised that the boys were teasing their brother.

"Well..." said Jack, "It wasn't exactly *playing* rugby, was it Ed."

Susan watched, as Edward shook his head. "No," he said, sounding resigned. "What my lovely brothers are trying to tell you Emily, is that I was, once, picked for the rugby team – which I believe is more than Neil ever was, by the way – but unfortunately, before the game got started properly, I had an accident..."

"In the changing room," added Ben, "he hadn't even made it on to the pitch, and he tripped over someone's sock..."

"I believe it was a shoe," corrected Edward.

"And fell, arse over –" Ben glanced at his grandmother, "and fell right over, bashing his head on a bench."

"There was blood everywhere," said Edward, as though hoping for sympathy.

"And we were all there," said Jack, "Mum had made us all go, even though it was a Saturday, because she was so proud that one of us had made it to the team. And we sat there," he giggled, "we sat there, trying to spot which one was Ed."

"But he never appeared," finished Neil. "He was patched up by the school nurse and had to read a book for the rest of the match."

"I believe I was sub, actually," muttered Edward.

Emily smiled, still looking bewildered. Susan saw her glance at Edward, then down at her hands, which were twisting in her lap.

Susan stood, knowing that embarrassing stories could last all afternoon, and was keen to stop them before they turned to less appropriate subjects.

"Let's have some cake," she said, handing a plate to Aunty Elsie.

The table was laden with plates of food. There were the sandwiches, and there were currant buns and cinnamon whirls. The birthday cake was chocolate, one of her favourite recipes, and she had grated swirls of milk, dark and white chocolate across the top. Thick butter icing oozed from the middle, and the sponge, when she cut it, was soft and fresh. Susan cut fat slices and left them on the plate, so people could help themselves, then started to pour tea.

Kevin was standing next to Susan, talking again. She thought he had hardly stopped talking since he had arrived, almost as if he was being sponsored, so many words a minute. He would, Susan thought, make a fortune, if anyone did ever sponsor him, as he darted from subject to subject without pause, and the only way to stop him was either to interrupt and speak over him, or to leave the room. He had moved from Clark's shoes to the decline of the high streets to the state of the economy, and was now discussing his hobbies.

Ben came to the table, and collected tea for his grandmother and Elsie, to save them getting up. Susan thanked him, and put a few sandwiches and cakes on their plates. They both had a sweet tooth, so there were more cakes than sandwiches by the time Susan had finished, and she watched Ben carrying them, hoping nothing would topple off.

"I've always liked chess," Kevin was saying, "though I'm more keen on physical games. I've started kite-surfing recently, have you ever tried it?"

"Oh, how lovely," Elsie said, interrupting Kevin as he described the kites he owned. Susan looked at her in surprise.

"I would love to do that. I always loved flying kites, it was one of the things I did with my father, when I was a girl. Gosh, I haven't flown a kite for years. Now, I'm not quite sure what 'kite-surfing' is — does that mean flying a kite next to the sea? Oh, I would love to do that, it would be quite perfect. Being old is so boring you know, people think you want to sit and do jigsaw puzzles all day. But I don't, I still want to do fun things. Will you take me one day? Would you mind?"

The room went quiet, and the family turned to her.

"Do you know what kite-surfing is, Aunty?" asked Jack, very gently, as if he was talking to a young child.

Elsie looked cross. "Well, I'm not entirely sure, like I said, but I think I do," she said, sounding annoyed. "I think my friend June from Bingo goes all the time," she added, sitting straighter. "I've always thought it sounded fun, and I would like to have a try. Will you take me?" Elsie asked again, turning to Kevin. "But I don't have a kite, could I borrow one?"

"Yes," said Kevin, clearly not sure what to say, "of course, that would be fine. Um, I'll let you know when I next go. Er — Do you have a wet suit?"

There was a splutter, as Edward coughed tea all over Emily. Susan passed him a napkin, wondering how to end the conversation without embarrassing her aunt.

"Oh I won't bother with that," said Elsie, "I have a swimming costume, I'll wear that."

Susan saw Ben glance at Kevin, shaking his head. She went across to them and whispered that she'd sort it out later, why didn't they have another sandwich? The two young men went to the food table, and began to talk in low voices. Their heads were together, and one of them giggled.

Susan was about to join them, when Neil suddenly stood, muttered something about going to see the cows, and he'd be back in a minute, and not to wait for him. Susan watched, confused, as he left the room. Then, before Susan could speak, or properly grasp what was happening, Elsie also stood, passing her an empty plate and patting her arm.

"You stay here, Susan dear," said her aunt, "I think I had better help with this."

Susan stood still, holding the plate, thinking that she really had absolutely no idea what had just happened, watching her aunt as she walked slowly, but with great determination, after Neil. The door shut behind them.

***

Neil was in the big barn, when Elsie caught up with him. He stood there, trying to sort out his feelings, to overcome the wave of helplessness that he had felt in the parlour.

When he had seen Ben and Kevin chatting next to the table, so close, so obviously a couple, he had felt something like despair overwhelm him. His brother, who would always be his little brother, however old they were, seemed to be hurtling headlong into a lifestyle which Neil felt was bound to damage him. Neil felt like he was in a nightmare, trying to save someone from drowning, and they were refusing to grasp the lifebelt, while the sea washed them ever further away.

Neil felt, deeply, that his little brother was wrong, was edging towards a life of immorality and Godlessness, but Neil had no idea how to help him. He understood that this birthday gathering was the wrong place to say anything, that he must respect his mother's decision – even though he wasn't at all sure that she had made the right decision by accepting Kevin. But Neil had listened to Kylie, he understood that it was his mother's house, and that he shouldn't be anything other than polite. But oh! How it hurt him, to see his brother in that situation, to be so impotent in saving him. To just sit, and chat, and pretend all was normal, while his brother plunged further and further into something that Neil felt sure was wrong. It had been too much, more than he thought he could bear, and so, before something snapped and he said something, Neil had left. His heart was beating very fast, and he felt slightly breathless. He wondered if he was having a panic attack, and went to sit on the pile of food sacks near the pen.

All the cows were outside now, would stay there until the weather turned wet. The barn felt empty without them, smelling of hay stacked ready for the winter, dust from the barley grinds

190

lingering in the air. Neil was perched on the heap of food sacks, staring into space, when Elsie found him.

"Ah, Neil, I found you," said Elsie.

Neil turned round, and saw his elderly great aunt as she walked into the barn, smiling. His heart dropped even further, she really was the last person who he wanted to see. He wasn't sure he had the patience to listen to her, not this afternoon, when he felt so tortured.

"Hello Aunty," he said, forcing a smile. "What are you doing out here?"

"Did you need a break?" said Elsie, approaching.

"Yes, yes, I did actually," said Neil, hoping she would take the hint, "I need a little bit of time to myself."

"Yes, well, it isn't a place I would choose to come," said Elsie, picking her way past a heap of something dirty. She waved a hand distractedly at a fly, and went to where Neil was sitting. She looked for a moment, at the space next to him, on the grimy sacks, but didn't sit.

"I came to see if you were going to be all right," Elsie said, "about Ben's friend, Kevin, and everything. It upsets you, doesn't it?"

Neil looked at her, but couldn't think of anything he wanted to say, not to Elsie, so he just went on sitting there, waiting to hear what she would say, trying to control his emotions.

"Now Neil," Elsie said, touching his arm with her hand, "I hate to see you upset. You're such a good big brother, so much better than my own brother..." For a moment she paused, and Neil guessed she was thinking about George, and all the torment he had caused over the years.

"I've seen you keep your brothers safe," Elsie said, "I know your mother could always rely on you, and even now they're grownup, I've heard you help them. Your mum was talking just the other week about Jack, saying she didn't know where he'd have got to without you helping him."

Neil looked at her, surprised. Elsie saw the look and grinned.

"Yes, well, she wasn't talking to me, people don't, as a rule, have those conversations with me. I'm the silly one, aren't I? But I've got ears, I hear what Susan tells her mother. I might be silly, but I'm not stupid!"

"No," said Neil, "you're not stupid."

"Yes, well, I know what people think," Elsie said, "but I know you boys, I've been watching you your whole life. Every weekend, when you were just a tiny tot, and your mother would plonk you down in the middle of the carpet, I would watch you. I've watched you learn to walk, and I've seen you taking care of your brothers when they came along, and helping your mother now you're older, and I think I'm right when I say, I know you Neil, maybe better than you know yourself!

"So, you mustn't keep worrying – about Ben, I mean. He'll find his way, whatever that might be. You can't make those choices for him. In fact Neil," Elsie leaned closer and peered into his eyes, "it would be very wrong of you to make those choices for him."

"I know that," said Neil, keeping his voice calm and polite. This was Aunty Elsie, he was never quite sure what she understood. But she was trying to help, to be kind, so he didn't want to offend her. For a moment Neil simply sat, listening to a bird outside, smelling the smells of the barn, waiting for his aunt to leave. But she didn't, she just stood there, as if waiting.

"But I believe what Ben is doing is very wrong," Neil said at last, "and I don't want stand by and let him ruin his life, not if I can save him."

"Yes," said Elsie. "You can, and you must. Because it's *his* life isn't it? It's not yours Neil; it's Ben's life. And he must do what he feels is right, not what you say."

Neil took a deep breath. He so wished he was not having this conversation, and if he was, with anyone other than Elsie.

"I'm not sure that you understand, Aunty," he began, using his patient, 'speaking to a child' voice. "You see, in the Bible it clearly says that what Ben is doing is wrong, but Ben doesn't seem to see it like that. He has convinced himself that what he's doing is okay, that it doesn't matter, that the Bible is saying something else. And I'm worried about him, Aunty, really worried. It so clearly says in the Bible that what Ben is doing is wrong."

"Does it?" said Elsie. "Does it say that clearly? And if it does, don't you think Ben can read it for himself?"

"I don't think I can explain this properly," said Neil, not liking to add: 'to you'.

But the words hung there, waiting to be said.

"People ignore what's written in the Bible all the time, or else they look to find someone who translates things differently, who makes it sound like the teaching isn't really saying what it seems to be saying. So, I feel I need to step in, to try and show him what the Bible *really* says."

Elsie folded her arms. "Yes Neil, and all sort of evil things have been done using that argument."

Neil was shocked, this was not the sort of statement that he expected Aunty Elsie to make. She looked at him, gave a slight smile, and continued.

"I know, you all think I'm past it, I never married, never raised children of my own, and now I'm this withered old woman. Sometimes when I look in the mirror, I hardly recognise myself, I don't know where the girl is hiding, the young woman that I *feel* I am is hidden in this droopy old body.

"But that's just the outside Neil, it's not who I am. And I know I'm a bit slow, can't quite keep up with things, and you all laugh at me – yes, you do," she said, when Neil started to protest. "But it doesn't matter, I don't mind, because I know what's inside, and I know who I am.

"Let me tell you something Neil. Something which I don't think even your mother knows, because at the time, it was considered shameful. Just like you think Ben is being shameful."

Neil moved slightly, and asked if she wanted to share the food sacks with him. He wasn't sure where this conversation was going, didn't know why his great aunt had followed him out, but she clearly had something she wanted to say, and it would probably be quicker if he simply listened, and got it over with.

"No, thank you dear, I'll keep standing. Those sacks look rather dusty and my dress is new. I'll be all right for a minute or two, I want you to listen to me, because this is important.

"It might surprise you," Elsie said, "but I was young once."

Neil grinned, and she smiled back.

"You'll have to use your imagination a bit, but, it feels like yesterday, I was a young girl and I was quite pretty; even if I do say so myself. The young men, they noticed me. There was one young man, in the forces he was, and he was very handsome. We used to walk out together, and he was such a lovely dancer, and his manners were perfect. A real gentleman he was, older than me, but that didn't worry us.

"Now, I was very young, and rather silly, and you don't need to know anything except he told me a lot of lies, and then suddenly went away, and after he'd gone, I found I was having his child."

Neil started, and turned to face her. But Elsie wan't looking at Neil, she was staring hard at the beam next to the barley store.

"Well, I was devastated, you can imagine, and I felt so silly, to have believed him and everything. It was different in those days, people didn't get themselves in the family way, not unless they were married, and it was shameful. Like what you think Ben is, being shameful."

"No, Aunty," said Neil, wanting to reassure her, "I would never think that. You were young you said, we all make mistakes."

"Let me talk, Neil," said Elsie. "I want to tell you this, and it will be too hard if you interrupt me.

"Now, after I found out I was in the family way, I needed to ask for help. I was disgraced you see, could've been turned out of home for what I'd done, could have lost my job and everything. But my grandmother – I lived with my grandmother when I was young, did you know that? Because my mother died when I was born – anyway, she stood by me, my grandmother, and so did Dot. We went away together, me and Dot, pretended we had work in Devon, where no one knew us, and we lived with our Aunty Sheila – she's passed away now, so you never met her – but we stayed there, together, until the baby was born. No one knew, you see, back home, what I'd done, how silly I'd been.

"After the baby was born, a little boy, they took him away. They'd arranged for him to go to a family, a married couple, who could bring him up properly. It was the hardest thing, you cannot imagine, holding that little warm bundle for a few minutes, knowing my heart was going to be wrung out with sorrow, when they took him away."

Elsie stopped, her voice not quite steady. Neil moved, to put an arm around her, but she moved, very slightly, out of reach, and shook her head.

"Now Neil, this is what I want you to think about," Elsie said. "I know people said what I did was bad, against what it teaches in the Bible. And perhaps they're right, though at the time, I was so in love with that young man, I could hardly think straight.

"And afterwards, when I had the baby, they could all tell me in very serious voices that the baby would be better off growing up in a family. They could argue all about God, and what was right, and how I should think about my baby and not myself. And perhaps they were right."

Elsie turned, and faced Neil again.

"But perhaps they were wrong. Perhaps I'd have loved that baby better than all the other mothers in the world. Perhaps we'd have done all right together.

"What I think, now I'm old and slow and have lived most of my life, is that that decision, whether or not I kept that baby, should have been my decision. No one else's.

"And what I think, is that although you want to protect Ben, and for him to live how you think is right, he has to live how he wants to. I can't give you lots of clever arguments about the Bible. But I do know it's Ben's life, and he has to make his own choices. And if he's wrong, if God wants him to change how he's living, don't you think God will tell Ben that?

"I know Dot loves me, and she always has. I know her and Grandmother were doing what they thought was right. But I think they were wrong, and I wish I'd been brave enough to say it at the time, because I've lived with it all these long years."

Her voice cracked, and the words stopped. One tear eased from her eye, and rolled down her face, over the wrinkled cheek, and hung for a moment, suspended, on her chin. She put up a hand and wiped it away, as though determined to keep inside the hurt, the anguish that had sat inside her for over sixty years.

Neil moved from his seat, wordless, he stood in front of his great aunt and wrapped both arms around her. He could feel her bones, as delicate as a bird's, her heart beating true and strong. She was tiny, and Neil rested his chin on the top of her head, and simply stood there, holding her, sharing her hurts. What she had told him, and her motives for telling him, had moved him in a way that no other argument could have done. Neil sensed what the telling of her story had cost her, and he realised that she had shared it because of a deep love for him, and for Ben.

He wanted to ask for more details about her story. Where was her son? Had she ever seen him again? Did she know his name? Where had he lived?

But Neil knew that Elsie had told him as much as she was able, he had sensed the pain of revealing that part of her history, knew it was a not topic of interest, not something he should ask questions about. She had told him as much as she wanted him to know, and that would have to be enough. He felt honoured, that she had chosen to trust him enough to tell him.

As Neil held her, this tiny relative who they were so accustomed to laughing at, he felt ashamed. Not because he had treated Ben badly, but because he had treated Elsie badly. He had never seen her, not really, never noticed her as a person, as someone with feelings and hurts. Someone with a whole story inside that had happened long before he was born, someone who knew things that he could never know, never experience – so easily dismissed as 'old', as 'silly'. Yet someone who felt very deeply, and had a wealth of knowledge: untapped, unheard, unknown.

Elsie took a deep breath and wriggled free.

"Well, it's not often I get a hug from a strong young man!" she said, smiling up at him. "Shall we go back inside? And will you let Ben live his own life?"

"I'll try Aunty," said Neil, meaning it. He put his arm around her shoulders, guiding her from the barn. His mind was full of things he couldn't say.

"Your story actually explains why I want to stop Ben," Neil thought. "I don't want to stop the 'keeping the baby' bit, I want to stop the 'sleeping with the boyfriend' bit, I want to protect him so he never knows those hurts. You knew it was wrong to sleep with your lover before you were married, but you chose to do it anyway, but the problem, the absolute modern-day problem, is that no one is saying that being gay is wrong in the first place. No one is warning people not to do it. And if it's wrong, and I believe it is, then I should say something, try to warn Ben, so he isn't hurt in the long run." He glanced down at Aunty Elsie. "No," he thought, "I can't say any of that. You wouldn't understand."

They walked back to the house. As they reached the kitchen door, it opened, and Jack came out.

"Oh! Hello you two, where have you been?" Jack asked.

"We were just having a little talk," said Aunty Elsie, "and now we want a nice cup of tea."

***

Jack held the door for them, then continued out, into the yard. He needed some space, some fresh air, and a rest from all the happy relatives and buoyant conversations. He decided to walk around the yard, go to see the yearlings that were in the outside pen, and get some fresh air.

"Mostly, I'm feeling better than I was," Jack thought, as he walked. "And some days, when I'm busy, I feel almost normal again. And I know I'm *behaving* normally, because even Mum hasn't said anything.

"But I do feel useless," he thought, a sigh escaping like a great wave of sadness. "I feel like a little boy whose dad is finding him jobs to do. I don't have much self-respect anymore. And," he paused, staring out across the corn field, "I'm lonely."

Jack felt another wave of self-pity, and took a deep breath, trying to expel the feeling. He wasn't sure if he was actually depressed – had always been rather scathing of people who claimed to suffer from depression – but there wasn't much happiness in his life at the moment.

"True," he thought, "that blackness has lifted a bit, and if I was choosing between life and death now there wouldn't be a question – so I'm better than I was. But I don't know, it all feels a bit pointless." He could act the part, tease his brothers, listen to his mother, laugh at his aunty. But inside, things were – if not completely black, then very grey.

Jack began to walk around the side of the barn. He kept to the right, the route his father had told him was for pedestrians. He knew there wouldn't be any vehicles, he was unlikely to turn a corner and meet a fast-moving tractor, but since his scare in the wheat field, he was obeying all his father's safety precautions, even the ones that made no sense to him. He looked up, seeing a patch near the top of one wall that needed to be repaired or it would leak if they had a lot of rain.

"I need to remember to tell Dad that," he thought.

In the near field, Jack could hear the cows, restless because they would be fed soon. They were checked every day, even the herd in the far field.

"It's easier when they're inside," thought Jack, "even if it's not so nice for them. It takes less time to feed them, to check them over, make sure none are lame or off their food." He could understand why large producers chose to keep their stock inside all year round.

"Not that I ever would," he thought, clapping his hands to stop a hen pecking at a smaller bird. "I like to see them outside, where they're supposed to be."

He stopped. At the perimeter of the yard, behind the stone wall, Jack caught sight of a movement. There was something furtive about it, something that told him it wasn't right. He stood very still, trying to see what it was. There was another movement, and he realised it was a head. Someone was standing in the lane, mostly hidden by the wall of the house, peering into the yard. There was something that told him this wasn't a hiker, looking in out of interest. This person was trying to avoid being seen, which made him curious as to why.

Very slowly, so as not to cause a movement that would be obvious, Jack backed up. When he was out of sight, hidden behind the barn, he turned, and sprinted. He could run behind the barn, squeeze between the chicken run and house, and come out right by the wall, where the person was standing. If he was quiet, he would catch them, find out what they were doing.

"I wonder if it's the arsonist," he thought, thinking of the trouble one of the neighbouring farms had had last year with haystacks set alight. "Or it could be thieves, looking for stuff to steal."

As he skirted the barn entrance, he saw a shovel, detoured in, picked it up. It was heavy, weighed him down, so he could run less fast. But he felt safer with a weapon, less exposed if the person wanted trouble. Jack adjusted his grip, so he was holding it in the centre of the handle, jogged with it at his side.

He reached the chicken coop, and stopped running. There was barely room to squeeze next to the wall, between the run and the side of the house, and he caught his knuckle on the brickwork, scraped away the skin. He was being careful to not let the shovel touch the house, not to allow it to scrape and make a noise. As Jack neared the wall by the lane he slowed, began to inch forward, keeping low.

He could see the shadow of someone. They were standing there, silent, still. As he edged nearer the shadow moved, elongated as the person stretched forwards.

"They're having another look," thought Jack. He pictured someone hard and rough, ready to fight, and gripped the shovel handle tighter. His hand hurt where he'd scraped it, he felt the sting and guessed it was bleeding, but didn't pause to look down. Jack crept forwards, his feet silent on the tufts of grass growing in the gap. A hen was in the coop, and it stirred and moved away, but nothing too loud, nothing to alert the watcher that Jack was advancing on them.

In one smooth movement Jack reached the end of the house and leapt forwards, shovel ready to be raised, feet apart so he could jump the wall and give chase if necessary. The movement surprised the watcher, who gave a squeak of alarm.

"Josie!" said Jack, lowering the shovel. "Whatever are you doing?"

"Jack! Oh, Jack, you made me jump." Josie had stepped back from the wall. Her face was very red, and for a moment Jack thought she might be about to cry, because her face was making strange expressions, her mouth moving and stretching in all directions.

She didn't though. She managed to get her face back under control, though not the colour, which was still very pink.

"I was, um, I was just passing," she said.

Jack frowned, not believing her.

Then she added, her voice hoarse, the words forced: "I wondered if your mother needed any help, I'd heard she was having a birthday tea and everyone was coming home."

Jack watched her face, the truth dawning on him.

"You heard that Ed was bringing Emily, and you wanted to see her, didn't you?" he said.

Now Josie really was almost crying. Jack saw her eyes glisten with tears, and her face grew even redder. She wiped a sleeve across her face, then stood very still, as though too embarrassed to move, as if wishing she could evaporate.

Jack dropped the shovel on the floor and jumped over the wall. He took her arm, and moved her, very gently, to the stile on the other side of the lane. She sat on it, pushing her hands through her hair, sniffing loudly. She lifted her eyes, looked at Jack. He noticed that she had worn make-up, and there were now black smudges around her eyes, making her resemble a damp panda.

"Embarrassing," she said, forcing a grin.

"To like Ed? Yeah, that's pretty embarrassing – shows very poor taste."

Jack moved next to her, not touching, but very close. He could smell her perfume, realised she had made an effort, wanted to look nice, in case by some tiny chance, she had seen Ed, been invited inside. She didn't look nice now; she looked flustered and smudged, and very young. He felt defensive, wanted to save her from the rashness, the casualness, of his brother's games.

"Listen Josie, Ed is fun to be with, he likes a laugh; but his track record with women isn't a good one. I don't know what he's told you, but I really think him and Emily will last, if only because she doesn't take any of his nonsense, and he sort of respects that. I'm sorry if he's been stringing you along, but really, you're better off without him."

Josie sniffed again. "Yeah, I know..." she said, her voice husky with emotion. "I do know that, I know I'm not his type...but, you know, I just wondered what she was like, his girlfriend... Ed always told me –" she cleared her throat, "he told me that Emily wasn't interested in the farm, that she never wanted to come down. So I thought...well, I was stupid, that's all."

She looked down, stared at the grass for a moment, and then looked rueful. "I know what you're thinking," she said. "I know you think I'm daft to keep waiting for Ed, and that I should find someone else. The trouble is..." she coughed again, a short grunt of embarrassment, and when she spoke her voice was harsh. "The trouble is Jack, no one wants Big Josie, do they? So when I thought Ed was interested, when I thought..."

She stopped, as if aware that she was saying too much. She turned away from him, and looked across the field.

Jack didn't reply. He felt embarrassed for Josie, sorry he had seen her when she was so vulnerable, and he wasn't sure what he should say. He simply stood there, leaning against the fence, waiting for her to recover, wondering if he should offer the used tissue he had in his back pocket, deciding that she would probably think that was gross. When he did speak, he talked about the farm, and the awful weather with not enough rain to be any use, and the price of hay. He kept the conversation impersonal, easy, until she had recovered, was her normal colour and the twitchy mouth had settled back into position.

"I'd better go back inside," he said. "Will you be okay now?"

She nodded.

"You've got a bit of black on your cheek – no, down a – yep, that's it." He looked at her, appraising her appearance. "You're okay, no one will guess anything's wrong," he said. "Will you go home now? Or did you want to come inside?"

Josie shook her head.

"Yeah, good decision I think," said Jack, relieved but feeling he'd needed to offer. "Come on, I'll walk down the lane with you."

"You don't need to. I'm fine now. Really. Just embarrassed that you saw me like that." She lowered her head, the colour rushing into her cheeks again.

"Oi! Stop being silly. We've known each other long enough, a little thing like this won't change anything." He stood up straight, took Josie's hand and hauled her to her feet. "Come on, silly, I will walk some of the way with you. I want to," he said.

They walked, along the lane towards her house. Flies buzzed around the brambles and they could hear the wind moving the trees, some sheep on the hills. For a while they walked in silence, their feet rhythmic on the tarmac, an angry bird fussing when they passed too near. It was beginning to get properly dark now, reminding them that it would soon be winter. Then Jack began to talk, telling her about the tea, trying to make her smile.

Jack stayed with her until they reached her driveway, chatting, listening, enjoying her company. Josie was laughing by the time he left her, giggling at his stories. He stopped when they reached her driveway, gave her a wave, and left.

As Jack walked back to the farm, he felt better too, inside. He realised the empty place didn't feel quite so empty, and when he thought about Josie, he smiled, thinking there was something comfortable about her, something sweet that made him feel protective. He hoped that Ed hadn't hurt her too deeply, that she would move on. She was, he thought, rather special.

Chapter Twenty-Two

Josie *was* hurt later that day, but it had nothing to do with Edward. She was devastated actually, hurt beyond repair, but it was her father, not Ed, who did the damage.

Trevor had been living on the edge for several months. The weather had been too dry, so his winter stores wouldn't last and he didn't have the money to buy in enough extra feed, especially as everyone would need to, so the price would be even higher than normal. Then he had lost two calves, both to neosporosis, so the mother would have to be culled too. *Neospora caninum* had been a problem for years, but Trevor had managed to avoid it until now. It was caused by dogs, when their owners didn't clean up after them, and their poo contained neospora eggs.

"And the dogs had every right to be there," Trevor thought, as he walked towards the barn. "The owners wouldn't know of course, and they would see fields full of cow muck, and think that cleaning up after their dogs was unnecessary. Countryside is meant to be dirty, a bit more muck from their dogs wouldn't make any difference. Not to them, at any rate."

His land had footpaths across every field, and although he'd applied to get them moved, had tried to explain the problem, the old laws in England made it practically impossible. But it was very one-sided, they wouldn't pay any compensation when Trevor lost stock, he was expected to just absorb the loss. He couldn't, not anymore.

Trevor walked the distance from the house – where he kept the gun locked in a cupboard – to the barn, where the cow was waiting. He didn't feel sad, more resigned, like all options had disappeared.

There was too much against him. The weather, disease, laws – he was powerless to change any of them, and although he worked hard, had worked hard his whole life, everything was slipping away. His family had leased Broom Hill Farm for generations, but he couldn't make it pay. Bit by bit, everything was sliding away, not so much an avalanche as gradual erosion, hardly noticed at first, but impossible to stop.

"And Claire isn't much help," he thought, feeling the weight of the gun in his hand, box of bullets in the other. "She's made a separate life for herself, with her interior design business."

All the wives worked now, gone were the days when the men worked the fields and the women kept house and baked, joining up for regular Union socials where they'd provide picnics and pot-luck suppers, keen to display their culinary skills. He'd liked those days, the simplicity of the farm being their whole life, one life, absorbing the whole family. Not like today. Today, all the wives – because, in Trevor's experience, it was mostly the men who ran the farms – had outside jobs to try and pay the bills.

Claire had started her own business a few years ago, and at first it had helped, but as her own job had grown and become more absorbing, so her interest in the farm – and Trevor – had waned. Both were now more a hindrance than anything, and Trevor knew that Claire would leave given half a chance; was surprised she hadn't left already to be honest. Josie was all grownup now, so it couldn't be some parental duty that kept his wife.

"And Josie..." Trevor's thoughts turned towards his daughter. Claire had always kept Josie away from the farm, tried to steer her into other jobs, to find some kind of career outside of the farm. Not that it had been very effective, nothing much seemed to interest the girl other than animals, and Trevor often found her in one of the barns, helping with the animals when she should have been going out with her friends. But he couldn't be thinking about Josie, not now. No, Josie was his weakness, and he needed to concentrate on the job in hand, not get distracted, in case he changed his mind...

Trevor reached the barn, the big door swung open, creaking on its hinges. He turned, shutting it behind him. This didn't need witnesses. The evening light was beginning to fade, and it was gloomy in the barn, everything reduced to shadows and grey shapes when the door closed.

He had put up signs weeks ago, telling dog walkers to clean up after their dogs; he even took a photo of one of his dead calves and stuck that up, hoping to shock them into action. He went round the farm, sticking them onto every gate, every stile. But it hadn't made any difference. Waste of an afternoon that had been.

When the dog mess infected hay that was used for bedding, or grass that the cows ate, then the parasites passed to the cattle. Even if he had managed to stop the dog walkers, there wasn't much he could do about the foxes, and if dogs were spreading the disease, then probably the foxes in the area were carrying it too.

An infected cow always aborted her calves, and there wasn't a cure. Trevor knew they would produce less milk too once they were infected, so not much use for dairy either. He couldn't afford to keep a cow that couldn't breed. Not even this one, with her creamy brown coat and long lashes. She was a beauty – but useless.

Mind you, he thought, the last lot of calves he'd taken to auction had come straight home again; the prices had dropped so much it wasn't worth selling them. They had been loaded into the trailer, paperwork all checked, a day wasted driving them all the way to the Ashford market. But when he'd seen what stock was selling for, how few buyers there were, he hadn't even bothered to unload them.

Trevor stood for a few minutes in the peace of the barn, with his cow. He ran his hand across her flank, comforting her, scratching behind her ear.

"You'll be okay old girl," Trevor said, his voice soft. He was fond of his cows, they'd never done wrong by him, he'd never had a bad one. Some days, when Claire was working late and Josie was out, the cows were the only living things he spoke to. It was a lonely job, farming, which he supposed made everything harder. He'd get up, spend all day spraying the fields, feeding the animals, mending a broken fence – just him, alone with his thoughts. Then he'd return home to a neat dinner on a plate, sealed in clingfilm, congealed in the fridge. Claire did her duty, he admitted that, but it was a cold, malnourishing duty. The cows listened to him, they looked at him with their dark eyes, touched him with their long grey tongues, moved against him. But it was no company really, there was no one to share his worries with, as he watched the farm gradually dip further into debt.

Trevor lifted the gun, loaded it, then faced the cow head on, imagining a cross joining her eyes and ears so he was aiming straight for the brain. He wanted to get this right, didn't want her frightened or in pain. He held her under the chin, keeping her head steady, still. She looked at him, her eyes calm, because she knew this man, this barn, everything smelt familiar, there was no need for alarm.

He shot her through the skull.

The cow's legs crumpled beneath her, thumping down with a bump and a strange groan, the air forced from the lungs as the body slammed onto the floor.

Then, because it felt like a solution at the time, and with barely a thought, he turned the gun on himself.

***

No one noticed at the time – shots were often heard around farms. Trevor's body was found later, by Steve who sometimes did casual work around the farm.

Steve threw up when he saw what had happened, and nearly fainted into his own mess. Then he pulled out his mobile and called 999.

By the time the police and ambulance arrived, Steve had recovered enough to wonder how long everything would take, and if there was a way to ask. He understood that until the cause of death was established, they had to keep the barn as a crime scene; but there was only so long he could wait before someone butchered the cow – otherwise the meat would be wasted. He watched the blue flashing lights sweep into the yard, the police march towards the barn. It was their uniforms, as much as their hard faces, that made Steve decide he shouldn't ask. Better to wait and risk losing the money. He figured the family would just have to cope with the loss.

***

Susan and Tom saw the lights, the blue pulsating glow in the sky, and they wondered what had happened. Susan listened, as Tom wondered aloud about walking over, guessing it was coming from Trevor's land; or phoning, asking if his neighbour needed any help.

"But if the police are there already, I guess he has all the help he needs," Tom said to Susan, pushing back his chair. "I expect it's joy-riders again, probably another burnt-out car for other people to deal with." He swore, letting Susan know exactly what he thought of selfish people who seemed to forget, or never cared in the first place, that someone was trying to earn a living, and fields weren't unowned places to abuse as they wanted.

"I think I'll have a quick drive round the fields, check everything's in place," he said.

Susan nodded.

"Shall I come?" asked Jack, looking at the remains of his meal.

"No, you finish eating," said Tom, whistling for the dogs. "I won't be long."

"There's cake for pudding," said Susan as Jack finished eating, "do you want custard on it?" She was tired after her birthday tea, though it had been lovely to see everyone.

It had all gone rather well, Susan thought, as she cleared her and Jack's plates. Even Kevin turned out to be a positive element, and it was good that she'd met him, at last. Ben and Kevin had left together, planning to stay in London for a few days.

It was strange having two boys back at home, Susan thought, carrying the cake from the larder and cutting two pieces. Jack was easy enough to have around, and it had been a help, with Tom's back being bad. But she rather liked when her and Tom were on their own, just the two of them. There was a certain restraint with having someone else there, even one of their boys. She wondered how long Jack was planning on staying, and when Ben would find a job and move into his own place.

"How big a piece do you want?" she asked.

There was a knock at the door. Susan passed the knife to Jack, so he could cut his own slice, and went to answer it.

Steve was standing on the step. Susan recognised him, because he did casual work on all the local farms, had been at their farm last year for a few weeks. He stood on the step, looking rather grey, and Susan wondered if he was drunk, and whether he was going to be sick on her step.

"There's trouble at Trevor William's," he said. Susan opened her mouth to say yes, they'd seen the lights, what was wrong, when Steve blurted: "He's dead. Shot himself through the head. Police are still there. Right mess. I need to get home. Their cows need sorting, and Josie and her Mum are in a right state, so I wondered, is Tom here, or could you...?" He looked across the narrow boot-room, into the kitchen, where Jack was sitting.

Jack was already out of his seat as Susan turned. His face had a determined, set look, and he barely glanced at her as he walked towards her and into the boot-room.

"I'll go straight there," Jack said, pulling on his shoes, reaching for his overalls and boots, ending the discussion. He looked up at Steve. "Thanks for letting us know. Don't worry, I'll help with anything that needs doing with the animals. Are you there tomorrow?"

"Well, no, I'm not meant to be. I can try to change things around a bit, but not sure..."

"It's okay," said Jack. "Dad can manage without me, at least for the morning. I'll make sure they're sorted."

Then he was gone, striding out the door, carrying his boots in one hand.

Susan turned back to Steve, and thanked him for letting them know. She thought about offering him tea, but decided she was too tired, so said goodbye and shut the door. She went back to the table and sat for a moment, looking at the remains of the meal. With a sigh, she began to gather the dirty plates.

***

Jack wasn't sure what he would find when he got to Trevor's farm, whether the police would let him in, whether Claire and Josie would let him help. But he hoped so, hoped he could do some good. He decided to take the tractor, as Broom Hill wasn't far, and he thought it might be more useful than a car.

He thought about Steve, how ill he'd looked. Jack felt ill too, a lump of undigested dinner churning in his stomach. At least, he told himself it was indigestion. He was trying to avoid thinking about Trevor, about why he'd done it. Nor was he keen to start thinking about that day in the harvester, how close he'd come to making the same decision. But somewhere, at the back of his mind, the part he couldn't control, there was a horrified scream, the petrified recognition that it could have been him. Could have, so easily, been him.

"The trouble is," he thought, driving down the lane, "it's too easy on a farm, too easy to end it all. And you live with death every day, so it feels sort of natural, not as big perhaps, as to someone living in a town, where their world is sanitised, and meat comes in a neat package and never linked to the animal it once was. When you stare at death all the time, either because you know the livestock has a limited life, or because culling a sick animal is just part of the job, it can seem like a solution.

"But it's not," Jack told himself, turning the tractor into Josie's driveway and heading up to her yard. "There's too much to live for, when you think about it rationally."

Jack slowed as he neared the farmhouse. There were two police cars; their lights revolving lazily, sweeping around the yard. A uniformed man approached as Jack drew near, waving for him to stop.

Jack scanned the yard, looking for Josie. There were lights on in the house, and a bright floodlight was in their barn across the yard, shining out into the dusk. He didn't want to think about why.

"Hello Sir," the policeman was saying, peering up at Jack. "Could you tell me why you're here and give me your name please."

"I'm a neighbour – Jack Compton – I've come to sort out the cows, get them settled for the night. Is Josie here? Or Claire?"

The policeman spoke into his radio, then nodded, waved Jack through, and he drove forwards, into the yard.

The yard was full of people who Jack didn't recognise, so he left the tractor next to one of the sheds, where he hoped it would be out of the way, and went to the front door. Claire answered on the second ring. Jack noticed her eyes were red, but other than that, she was immaculate, and could have been dressed for a day out.

"Hello Claire," said Jack. "Steve called at the farm, told us the news. I'm terribly sorry." He paused, wishing he had planned this part a little, trying to decide what he should say.

Claire was staring at him, not speaking, giving no clues as to what she was thinking.

"I am very sorry for your loss," Jack said at last, worrying the words sounded contrived, adding: "Mum sends her love," and then, in a rush, keen to get to the real point of his visit, "I wondered if you needed any help, with the animals?"

"Thank you," Claire said. She stood in the doorway, her eyes glassy, not moving, not speaking.

Jack wasn't completely sure if she understood what he was saying. He needed some more details if he was to help. Perhaps she was still in shock.

"Is Josie there?" Jack said at last. Perhaps she would be more coherent.

Claire still didn't answer, but she moved to one side, as if to let him in, so Jack walked past her, into the hall.

The floor was white tiles, and Jack wondered, too late, if he should have removed his shoes before entering. The walls were dark red, and the light was dim but he could see paintings in gold frames at regular intervals. It was several years since he'd been inside Broom Hill farmhouse. The hall was cold, seldom used as, like most farms, people tended to enter through the back door. Jack wondered if the back of the house felt more like a farmhouse, and less like a stately home.

There were lights on upstairs, and after waiting for moment, and realising that Claire was not going to direct him, he decided to take the initiative. He went to the stairs and called up: "Josie, are you there? It's Jack. I've come to see if you need help with the cows."

Jack waited, unsure if he ought to go up, deciding that might be an invasion of privacy. He hoped Josie had heard him, and Jack was about to shout again, when there was the creak of a floorboard, and a bang as if something fell to the floor. He heard one of the doors open.

"Jack?"

"Yes, Jack Compton. Sorry about your dad...sorry for your loss." *Thinking, it still sounds stupid,* then calling, "Is there anything I can do? Steve came to our farm – he thought you might need help with the cows – getting them sorted for the night? Otherwise I'll go, leave you in peace."

He was feeling embarrassed now, thinking that perhaps he shouldn't have come. The urge to be there, to see Josie, to help, had made him act without really thinking. Jack wanted Josie to know that he was there for her, that she didn't have to go through this on her own. He hadn't stopped to consider whether it was appropriate, he'd *needed* to come. Josie had looked so vulnerable the last time he'd seen her, and it had woken something protective in Jack. But now he was actually here, in this cold quiet house, he began to think that maybe he was in the way, intruding at a time when they should have been left alone.

Josie appeared, and came down the stairs. In contrast to her mother, she was very crumpled. Her face was blotchy, her eyes puffy from crying and her nose swollen. Her hair, never tame at the best of times, was damp and wild, curling in all directions, and she looked as if she had slept in her clothes. When she spoke, her voice was hoarse, little more than a whisper.

"I don't know," Josie said, "I can't think. I think Steve checked the herd in the field before he left, but we've got some young ones. They need feeding, but I haven't got round to it yet. What's the time? I can do it..." Her voice trailed away, and she glanced around, as if confused.

"It's seven o'clock," said Jack. She didn't look in any state for lugging heavy buckets around.

"I'll help you, seeing as I'm already here," he said, making the decision for her.

Josie nodded. She wandered through to the kitchen, walking as if she had been awake for several days and was disorientated. Jack followed her, ready to catch her if she fell. He wasn't at all sure that she was up to feeding the calves, but he needed her to at least show him where they kept everything. It all needed to be done in the same way, otherwise the young cows would sense things were different, and would refuse to eat. The last thing the Williams needed were sick cows. And Jack thought it might do her good, to have something else to think about, some routine.

"Are the police still in the big barn?" Josie asked as she pulled on her boots in the porch.

Jack nodded. "Are any animals in there?" he asked.

"Not alive ones," said Josie, her voice grim. Her eyes filled again.

"Sorry," said Jack. He didn't know what else to say, so he passed her a coat that was hanging by the door. "It's a bit chilly," he said.

Josie struggled into the coat, which was too big, and Jack wondered, in a horrid rush, if it was Trevor's.

They crossed the yard, neither of them looking towards the floodlit barn, ignoring the low voices of the police, the arrival of a low white van. Jack saw one of the officers go across to the house, and he thought he would try to keep Josie with him for as long as possible; let Claire deal with all the horrid details.

Josie showed him the food store, and together, they mixed feed, scattered hay, and made the cows comfortable for the night. They barely spoke, moving around each other as they worked, Jack checking Josie from time to time, trying to gauge how she was feeling.

Jack noticed Josie was trying to keep her face averted, only spoke when she needed to give an instruction or explain where something was. But she let Jack help, let him do most of the lifting and carrying, all of the thinking.

When the calves were all fed, their whole being concentrating on sucking the milk, Josie and Jack stood for a moment, watching. It seemed as if Josie couldn't quite summon the energy to go back inside, and Jack wanted to stay with her, felt that she shouldn't be alone. They stood, side by side, hands resting on the metal fencing, watching the animals.

Jack was watching Josie in the corner of his eye, trying to guess her thoughts. He knew the barn, with all the smells and sounds of the farm, would remind her of her dad, and he guessed it would be hard for her to be there. He looked back to where the animals were eating, wondering if he should suggest they went back to the house.

Without warning, a sob rose from deep within Josie, a guttural, animal sound, something wild and wretched. The calves jumped, the ones nearest to Josie shying away, pushing each other to move further from the unexpected noise.

Jack jumped too, before stepping closer and folding Josie into his arms. She didn't pull away, didn't push him off, she simply stood there, completely still. Jack held her, not moving, not speaking, simply waiting for the warmth of his body to somehow reach her. After a few minutes, he felt a change, as she began to relax, to lean in to him, and he stayed there. He wanted to stroke her hair, to move it from her eyes, to adjust his hold. But he worried that if Josie became aware of him, thought about who it was, she might move away. So he kept very still, his arms around her, waiting.

Josie whispered something, her voice hoarse and low, so Jack had to bend to catch the words.

"How could I have not known?" she said, "He was my dad, and I never knew, I never knew how he was feeling. I never tried to help, I didn't do anything, I was so wound up in my own stupid little life."

Josie pulled away from Jack slightly, and he adjusted his grip, so he was still holding her, still supporting her, but with a single arm round her, so Josie could turn from him. She was staring round the barn, gazing at the beams, the pens, the walls.

"I can't feel him," she said, as if talking to herself, almost as though she had forgotten that Jack was there. "He was always in this barn, it was where he came to think, but I can't feel him. There isn't even a whisper of him..." Jack felt her shudder.

"He's gone, isn't he?" she said, her voice full of despair. "He's left me, and totally, totally, gone. None of him is left, nothing. There's nothing here...Dad?" she called, looking towards the dusty beams, "Dad?"

There was no answer. All was still, empty. Jack pulled Josie close again, trying to reach the centre of her, to show that she wasn't alone, knowing that she didn't want him, she wanted her dad. But her father was gone. As she had said, there was not even the whisper of him.

Gradually, the calves began to move nearer again, to resume eating. The barn was quiet, only the sucking of the calves and the stomp of their feet as they moved. Through the open doorway they could hear voices, footsteps, the sound of a motor. Everything outside was business-like and cold and stark. They stood there, surrounded by the heavy smell of drying hay and animals, two people joined by the need of not being alone.

Afterwards Jack couldn't say how long they had stood there, but it felt as if time stood still, as if for an eternity it was just the two of them. When Josie eventually broke away, moved back a step and looked up, her face red and her eyes doubtful, he smiled, very gently.

"This has to be the worst of it," Jack said. "If you can survive this, then it can only get better from here."

She nodded silently, her eyes wet again, as if not trusting herself to speak.

Jack reached out a hand, moved a strand of damp hair away from her cheek.

"There's nothing I can say, to make it better," he said. His mind touched briefly on how he would feel, if it was his own father, then it whirled away instantly, as if burnt. No, he couldn't go there, he needed to keep focussed on Josie.

"But I can be here, I can help – if you'll let me – with the farm. Dad..." Jack stopped, cleared his throat, tried again. "My dad can manage without me for a bit. Shall I come back tomorrow morning? In time to help with the first feed? We can take it from there, decide what else needs doing, to keep things ticking over. You can have a proper think later, there's no hurry, decide what needs to happen. But for now, for the next couple of weeks, you, we, just need to keep things stable. Don't you think?"

Josie nodded again.

"Does anything else have to be done tonight? No? Well I'll walk you back to the house and then I'll be off. I'll be back first thing, but you can phone, in the night, if you need to. I won't mind."

Jack took hold of Josie once more, it felt comfortable now, easy; he steered her across the yard, back to the house. He opened the back door, guided her inside. She undid the buttons of her coat and he eased it from her shoulders, returned it to the peg. Then he reached down, took hold of a wellington and helped to pull it from her foot. She stood there, like a child, letting him help. It was as though something inside had folded up, making her incapable of anything other than obedience.

Jack wasn't sure what to do then, once she was standing, ready to go into the kitchen, but not moving.

"Do you want tea? Some brandy?" he asked, wracking his brain for things you were meant to say in these situations, feeling awkward. In the barn he had been in control, it was familiar territory. But this house, with its shiny tiles and fabric bows on the doorhandles and carefully placed furniture, changed everything. He wasn't sure of his role now, not in here.

Josie took a breath, summoning energy.

"No, thanks. I've drunk enough tea to last a lifetime, and I don't like brandy. Dad's the only one who..." Her eyes filled again, the tears pouring down her cheeks. She wiped them away roughly, almost angrily. "How many tears is it possible to cry?" she asked, her voice thick, "I thought I'd have run out by now..."

She sniffed, and wiped her face on her sleeve, looked fully at Jack. "Thank you. Really, thank you. I think I'll be okay now. I just need to go to bed I think, get some sleep. Like you said, this has to be the worst of it.

"But tomorrow, if you could come, that would really help. I'm not sure I'll manage otherwise..."

Her voice cracked again, and she stopped.

"Right, that's sorted," said Jack. "You get some rest, and tomorrow I'll be here to help."

He thought about kissing her cheek, or hugging her, decided it was best not to. He gave a small wave and turned away, opening the door. "Bye then."

As Jack crossed the yard he saw the knackers van drawing up next to the barn. Claire must have phoned them, sorted out the removal of the carcass. She was managing to be some help then, Josie wasn't completely on her own.

He climbed back into the tractor, started the engine, and drove back home.

Chapter Twenty-Three

It was towards the end of October, and as Susan filled the chicken feeder and half the pellets missed the opening and scattered on the ground, she realised she was stressed. She stood there, lifting her face to the autumn sun, trying to relax her body. The air was tinged with the acidic tang of freshly ploughed fields, the strewn lumps of muck now turned into the soil, fat furrows waiting for the final fine plough of the season. All around her was order, everything prepared for the onset of winter; but her own mind was in turmoil.

The problem – which Susan knew was silly – was the barn dance, and all the things she needed to do before it happened. Her brain was a whirl of brown and orange invitations, and hay bales that needed moving into place, and trestle tables needing positioning.

Her friend Esther had persuaded Susan to host the barn dance several months earlier. Esther, the wife of Rob the minister, was enthusiastically raising funds for a charity she supported in India. Her conversation was often smattered with updates about the plight of trafficked women, the need to rescue girls trapped in the sex trade, and how money from England was helping to break the cycle of poverty facing the poorest people in the world. Susan always listened, nodding and smiling, showing her friend that she was interested and supported her with what was, undoubtedly, a good work.

However, Susan had not expected to become personally involved. It was one thing to listen, to put her loose change into a collecting box and to appear sympathetic. It was another thing entirely to spend many hours organising a fund-raising event. But when Esther suggested the barn dance, said she knew it was a bit late in the year – and they had thought about making it part of the harvest celebration at church, but maybe more people would be prepared to attend if it was off-site, held at the farm – Susan had nodded warily and agreed to ask Tom if they could clear one of the barns. Susan hoped he would say it was too much work, and there was nowhere to put the winter feed, and they ran a farm, not a community hall. He hadn't. And now, in less than a week, an unknown number of people would be coming to the farm, tickets in hand (all proceeds to be sent to India) hoping for an evening of entertainment.

Of course, even at that stage, when Susan had first told Esther they could use the barn, she viewed the project as Esther's event. Susan was merely the provider of a space. Gradually, she found herself on a committee, and then one of the main organisers. So that when, a week ago, Esther had gone down with a nasty bout of food poisoning, everything had fallen to Susan as the natural person to take the lead.

She took a breath, trying to relax her shoulders, to put everything into perspective. In the grand scheme of things, it really didn't matter. There was poor Claire, coping with the aftermath of Trevor's suicide. Jack was racing off to Broom Hill at every opportunity, helping to keep the farm running until Claire decided what she wanted to do.

"She'll move out probably," thought Susan, as she walked back to the house, "I can't believe Claire will keep the lease, and I doubt Josie could run the farm on her own." Susan shook her head, forcing herself to think about her neighbour's problems, to acknowledge that the barn dance didn't compare.

"The trouble is," she thought, pausing to pull off her boots, "I have all these people coming, and I cannot raise the enthusiasm necessary. And there's the pressure of raising enough money to cover the cost of the band, and the advertising. Never mind that we're supposed to be raising money for India."

Susan went into the kitchen, pulled a folder of papers in front of her, and forced herself to think. She stared at a flier, which promised two hours of fun, dancing to a live band, with a bar selling drinks. There was a picture of a couple dancing, surrounded by a whirl of autumn leaves. All very artistic, printed in runs of 250 and distributed around town. She knew they had sold about 70 tickets, and they should probably expect a few people to turn up at the last minute. They would all have to park in the lane, and they were using one of the barns in the far field, where the noise wouldn't disturb the cattle. The original plan had been to park in the field, "But it's too wet for that," thought Susan with a sigh. Even the weather was against her.

She moved to the kettle and filled it with water. The door opened and Jack came into the kitchen, his face flushed from the wind, his hair unruly. He looks happy, thought Susan.

"You making tea?" said Jack, "I'm gasping. I've finished moving the cows from the far field. Some plonker arrived when we were halfway along the lane, and started trying to edge round the tractor. Honestly, some people! He'd have made a fuss if one of the heifers had put her foot into his door. As it was, two of them ran into Mrs Brown's garden, and the dogs had a right job chasing them back into the road."

"Did you knock?" asked Susan, pouring boiling water into the teapot.

"No, she won't have noticed, too early for her to be awake. She might wonder about the footprints on her flower bed, but this time of year there wasn't much to damage.

"What's this?" he asked, picking up the flier from the table.

"Stuff for the barn dance," said Susan, pulling mugs from the cupboard and sniffing the milk in the fridge door. It seemed ironic to her that occasionally, even surrounded on all sides by cows, they sometimes ran out of milk.

"I'm really worried about it, to be honest. I don't know how many people will come, and I'm not sure that I'm going to have enough helpers from the church to move all the hay for people to sit on, and to serve behind the bar, things like that. I'm trying to make a list of all the jobs that need to be done."

Jack picked up her list from the table. He read: collect money, bar, coats.

"Not much of a list so far," he said, putting it back. He reached for the mug of tea she was pouring and sipped it. "That's good, I needed a drink. I'm off to Broom Hill for a couple of hours, told Josie I'd help with the seed drill. Dad knows. I should be back for lunch."

He stood, carrying his tea so he could drink it while he pulled his boots back on.

"I wouldn't worry about the barn dance," Jack called as he left the room, "you could always ask the family to come and help, be your back-up. It might be fun." He turned, grinning at her from the doorway. "Why don't you ask Ed to run the bar? And Ben could bring Kevin for another visit. What could possibly go wrong?"

***

It was while they were driving to the farm, the day before the barn dance, that Neil mentioned to Kylie the conversation he'd had with Aunty Elsie during their last visit. Kylie had been sick several times already that morning, and was sitting next to him, holding an empty ice-cream container on her lap, 'just in case'. Neil glanced at her, and she smiled back. He thought she was looking a bit better now she was out of the house. Mornings were always the worst time for her, but she was, she said, after five long weeks, beginning to be accustomed to it; although the tiredness continued all day – a deep tiredness, unlike any she had ever known before, one where her very bones felt tired.

Neil knew that once she was feeling better, she preferred to ignore the fact that she had been ill, and carry on with her day; he decided to tell her about his conversation with Elsie.

"I didn't really know what to say," Neil said, "the last thing I wanted to do was hurt her feelings. But she really doesn't understand, she doesn't realise that the situation with Ben is totally different."

"Is it?" said Kylie, raising an eyebrow. She leant against the headrest, looking wretched.

They had turned off the main road and were weaving their way along increasingly narrow roads. Neil slowed, knowing that at each bend he might meet wide farm machinery or the back end of a horse. He was driving as steadily as he could, not wanting to jolt Kylie. She had insisted on coming, said she was fed-up with being confined to the house all the time, but he was keen to protect her where he could.

"Well yes, obviously, the situation with Ben is completely different to Aunty Elsie. I'm not trying to tell Ben what to do, I'm trying to protect him from something that's wrong, so he doesn't get hurt in the long-run."

"If it is wrong," muttered Kylie, staring at the high green hedges.

"It is," said Neil, gripping the steering wheel with both hands. He knew Kylie disagreed with him on this, and wasn't

219

sure why he was even telling her. But they tended to tell each other everything of significance, and Aunty Elsie's revelation had certainly been that. Neil had hoped for a discussion about Elsie, not the rights or wrongs of being gay, but Kylie wouldn't let it drop.

"Listen," said Kylie after a pause. She sat up straighter, as if determined to have her say before they arrived at the farm.

Neil glanced across at her. He decided she was still looking queasy, but having the discussion might be enough to distract her, might help her to feel a bit better.

Kylie took a breath. "Suppose you're right, suppose we ignore all the evidence that points to the passages you like to quote in the Bible meaning something other than monogamous loving gay relationships. And there is, by the way, lots of evidence that suggests the word that our Bible translates as 'homosexual' meant something *entirely* different when the Bible was written – but we'll ignore that for a minute. Let's, for the sake of argument, say that gay relationships are wrong, against what God wants. That still doesn't give you the right to say the things you're saying, or to interfere in Ben's life."

"But I'm *not* trying to interfere," interrupted Neil, "you know that, I'm only trying to stop him making a wrong choice."

"Hear me out," Kylie snapped, "this is important, and you don't seem to be getting it."

Neil felt himself tense up, wanting to defend himself. He stared hard at the road ahead, telling himself that Kylie's hormones were all over the place, she was bound to be snappy.

Kylie turned, and Neil could feel her staring at him. "I'm not managing to explain this very well," she said, "but please let me try."

Neil nodded, and waited. For a moment, there was silence, just the sound of the wheels on the lane and the squeak of the windscreen wiper when he washed a fly from his window.

"Okay, so let's assume that gay relationships are wrong," Kylie repeated. "I would still think that Christians, however well-motivated, should not be preaching that. I think they should be copying what Jesus said on the subject."

Neil gave a wry smile. He'd heard this argument many times, knew that the Bible included no accounts of Jesus ever saying anything about homosexuality.

"But Jesus did, often, tell people to stop sinning," he said, swinging the car to one side to avoid a pheasant that had appeared from the hedge. He slowed, as another pheasant appeared in front of them. The birds appeared to be a couple, and the hen was running down the middle of the lane, in huge panic, not having the sense to run into the hedge and instead charging forwards along the road.

"Stupid bird," he muttered, inching forwards, waiting for it to move to the side. The bird knew only that it needed to run from danger, was incapable of thinking logically, unable to turn to the side and let the car pass. It used its wings to run faster, veering from side to side, the epitome of panic.

"Well, yes," conceded Kylie, "but his main message was about love and acceptance. In fact, the only people he really bashed up for their sin were the teachers. He was always telling them to stop interfering with other people's faith, to stop making rules for them, stop trying to pronounce how they should live..."

She didn't add: "Like you are," but Neil knew it was what she was thinking.

The pheasant was still running ahead of them, not looking to either side, intent on outrunning them. Wings flapping impotently, squawking in alarm, it rushed forward, its only instinct being to run faster, to not be caught.

"Think about the time when he was confronted with the woman who'd been caught having adultery – a clear sexual sin – what did he do when asked to judge her?"

"He scribbled in the dirt," said Neil, wanting to show he knew the Bible as well as Kylie.

"Yep, and why was that significant?"

Neil frowned. He didn't know, he only knew that Jesus then told the teachers that whoever had never sinned themselves should throw the first stone.

"It's because it was the Sabbath," said Kylie, "and one of their picky rules was that the only writing you were allowed to do was writing that wouldn't last, that would be blown away. So Jesus was showing that he knew their picky rules, he knew the law better than they did. And the thing he thought was important, was that they sorted out their own relationships with God, not stood on judgement against the immoral woman. He didn't want them correcting other people – that is God's job – he wanted them to correct themselves.

"And I think, that is the message for churches today. They need to be doing what God wants *them* to do, which is telling people about his love, and acceptance and huge *God-ness*.

"*If* people are making wrong choices, then that is up to God to tell them, not the church. The church's role – your role – is to be as good and loving and accepting as you can be, and point people towards God, help them develop their own relationships with a God who loves them – right where they are. He never makes people change before he will accept them. If later, things need to change, then God will sort that out. Not us, not people. You need to let Ben sort out with God how he should be living."

They both watched the pheasant, still charging down the road, still refusing to move to the side in spite of the danger behind it.

"The trouble is," said Neil, feeling that her argument, although sounding plausible, was still wrong, "I don't entirely trust Ben, or anyone else who claims to be gay, to necessarily sort out that side of their life."

"No," said Kylie. "The trouble is, you don't entirely trust God to sort out that side of their lives. Which really, is my whole point."

Neil gripped the steering wheel very tightly, determined not to respond to her barb. He was, he was fairly sure, not like those early teachers at all. He was only trying to stand up for what he believed was right. What *is* right, he corrected himself.

The pheasant finally plunged into the hedgerow, and Neil accelerated to a normal speed again. For a long time, he was silent. He wasn't sure whether Kylie was right or not. It was a good argument though, and they had managed the discussion without getting heated, which was rare for them, especially now. He could think about what she'd said later.

"We're nearly there," Neil said. "Have you thought any more about whether or not we should tell them?"

"Not really," said Kylie, sounding miserable. Neil knew she had wanted so much to wait, to mention nothing to anyone until the pregnancy was at the three months mark, when things were more secure. But she had been so ill, it was so hard to carry on as normal. He was pretty sure his family would guess anyway, but it was Kylie's choice, he'd do what she wanted.

"Perhaps, if they comment, you should tell them," she said, "but otherwise let's leave it until another time, when we can tell them properly. It's hardly the right occasion, is it? They'll all be busy, and tired, and I don't feel well enough for some big announcement. But we shouldn't lie, if they ask, then we'll tell them."

Neil nodded. He didn't agree with her logic, but they were arguing a lot at the moment, and he wanted to arrive at the farm with no tension between them.

"I wonder if Josie will be at the barn dance," he said. "It's the sort of thing she would've come to, but I don't know if it's too soon, after her dad and everything. How long do people wait, do you think, after something like that happens?"

***

Whether or not he should invite Josie was something that was bothering Jack too. He had spent the last few weeks going to Broom Hill Farm whenever he could, helping to keep the farm running. He still helped at home, but he wasn't needed full time, and he felt useful when he was at Broom Hill, he knew they honestly needed him.

It also meant he saw Josie most days, and he spent a lot of time thinking about her. There was something about her, her mix of strength and vulnerability, that appealed to Jack. Josie had been around, on the periphery of his life, trying to be noticed by Ed, for as long as Jack could remember. But Jack had never really noticed her before, never considered her as a person. He felt that he was seeing her with new eyes now, and he very much liked what he was seeing. Josie made him feel needed – manly, he supposed – and he wanted very much to protect her. There was something warm about her, something genuine. He loved to make her laugh, loved seeing the sadness disappear from her eyes occasionally. And she had a good laugh, a real deep chuckle that made you want to hear it again. He liked that she cared about the same things that he cared about. He watched her with the cattle, her gentleness towards them, and her determination to be the boss, to ensure they were safe. And she was a hard worker, there was no doubt about that. Since Trevor had gone, she had put in all the hours she could, she was often awake and out in the fields when Jack arrived first thing.

"And she's kind to her mum," Jack thought, "kinder than I would be."

Claire was completely disinterested in the farm, and had told Josie she planned to sell the business as soon as probate came through. There had been no Will, of course, so she couldn't do anything for now. Josie was hoping to turn things around, to pay off some of the debt, show that the farm was still viable. Then she was going to ask her mum if she could stay there, keep the lease going, run the farm herself. Jack was very much hoping to be part of that.

"But how soon can I make a move?" Jack thought, walking towards the barn where the dance was to be held. "If I could get Josie to come to the barn dance tomorrow, away from the farm, in a social setting, maybe there would be chance to say something then. I don't even know if she likes me, not in that way. She might just see me as an old friend, someone who's just there. I don't know what she thinks; she's not the sort to flirt, is she?"

He reached the barn, and swung open the big wooden door. The floor was covered in spilt grain and dried cow dung. He'd need to sweep that before anything else could be done.

"Is it too soon?" he wondered again, "Or could I invite her? It would do her good to have a break, be away from her farm for a couple of hours, and she might come, seeing as it's for a good cause and all that. Perhaps I'll mention it, when I'm there later, and see what she says.

"And maybe," Jack thought, pushing the broom through the muck, raising great clouds of dust that billowed up into his eyes, rushed into his lungs, making him cough. "Maybe, there'll be a chance to say something about us, move things on a bit. Might be worth a try, anyhow."

***

On the afternoon of the barn dance, Ed arrived at the same time as the band. Susan had phoned him, and whether he could tell from her voice that she was stressed, or whether he thought it might be fun, Susan didn't know but to her surprise he agreed to come and help man the bar. Susan had ordered lots of bottles on sale-or-return from the local wholesalers, and bought a supply of plastic tumblers.

"Esther wanted me to borrow proper glasses, from the supermarket," said Susan, showing Edward the bar they had made at one end of the barn. "But I'm sure some will get broken, and Dad didn't want the worry of searching for fragments of glass when he's using the barn, so I said no." Susan frowned. There had been a lot of ideas that she had said no to.

"The trouble is," she said, continuing even though she could see that Ed wasn't listening, and was in fact already moving away to inspect the alcohol. "The trouble is, people at church forget that this is a business. They tend to see the farm like their gardens, a place that's fun to use for church events, and it doesn't really matter if things get spoiled a bit. But it does matter, it costs us money, and we can't afford that.

"Oh, who's that arriving?" Susan turned at the sound of cars pulling up in the lane. "It must be the band. Good, I'll get Neil and he can show them where to set up. Ah, here he is."

Neil and Jack appeared in the doorway, and came across to say hello to Edward. They all moved to the doorway, looking down towards the lane so they could see the band as they hauled their instruments towards the barn. They stopped, and stared.

"Oh man," said Neil, "I've seen everything now!"

"Please tell me no one else is going to have that idea..." muttered Jack.

There, his arms wrapped around a fat accordion case, was a cowboy. Or at least, a man in his late fifties who had decided it was appropriate to dress as a cowboy.

"He even has spurs," said Ed, beginning to giggle.

"Left his horse in the lane, I expect," said Jack.

"We're raising money for India," said Ed with a chuckle, "do you think anyone will decide to come in ethnic costume? Cowboys and Indians!"

"Stop! All of you," said Susan, beginning to giggle herself. "They'll hear you. Now behave!"

The man walked towards them. They could see the breeze catching his hat, and he kept his head lowered as he walked. He was walking very slowly, in his high-heeled boots, at one point nearly falling when he stumbled on a tuft of grass.

"Do you think that's his wife's blouse?" murmured Jack.

Susan stared at the pink chequered shirt billowing in the wind, and thought that it might be. He was wearing brown suede chaps – with a fringe edging for added authenticity – and the matching frilled waistcoat. "At least he didn't come without a shirt," she said, giggling properly now. "He'd look like a stripper!"

"Hello," said Neil, as the cowboy approached.

"Have you come for the barn dance?" asked Ed, his face completely straight.

Jack began to laugh, and moved back, out of sight.

"Howdy!" called the man. "Pleased to meet you, I'm Alan White. Where do you want us to set up?"

The rest of the band appeared in the doorway behind him. They were dressed, Susan was relieved to see, in jeans and sweaters. She could see a violin case, and a slim box that probably held a flute. A fourth man was carrying a microphone and amplifier.

"I'll show you where to go," said Neil, leading them to where there was a power socket. Susan left them to it, she did hope no one else would decide to dress up.

***

At Broom Hill Farm, Josie had no idea what to wear. She was sitting on her bed, in her underwear, head in her hands, feeling slightly sick.

Jack had invited her to the barn dance yesterday, and at first she had refused, said she wasn't ready to start socialising again. Although she no longer cried all the time, and the first agony had dulled to a constant ache, tears were never far under the surface. Especially with some people, those friends who offered sympathy but seemed to want to talk, on and on, reminding her of her pain, until the tears started to flow – almost as if they *wanted* her to cry – as if it was part of some strange deal whereby they came to offer condolences and in return, she should appear distressed.

Josie had thought she would feel better after the funeral, after that desolate day when she had followed the coffin with her mother, knowing that everyone was watching them, feeling their judgement. But she hadn't felt better, she had felt worse, because whilst everyone else moved on, carried on with their lives, Josie was left with a gaping hole and knew that this was what constituted 'normal' now. Her dad was never coming back. Therefore, although she was coping, although she was 'getting on with it', as her dad would have said, she did not feel, in any way, like attending a dance.

But Jack had persisted, and Claire had joined in, telling her it would be good for her, and it was for a good cause, raising money to help trafficked women in India. Josie had tried protesting, saying that she hated barn dances, she couldn't dance anyway. Jack had said that was fine, they needed some help with the bar and refreshments, couldn't she come and help Susan?

So Josie had agreed, said she would come to the farm and help Susan in the kitchen with sausage rolls and bowls of crisps. But she wasn't dancing, she would only watch.

Jack had grinned at her, that grin which she was beginning to look for, the one that warmed her insides.

Jack was coming to Broom Hill every day at the moment, and Josie found she was relying on him more and more; she didn't like to think that there might be an end to it, a day when he stopped coming. It wasn't just for his help around the farm; there was something about Jack, the way he never pressured her, the quiet manner that he worked beside her. Plus, if she was honest with herself, he made her feel special, like he noticed her. He seemed to enjoy her company, and he told her things, like that she was brave, and a hard worker, and he admired the way that she dealt with the animals. No one had ever said things like that to Josie before, and she found she rather liked it. So although initially she declined the invitation to the dance, she was secretly glad that he pushed her, was looking forward to spending some time with him when they weren't both moving cows or humping manure around.

Until now. Now she wasn't feeling pleased. She was, Josie thought, feeling terrified. Because, quite simply, she had no idea what to wear. It was easy enough when she was working, everything got splattered with mud anyway, so anything other than jeans and an old coat was unnecessary. And she had formal clothes: a slightly too tight smart suit that her mother had bought for her a few years ago; and a long skirt – which completely hid her horrible legs if not her bulging tummy – for more casual occasions. But could she wear that to a barn dance?

Josie heaved herself from the bed and swung open the wardrobe door. Her clothes hung there, taunting her, looking like tents dripping from the hangers. She reached for the long skirt and a sweater, pulled them on, went to the full-length mirror on the landing.

"I look like a hippo," she thought, turning sideways and trying to pull in her tummy. The clothes made her completely shapeless, "Like a sack of potatoes," she thought miserably. She tried fastening a belt over the sweater. It didn't help much. She went back to the bed.

"I don't want to go and be seen by all those people," she thought. "It will be full of skinny people, in tight jeans, skipping around, and I'll be the heffalump in the corner. And Jack will notice, he'll realise that I might be a good worker, a great farmer, but as a woman..." Josie stopped. Something like a shudder was rising up inside of her. "I'm not really a woman," she thought. "There is nothing even faintly desirable about me, so I may as well get used to the idea. It's stupid to even try."

She went to her dressing table, and pulled a comb through her hair, flinching as it pulled at the roots. Then she pulled it back and secured it with a hairband. She glanced at her make-up bag. Was it even worth the effort? She thought of Jack, with his eyes – green where Ed's were blue – and kinder, softer, laughing with her, whereas she was never sure if Ed had been laughing *at* her. Ah yes, Ed, she thought. He would be there too, with his knowing face and pushy ways. It would be embarrassing, seeing him again, but not overly so. She'd thought a lot about their relationship in the last few weeks, and realised that it never had been a relationship, not really. Not like the friendship she was developing with Jack and his green eyes. She would like, very much, for those eyes to notice her, to not simply think of her as a farmer. She sighed. No harm in trying.

Josie slid onto the chair and peered at her face. She had nice skin, and wide eyes. "If you don't look at the body," she thought, scrabbling in the make-up bag for an eyeliner, "the face isn't too bad."

She drew a thin brown line around each eye and flicked mascara over the heavy lashes. Then she stared back at her reflection, critical, looking for flaws. With a sigh she got up, and went downstairs to find her coat.

Her mother met her in the hall.

"Is that what you're wearing?" Claire asked.

Josie wanted to go back upstairs, and admit defeat. Instead she forced herself to smile at her mother's slim, neat, form.

"Yep," Josie said, and took her coat from the peg. "I won't be late," she called, as she walked through the door.

Chapter Twenty-Four

By 8 o'clock, the dance was in full swing. A man called John stood on a hay bale, shouting instructions as the band played the *Alabama Jubilee*, and *Bird in the Cage*, and *OXO Reel*. There was a good crowd, thought Ben, as he stood near the bar sipping warm beer from a plastic cup. He leant back, against a rough wooden beam, and watched.

The barn was, Ben thought, looking good. Bunting hung from the rafters, and the floor was clear of debris. They had set up a ring of hay bales for people to sit on, with an area to one side for the band and the caller. Couples were dancing in the centre, sometimes almost skipping into where people were sitting. Near the barn door was a long table, lined with plastic cups and bottles. Ed was running the bar from there, and Ben noticed Kylie, uncomfortable in heeled boots, scowling in the background, as she separated plastic cups from the stack. Ben grinned, thinking that a village barn dance was probably not her idea of a good night out.

Neil was by the door, checking tickets as people arrived, and pointing out the bar, and where the Portaloos were, and suggesting that if people enjoyed the evening, they might like to make a further donation to the India charity at the end. There had been a long discussion about whether they could sell raffle tickets, which was always a good fundraiser, but a few of the older people in the church considered it to be a form of gambling, and therefore inappropriate at a church event.

There was another table, also near the door, covered in a paper cloth and laden with plates of food and napkins, and a whole range of non-matching tea-plates – which someone, at some point, had thought would be a good idea for the church to buy from charity shops so they could save the environment and avoid using paper plates at events. Ben thought the person with the good idea had almost certainly not been the person who usually helped to wash-up after events.

A few people had brought children, and they were doing their best to keep up, whilst almost being stepped on by charging adults. You could see, thought Ben, the resignation in people's faces, when they were called to start a new formation, and one of the kids appeared in their group, all eager faced and full of energy. They were a pain really, he thought, it was stupid of the parents to bring them. Everyone had to slow down a bit, make sure the kids were moving in the right direction, pretending to duck under their arms when the men were turning the women.

A whole assortment of people had come, though Ben guessed most were probably from the church. Susan's friend Esther was still not well enough to attend, but her husband, "Black Rob," as Gran called him, was there, mingling with his flock and skipping in circles. "There's a lot of skipping involved," thought Ben, watching as a group linked arms and skipped in a circle, the men trying to speed things up, the women looking slightly lost, one man counting each step, but not in time to the music. More women than men wanted to dance, so several couples were made up of women, the taller ones dancing the steps intended for the men.

Alan White, his cowboy hat perched on the back of his head, was playing enthusiastically. His whole body seemed to be squeezing the air in and out of the accordion, his red face beaming. Between each dance he bent down and picked up the beer beside him. While Ben was watching, Ed appeared with a fresh pint, placed it next to the nearly empty cup on the hay bale. Ben wondered if Ed was trying to get the cowboy drunk.

Kevin appeared at Ben's side, reached for his cup and took a long sip.

"That's better," Kevin said, handing it back.

"And now for the *Gay Gordons*," shouted the caller. "Come along ladies and gentlemen, bring your partners."

"I don't think he means us," grinned Kevin.

"Here, you take this," said Ben, passing him the empty cup. "I'm going to ask Mum to dance."

Ben wound his way through the middle-aged people trying to catch their breath, and past the group of teenagers standing awkwardly at the side. He saw his mother appear at the barn door, carrying a heap of sausage rolls. Ben saw one of the sausage rolls slide off the plate, onto the floor, then watched Susan kick it deftly under the table, where it wouldn't be seen.

"Do you fancy a dance?" said Ben.

Susan looked up, and smiled. "Not even slightly," she said. "Why don't you ask Josie?"

Josie was behind her, bowls of crisps and dips in each hand. She heard what Susan said, and shook her head in panic.

"Or Laura?" suggested Susan, seeing Josie's reaction. Laura was a pretty geography student who attended the church, and she frequently asked how Ben was, and had specifically checked he would be at the barn dance before she bought her ticket.

"Rejected, by my own mother," muttered Ben, and went off to find Laura.

The dance was already underway as Ben and Laura joined the ring of dancers, Ben looking at other couples so he could copy the hand-hold.

The caller was yelling: "Forward 2, 3, 4, reverse 2,3,4, men turn the lady..." People skipped and stomped and stood still looking confused as other couples swept passed them.

"Forward, 2, 3, 4...try and keep it steady please musicians," chanted the caller.

Cowboy Alan glared at him. Ben wondered if the musician had tried to speed up the dance a little, and was annoyed the caller had noticed. The accordion paused while the man took another drink, the other musicians frowning at him.

Ben and Laura managed to keep up with the music, giggling when they went wrong. Ben caught sight of Kevin, dancing wildly with a middle-aged woman he recognised from church. The woman was counting and nodding her head, concentrating on the rhythm of the music, stepping with military precision; Kevin was skipping with exaggerated bounce, knees high, head up, laughing. Ben saw that Laura was watching Kevin too, and felt her giggle beside him.

"That boy looks a bit gay, doesn't he?" she whispered.

"I suppose he does," said Ben with a smile.

***

Later, when she was in the kitchen helping to clear dirty plates, Laura repeated her comment to Josie.

"Do you know who the new bloke is?" she asked, "The one who dances like he's gay?"

"I think you mean Kevin," said Josie, "and he is. He's Ben's partner."

"Oh!" said Laura. Josie saw her frown.

Laura continued tipping leftover pastries into the bin, putting the plate into the dishwasher, screwing up used napkins. "I didn't know – about Ben, I mean." Then she added, "But Jack isn't – is he? He likes girls – right?"

Josie's eyes narrowed. She took another knife, plunged it into the soapy water and ran a cloth along its length. Laura was clearly on the lookout for a man, and the Compton boys, strong and good-looking, had obviously caught her eye. Whilst Josie knew she had no claim on Jack, knew their friendship was platonic, Josie was suddenly aware that she did not want other women noticing him. She felt something sharp inside, something very like hatred towards Laura. She turned to look at her.

Laura had moved to where some crumbs had spilt, and was wiping the floor with paper towel. Josie watched as Laura's blonde hair swung over her face like a curtain, she noted the other girl's slim bottom in tight jeans, the tiny waist. Josie scowled at her. No, she didn't want this girl noticing Jack.

"Oh," Josie said, turning back to her sink full of dirty knives, her voice nonchalant, "you don't want to start looking at the Compton boys. The only one who's at all decent is Ben, and as I said, he's gay, so you won't get anywhere there. As for the others – well, I wouldn't trust them an inch. They're much too sure of their own superiority." She paused, thinking about how Ed had treated her. "They use people for their own amusement and then move on," she said, her voice growing louder as her feelings grew warmer. "They might look nice, but they think *way* too much of themselves..."

Josie turned and stared at Laura, wanting her barbs to hit their mark. "No, you'd better forget the Compton boys, the whole lot are just selfish and big-headed. Not worth pursuing, trust me."

Laura stared at her, as if surprised by the outburst. She shrugged, and reached for a tea-towel, and then began to chat about the weather.

Josie continued to wash the plates and bowls, bending to the too-low sink, feeling an ache in the small of her back. She glanced at the clock, her mouth stretching into a yawn, thinking that her evening of ferrying plates of food had been long and boring.

"I'm not sure whether it was worth coming really," she thought, moving to the table to collect another heap of dirty plates that had been dumped there. "All I've done is carry food to the trestle table in the barn, and ferry dirty plates back here to wash up. I've hardly seen Jack at all, and now Laura has clearly got her eye on him..."

The door burst open.

Josie glanced up, saw Jack, and stopped. He stood in the doorway, not speaking, just looking at her, a stack of plates in his hands. For a moment, they both stood there, as if statues, staring at each other. Josie felt as if her heart stopped beating – certainly she couldn't move, couldn't breathe, as she watched him.

The spell broke, and Jack came into the kitchen, dumped the dirty plates on the table.

"The last of the plates, I think," he said, his voice sounding strange. He gave a sort of smile, almost a grimace, and then turned, walked out, and shut the door, very carefully, behind him.

"Do you think he heard?" whispered Laura.

"*I don't know, I don't know, I don't know,*" thought Josie. But she said nothing, simply shrugged, and began to wash another knife.

***

In the barn the dancers were beginning to tire, and people were glancing at their watches. Tom was leaning against the wall, watching, wondering when they would finish. He would be awake early tomorrow, the same as every other day, and he wasn't especially keen on late nights. But he could see people were getting less enthusiastic, he thought things would wind up soon.

Alan, in his cowboy regalia, had started to improvise, and was adding strange notes and rifts to all the tunes. His alcohol consumption had increased, and Ed was bringing him a fresh beer after every dance. The man playing the violin suggested he should slow down a bit, but Alan just growled at him, reminded him that they weren't being paid very much, they had every right to enjoy the evening, and if he had a problem, perhaps he'd like to come outside and sort it out properly. Alan stood there, tall in his heeled boots, puffing out his chest, his face belligerent and flushed from the alcohol. The man went back to his violin.

The caller, John, clapped his hands and called everyone to silence, so he could make an announcement. Tom hoped it was to announce the end of the dance, and that there wouldn't be a speech.

"Ladies and Gentlemen, we have two more dances, so choose your partners and come to the centre. Then we'll finish for the night.

"Thank you everyone for attending, and I know your generous donations will all go to a good cause..." He stopped, and Tom wondered if the man knew what the 'good cause' was. Tom watched, as the caller scanned the room, as if looking for someone who he recognised. Tom grinned to himself, knowing that Esther wasn't there, and Susan would be hiding in the shadows in case she was asked to say something.

People were staring blankly at each other, waiting for the caller to continue.

"I know your tickets and the profits from the bar will all be put to good use – I believe Esther and her team are supporting a charity that helps girls in India..." John's voice faded, he paused, and then added: "and there is a bucket by the door for further donations."

"We also thank Tom and Susan for hosting us this evening," he nodded towards Tom, "and I know you'll be welcome to stay and chat for as long as you like after the dancing finishes."

Tom frowned. He was hoping everyone would go home now. The last thing he wanted was a group of merry people hanging round the farm. He couldn't go to bed until they'd all gone, he couldn't trust people not to do something stupid. Tom stretched his back, and reminded himself he'd agreed to this, it was for a good cause, and it would end eventually.

The music started up again, and most people found a partner and joined the dancing ring. Tom slipped outside. He wanted to stand by the door as people left, make sure that no one decided to wander round the farm, upset the cows. He didn't mind hosting the barn dance, it was good to use the barns for village events occasionally, but he was always worried about the damage. Some people treated animals like toys, thought that wandering through the cowshed would be an okay thing to do. They didn't consider how the cows would feel, having lots of strangers traipsing through.

Tom was still outside when the dancing finished. The first person to leave the barn was dressed as a cowboy. He lurched outside, unsteady in his heeled boots after so much beer, and went to the corner of the barn, in the shadows. He didn't notice Tom, and seemed intent on pulling his lighter and cigarettes from his waistcoat pocket.

Tom saw the flame, realised what was happening, and moved forwards.

"Hey, put that out!" he shouted. "You can't smoke here, you'll start a fire."

The man turned, glanced at Tom as if he was a person of no consequence, and turned away again to light his cigarette.

Tom was furious. This was just the sort of thing he'd been worried about, people not respecting the farm, treating it like a community centre. There was too much dry hay and foodstuff nearby, a cigarette stub could easily set the whole lot aflame. Tom could see the man was drunk, and decided to act, charging forwards, shouting. He reached the idiot dressed as a cowboy, and grabbed his shoulder, intending to grab the cigarette and stamp it out.

As Tom touched the man's shoulder, he reeled around, and a fist came up. The aim was wild, but the man leaned his weight into the blow, and it made contact, slamming into Tom's cheek.

Tom staggered back, shocked. His hands curled into fists as he took a breath. He considered punching the man, but fought to control the feeling, knowing the man was drunk.

"You need to put that out, and leave," Tom shouted, his voice louder than he'd planned.

In the barn doorway, another man appeared, and Tom recognised him as the caller, the man who'd been in charge all evening. He was frowning, obviously having heard the shout. The drunk man was standing, fists up, poised for a fight, and Tom thought he looked rather comical. Tom stepped back, rubbing his cheek, waiting to see what the caller would do.

"I think we all need to calm down out here," said the caller, moving towards the drunk man. His voice was loud and authoritative, as if trying to establish that this was a church event, and he was in charge. Tom heard him add: "Perhaps we should have a little prayer," and watched in surprise as the caller began to bow his head.

The drunk man seemed to recognise the caller, and Tom saw him sneer, then before he could react, the man pounced, lurching forwards, punching the praying caller in the face. The drunk seemed to be enjoying himself, and gave a shout of laughter.

Taken by surprise, the caller staggered backwards, lost his footing, and thumped into a heap on the floor.

A movement at the barn doorway caught Tom's eye, Neil and Edward appeared, took stock of the situation, and grabbed the drunk man, each holding an arm.

"You okay Dad?" said Edward, "We heard you shout."

Tom strode forwards and snatched the cigarette, amazingly still dangling from the man's mouth, and ground it into the mud.

"Like I said," he said to the pinioned man, "you can't smoke here, you'll start a fire."

The caller was clambering to his feet, dusting his trousers. He looked slightly sick, but Tom thought it was probably shock more than anything. The man coughed, as if testing his voice.

"I think, perhaps we need to all go home now," said the caller, seeming to want to take control again, to show that he wasn't upset, was taking all this in his stride; but his voice was trembling as much as his legs, only Tom heard him.

There was now a crowd in the doorway, as people heard the commotion and rushed to see what was happening. The caller's wife ran over, and he put a hand on her shoulder. Rob, the pastor, squeezed his way through the crowd, and came to the front. He walked up, and spoke quietly to the man held by Neil and Edward.

"Shall I drive you home Alan? It's probably best you don't drive." His voice was steady, Tom saw the man nod, then hang his head as if in defeat.

Neil and Edward released their prisoner, and Tom watched as he shook himself, and then walked with the pastor back to the lane.

Everyone watched them leave, not speaking until they were out of sight.

Neil and Edward walked together back into the barn, and began boxing the left-over bottles. Neil noticed the abandoned accordion, and asked one of the other musicians to make sure it was returned. Everyone felt subdued, as if something significant had happened.

Susan came to Tom, and asked if he was all right. Her words and expression were sympathetic, but Tom could see her eyes were merry, and knew she had found the incident amusing.

"Don't you laugh," he warned her, smiling, "or I'll set the boys on you too!" He looked across to where Jack and Ben were helping to carry dirty plates back to the farmhouse. People were collecting their coats from where they were slung across bales, throwing change into the buckets, queuing for a last visit to the Portaloos. Tom went to help clear up, glad that the farm would soon be back to normal.

***

It was later, when all the visitors had gone, and the family was doing the last of the clearing up, that Ed made his comment. Jack was in the barn, with Ed and Neil, and they were carrying the bales of hay between them, moving them back to the heap in the corner. People were still doing trips to and fro from the kitchen, and Tom had gone to check the animals. Ed caught sight of Josie, leaving with one of the trestle tables under her arm, and the size of her, as she walked next to Kylie, must have struck him as funny, because he turned to Jack, laughing.

"So, I didn't notice you dancing with Josie this evening. I guess *do-si-do* with a carthorse should carry a health warning!"

Jack stared at him. He was tired, and since he'd overheard Josie criticise him in the kitchen, he'd felt shaken. Now, as he heard his brother mock Josie, all the tension came together, and dropping the bale they were carrying, he moved roughly against Ed, shoving him hard. Ed, taken by surprise, moved backwards, his foot caught in the hay, and he fell heavily on his side.

"Hey!" he shouted, surprised by the ferocity in his brother's face.

Jack stood over him, his face red, breathing hard. He wanted to hurt something, and Edward was within reach. Before he could shout, tell his brother what he thought of him, he felt someone touch his arm, and looked down to see Josie, standing beside him, shaking her head.

"Don't Jack," she said, "just don't."

She took hold of his arm, started to pull him away, further from Edward, further from where he might do something stupid.

Jack allowed himself to be led away, then turned, and marched from the barn, away from the house, towards the lane. His feelings were racing, a muddle of thoughts and anger and wanting to hurt something. The futility of the situation angered him, his hopes extinguished by the overheard conversation, his brother's mockery rubbing salt in the wound. He walked blindly, not knowing where he was going, only knowing that he wanted to be away from the farm and his family. As he strode into the night, he heard a noise behind him, and became aware that Josie had followed him, was trying to keep up. He slowed, let her walk beside him.

"It doesn't matter," said Josie, and he heard her catching her breath as she came level with him. "What Ed said, it doesn't matter."

"It matters to me," said Jack, his voice curt. He didn't know why she was there, if she thought so little of him, didn't know why she was bothering to get involved.

He stopped, and turned to her. His anger, so fast to flare, was beginning to fade, and he decided he would rather know, for sure, if he'd heard correctly. He thought he might try and challenge her view, tell her it was unfair. He didn't think it would achieve much, but he would feel better if he could defend himself, and he knew that he might never have another chance. If he didn't sort it out tonight, he might never know whether, had he tried harder, he might have had a chance.

Jack's voice was hard, his anger and hurt bubbling back up as he thought about the overheard conversation, and he sort of spat the words at her:

"And I heard what you said, to Laura, in the kitchen – about me. Is that what you really think? That I'm the same as Ed? Because I'm not, you know, and I think it's pretty poor that you would think that. I've never done anything to hurt you Josie, not knowingly. Why would you say that?"

He stared at her as they stood facing each other in the dark country lane. There was a moon, casting grey and purple shadows over the road. Everything beyond the dark hedge that loomed beside them was a blank, hidden in the folds of the night.

Josie opened her mouth, then closed it again.

The wind was stirring the trees above them, the branches swaying, casting shadows in the moonlight that rushed, forwards and backwards, across the grey lane. Somewhere, an owl hooted.

Jack waited. He saw her bowed head, and guessed Josie was too embarrassed to say anything, that she *had* meant to criticise him; her honest view was that Jack too was untrustworthy. He was angry again, with her, with Ed, with his whole stupid meaningless life. He'd thought she liked him, thought they were friends, that it could develop into something deeper. He'd seen a role for himself at Broom Hill, thought he was getting somewhere. Now he realised, in a cold rush of self-awareness, that although Josie appreciated his physical help, she had no use for him as a person. Jack the failure was failing again. It was like a slap, an icy shock.

He spun on his heel, began to move away, to walk back to the farm. There was nothing else to say.

"Please don't go," said Josie, so quietly he barely heard her above the sound of the trees.

He stopped, though didn't turn. He looked straight ahead, his head up, shoulders square, waiting. He would listen, he decided, but he wouldn't let her know how much he was hurt.

"I'm sorry I said those things," he heard. Josie was speaking very softly, her voice hoarse with embarrassment. "I didn't mean it, I didn't mean any of it; it was stupid – but I was scared that Laura liked you, that you'd like her, that you'd stop..." She paused.

Jack waited. He wasn't breathing now, his whole being suspended while he strained to hear what she would say.

"She's so pretty," Josie continued. She was whispering now, so Jack had to turn and lean closer to hear.

"She's thin and pretty and funny, and I knew, if she made a move, you'd like her. And I'm sorry, I had no business to be nasty. It's just that, just that..."

"Just that what?" said Jack, frowning, his voice rough, almost cruel. She had hurt him, and now he needed her to explain exactly *why* she was sorry. Was she sorry because he'd overheard her words, or did she mean what he was now hearing? Did she, could she, have feelings for him? Josie was facing the moon, her face lit in the silver light, and Jack could see the agony of embarrassment as she forced herself to speak.

"Just that...I want you to like me," she finished, as if the words were being ground out of her, the last of her pride in shreds.

Jack heard her take a breath, and he realised, as his own hurts fell away, what it was costing her to admit her feelings. He recognised again the strength within her as she forced herself to speak, felt something stir within him, wanting to protect her. Her words were coming in a rush now, and Jack could hear the tears in her voice, the desperation.

"And I know it's silly, I know that I'm big and ugly, and that you can choose whoever you want, and you'd never choose me, but I couldn't help it. And Ed's right, I am a carthorse, and I should just get used to that and stop interfering, and..."

Jack moved close, stepping into the gap between them, he put his arms round her, pulled her to him. "Shut up," he said.

He put his hand under her chin, searching her eyes, making sure he'd understood. She gazed back at him, her grey eyes pools of embarrassment and longing and uncertainty.

He kissed her, slowly at first, tentative, still checking he wasn't making a mistake; then when she responded, melted into him, he kissed her deeply, firmly.

He felt her – shy at first, becoming more certain, then clinging to him; and Jack felt again that desire to protect her and hold her and keep her safe.

Jack pulled away. "You're not a carthorse, you're beautiful," he said.

"But I'm big," said Josie.

"I like big," said Jack, kissing her again. "And I like strong, and gentle, and kind, and determined." He held her head in both hands, forcing her to look at him.

"I like you Josie. No one else, just you. Do you like me?"

She nodded, as if not daring to speak, not wanting to break the spell.

"That's sorted then," said Jack, smiling into the night.

Chapter Twenty-Five

They walked back to the farm, Jack's arm firmly around Josie's shoulders, holding her close. Susan saw them return, noted the look in Jack's eyes and decided to not comment. She turned away with a smile, there was something distinctly right about the relationship, something which made her feel it had been established long ago, and had merely been waiting to blossom.

Susan carried the last few items into the kitchen, and dumped them next to the sink. She felt tired, and thought she might leave the last of the washing up until tomorrow. Behind her, the door opened, letting another wave of cold air into the already cool kitchen, and Neil came and stood next to her.

"I think I need to get Kylie home Mum," he said. "Sorry to abandon you, but I'm worried about how tired she is, and she's started to feel sick again."

"Has she eaten something bad?" said Susan, full of concern, her mind whirling to the pizzas pieces and nibbles they'd served, wondering if something could have been off.

"No, actually," said Neil, his face glowing.

Susan saw his huge smile, something joyful leaped inside her, and she gasped.

"Is she...?"

Neil nodded. "Yep," he said, sounding very satisfied. "It's early days, so we weren't going to tell people yet, but she's been so ill, I think everyone who knows us has guessed anyway."

"Guessed what?" said Ben, arriving from the barn with Edward.

"Kylie's pregnant!" said Susan, beaming. The whole world seemed happy suddenly.

"Oh, well done mate, not firing blanks after all," said Ben, moving to shake his brother's hand.

"Ben! That is a terrible phrase," said Susan, laughing.

"Will you tell Dad for me?" asked Neil, "I really ought to get Kylie home."

Susan paused. "No," she said. "He's in the barn, it will only take you a minute to pop out. He'll like to hear it from you."

Neil nodded, and turned to go and find his father. Susan smiled around the kitchen, her tiredness after the barn dance dissolving to a happy mist of wonder. She grinned at Ben and Edward, who were loitering near the sink.

"Isn't that fabulous?" she said, hugging the news to herself.

"I guess," said Edward, as though he wasn't sure that he relished the thought of a baby very much. "But it's nice to see you happy Mum. You can start knitting bootees or something..." He looked round the kitchen and yawned. "I think I'll be off now. You all seem very happy anyway..."

Susan glanced at him, surprised by the bitter resignation she could hear in his tone. She wondered if he was jealous.

"Thank you for all your help," she said, hugging Edward and kissing his cheek before he left.

When Tom arrived in the kitchen, Susan could see that Neil had told him the news, there was something about the way he walked, lighter somehow, and his face, although bruised on one side from Alan's fist, was creased into tired smiles. They didn't talk much, as they tidied the last few items, and when Susan announced she was knackered, was going to bed, Tom went with her.

Later, as she curled around him under the covers, he kissed her hair and sighed.

"Never been easy, being a parent, has it?" said Tom. "But I sometimes think, after evenings like tonight, that maybe we haven't done too badly."

"No," said Susan, smiling into the darkness, thinking of baby clothes and new life. "It hasn't been easy, not always, but I think perhaps it will start to get easier now. And even when it's been difficult, it's always been worth it, hasn't it?"

But Tom didn't reply. He was asleep.

***

Three weeks later, Susan was scrolling through her phone, looking at photographs of the barn dance. Most were blurry, snatched images taken in the odd moment when she remembered, and happened to not have her hands full of food or dirty dishes. But some of them were clear, and they allowed her to glimpse the things she had missed.

Laughing faces, clapping hands, people turned towards each other as they chatted. She had been too busy to notice many of the scenes at the time, and it was nice now, while she had time, to sit and look; to smile afresh at Kevin's big feet as he pranced, at Edward's stare of concentration while he poured beer, at Tom looking uncomfortable when cornered by one of the church ladies. There was Kylie too, hidden in the shadows, looking 'thin and spiteful' as Dot would say – her general description of anyone struggling through the early weeks of pregnancy.

Susan continued to scroll back, losing all sense of time as she looked at earlier photographs. There was Elsie, eating cake at her birthday tea. Susan thought about her aunt, remembered her childlike qualities, her desire to be part of everything, her eagerness to share in family events. There was something about the last stage of life which gave a certain security to younger people, almost an anchor. Her mother and Elsie were sometimes dismissed as peripheral to occasions, but in reality, they provided the stability, the balance, that would be missing if they were excluded.

There was a photograph of Ben, looking embarrassed as he wore a mortarboard at his graduation. That day had signified the end of another era, thought Susan. Ben was searching for jobs now, hopeful that his last interview would be successful, that he would soon be looking for digs in London to be nearer his workplace.

Susan turned from her phone to gaze out of the window as she pondered the man that Ben had become. Ben, the baby, the one who had always quietly fitted in at the end, following his brothers; now an independent man, making his own choices, in a relationship. Even if, thought Susan, that relationship is far, far removed from the one I was expecting him to have.

She thought of Kevin, who was gradually becoming part of the family. Susan knew that her own feelings had evolved, a germ of affection was developing towards the boy. Her views were still muddled, she wasn't sure she could explain them very clearly if asked. But if she put the theology to one side, if she concentrated on her own role, then she knew that accepting this boy, this man who mattered so much to her son, was the right thing to do.

"Perhaps Pastor Rob was right," Susan thought, "perhaps I need to concentrate on what God wants for me, and leave the muddle of everything else to him."

She looked back at her phone, and found a photograph of Neil smiling at Kylie, and found she was smiling back. Perhaps it didn't matter that Kylie was so very different to herself, it was Neil's life, Neil's relationship, and he was happy.

"If I have learnt anything this year," thought Susan, standing and walking to the window, "it's that I still don't know everything! My sons have chosen partners who fit them, and if they don't fit me, it is me who must adapt, not the partners. And if I listen, if I try to get to know them, then maybe I will find the special something which attracted my son, and I will learn to appreciate them too."

She was still unsure about Edward and Emily – didn't know if the relationship was a good one. But Edward had never been easy to raise, Susan had always sought to influence him rather than steer. He was like the joker in the pack, you could never be quite sure which way he would turn; but he usually managed to come up trumps. He would go his own way; they all would.

As Susan stared out of the window, over the fields to the hills, she could just make out the red tractor, in the distance. She knew Jack was driving, and her face relaxed into another smile. Jack and Josie seemed a perfect fit, and the relationship had given Jack a whole new sense of purpose. Claire had agreed to continue the lease on Broom Hill Farm, to allow them time to change things. Jack and Josie were working together, making plans, full of optimism. Susan hoped it would work for them, it wasn't an easy life, but they had both been born to it, they knew the cost. They were full of plans to try new crops – soya might be the way to go – and to streamline some of the methods the farm used. Jack was diligent with the figures, pouring over columns of numbers at the weekends, almost as if, thought Susan, he was trying to prove to himself that his debts of earlier had been a lesson well-learned; perhaps he could redeem his earlier failings by clearing the debts created by Trevor.

Yes, there was a cost to working the land, raising animals, thought Susan. It could sap all your resources, your energy, your money, your time. But there was something secure about being so close to nature too, something which seemed very right, very wholesome. Something about the natural rhythm of a farm gave structure and meaning. Seedtime and harvest, cold and heat, day and night, repeating year after year, generation after generation. Now there was to be a new generation, they would all shuffle naturally into new positions to make way for the new life, and Susan and Tom would be the grandparents, the slightly outdated, adoring anchors for the new arrivals.

Susan gazed across the farm, watched the trees move in the wind, the sky darken to almost indigo. The window rattled as a gust of wind pushed against it, flinging a light rain so the pane became misted and damp. Then as she watched, a sunbeam shone down, the clouds parted and the shaft of light divided into a rainbow. It curved across the sky, the colours deepening, a colourful arc against the blue-grey sky. There was something thrilling about rainbows, the whisper of their promise, the reminder that life, with all the seeming turbulence and randomness, was still controlled, in safe hands. The farm had a natural rhythm, and the family seemed to fold in various directions, but the heart of it, of all of them, was safe.

Acknowledgements

Thank you to my friends and neighbours who answered a million questions on all things farming. I send a special thank you to Nicki, Sarah, and John, who took time out of their busy schedules to show me their farms and cattle, and explain something of what it means to work on a farm. As ever, everything that is correct is thanks to them, all mistakes are my own.

Thank you to my beta readers for their invaluable input, and my editor who tells me what I need to change.

As ever, thank you to my family, who continue to support me and cheer me on when I feel like giving up. There is perhaps a whisper of our family humour in this one...I hope you enjoy it.

I would also like to thank you, the reader. It takes about a year to research and write a novel, and always it is done with the hope that people will read it. I hope that you enjoyed the story, and please, will you tell someone else about it?

Anne x

Also by Anne E. Thompson:

Hidden Faces

Invisible Jane

Joanna - The Story of a Psychopath

Clara - A Good psychopath?

Counting Stars

Non-Fiction

How to Have a Brain Tumour

The Sarcastic Mother's Holiday Diary

Due 2019

Sowing Promises

Coming Soon:

The story of Netherley Farm continues in Anne's exciting new novel:

Will Jack and Josie's relationship last...and can they save the farm?

What is the reaction of the church when they hear of Ben's orientation?

Who is rushed to hospital, fighting to survive?

Sowing Promises

To be published 2019

You can follow Anne's blog at:

anneethompson.com

Printed in Poland
by Amazon Fulfillment
Poland Sp. z o.o., Wrocław

54378720R00150